RECKLESS CHANCE

LOVE OVER MURDER
BOOK THREE

J. D. CAROTHERS

DREAMLIFIC PUBLISHING

*To my husband for his continuous
support and belief in me
and my writing*

1

SEAN

She's coming back. That's unexpected.

I lean backward in my leather chair and close my eyes, reliving memories of our one weekend together—pressing my weight against her, tugging on her long, coppery-brown hair, nibbling on her red-hot lips ... and, so help me, hearing her moans.

When she focused on *my* pleasure and had me screaming her name the first time, Lowri smacked my ass. She followed that with a sassy explanation. She may be a lawyer, but it's not *Law*-ree. It's *Low*-ree. Names deserve respect. I won't make that mistake again.

Her spunkiness is sexy as hell though.

Passion, smarts, and a little attitude—all wrapped in a picture-perfect package. I'm about to lose it remembering how that feisty woman fired me up.

A mischief-filled grin washes over my face as ideas swirl in my head, and a rising need grows elsewhere. If I have my way, she'll be rocking my bed again *very* soon.

It doesn't matter that we agreed there would be no repeats. We can change our minds. We're adults. Why not make the most of the nights she's here in Vegas?

What harm can it do? Neither of us believes in commitments. It's not as if walking away from each other again will be hard.

Enough of that. There's no time for such distractions at work. I shouldn't have let the news she's on her way sidetrack me. That's not the reason Evan called. I sit up, straighten my cuffs under my suit jacket, and hit play again.

Sean, mate, this is Evan. Sorry I missed you, but hopefully, this message will work. I need your help throwing a party for Cassandra. I'm coming to Las Vegas while she's your guest chef at Pinot & Pie. Her best friend, Lowri, is on her way to the Grand Athena to help with the celebration. Cassandra and I will see you in three days. I'll send an email with the details for the party. Thanks for your help, mate.

Shaking my head, I'm puzzled at how Cassandra, or Cassie as I know her, upended my best friend's life so quickly. Evan, a confirmed bachelor and spare prince of Catalinius, turned into a lovesick puppy after meeting her at the Grand Athena about five months ago. But no worries, if he wants to throw a party for her at my hotel, I'll make sure it's spectacular. That's what best friends do.

Besides, Evan isn't the only one whose life drastically changed overnight due to unexpected events. Mine was turned upside down two years ago when my father collapsed on the casino floor. He never made it to the hospital. In that moment, I became the owner of the Grand Athena, one of the most luxurious hotels and casinos on the Las Vegas strip. My father trained me for this life, but I never expected to lose him and take over the family business in my early thirties.

Now at thirty-five, as one of the most powerful men in Las Vegas, I'm a target. Everyone wants something from me, particularly women. But I won't make Evan's mistake of falling for one. Nope. I'm keeping my love life simple.

No commitments. No regrets. Only fun.

2

LOWRI

Evan's words, "I need your help for Cassie," sent my heart racing and conjured a sense of foreboding. Something must be incredibly wrong for Evan to call me from Cassie's phone. Otherwise, she would call me herself.

After a full five minutes of reassuring me that my best friend was safe, Evan explained he didn't know my number, so he grabbed Cassie's phone and snuck off to call me.

Okay, I overreacted a smidge, but not without justification. Who could blame me? Cassie has a history of getting into dangerous predicaments. The last time I got a call when she was on an adventure, she'd been wrongly accused of murder and had almost been killed at a cooking competition. But that's another story.

As my pulse slowly returned to normal, Evan was still talking a mile a minute in his deep British accent. His excitement was contagious. He'd finally worked out a way to spend time with Cassie while she's in Las Vegas for the next six weeks.

By the end of the call, Evan's plan was clear. Cassie's a lawyer, like me, but her dream of being a chef is finally coming true. Evan is determined to kick off her experience perfectly by throwing a party in her honor.

He needs my help planning it because he doesn't trust Sean to manage the arrangements alone. Yes, he knows Sean has a hotel full of qualified staff to oversee the details, but Evan doesn't want just any party. He wants to make sure it's specifically designed for Cassie, so she'll always remember it. He's convinced that my unique insight as her best friend will ensure success.

Listening to him talk, I was in awe. It's inconceivable to me that a man could exude such devotion to a woman. Clearly, Cassie found a one-in-a-billion guy.

The next part of Evan's arrangements took me by surprise though. He and Cassie arrive in Vegas in three days, and the party will be that first evening. He wants me to fly to Las Vegas tomorrow —yes, *tomorrow*—to work with Sean Cartwright in person. He came up with this supposedly brilliant plan because he remembers that Sean and I "got along extremely well" when I was there the last time.

Evan has no idea just how well Sean and I got along.

While my best friend Cassie was busy falling in love with a prince, unbeknownst to her, I slipped between the sheets with her prince's best friend. I couldn't resist Sean's tall, gym-hardened body, thick, blond hair laced with whiskey highlights, and intense, azure eyes. And his bad-boy smirk promised as much fun as I could handle.

Did he ever deliver!

My pulse is racing as I remember the way he played my body like a maestro conducting a symphony, bringing crescendo after crescendo. What a weekend!

When it ended, it was clear that our best friends were a serious item. Our paths would likely cross again. If we weren't careful, future misunderstandings or hurt feelings between Sean and me could lead to awkwardness around Cassie and Evan. We agreed there was only one safe solution. We don't do relationships anyway, so we were done. No repeats—not even casual ones.

It's disappointing that we need to keep our distance though. I wouldn't mind letting him treat my body to another *concert* while I'm in town.

That's irrelevant though. There's a bigger problem to deal with. Prince Evan has lost his effing mind! When he asked for help planning a party, I assumed it would be closer to when Cassie makes her debut as a chef in two weeks, but no. The party's in three days!

Evan shouldn't have waited until the last minute. I'm the queen of spontaneity, but what normal person can pack up and fly to Vegas for three weeks with less than twenty-four hours' notice?

I already promised Cassie I'd be there for the opening week of Pinot & Pie. That's when I've scheduled my vacation time, my plane ticket, and my hotel reservations. I explained to Evan that it's not easy to rearrange work and everything to arrive two weeks early and stay that whole time. It's expensive too. He assured me he is taking care of the hotel, leaving me to deal with work and my plane ticket, which, fortunately, is changeable.

I left out that I'm also a bit nervous about seeing Sean again. I'd counted on a couple of additional weeks to adjust to the idea.

What if sparks still fly between us? If so, will it be torture knowing we can't do anything about the attraction?

This line of thinking is ridiculous. That's one of the reasons we agreed to no repeats—to ensure our future encounters wouldn't be awkward. Besides, our chemistry was like a fire made of dry wood that burns fast and flames out quickly. It's over. We haven't spoken or exchanged texts. We've both moved on. I doubt that Sean has given me a second thought.

I'm worrying about nothing. There are no expectations on my part. There won't be any on his either.

So why am I having this internal debate? It's out of character for me to worry about running into someone from my past. I'm careful not to date anyone related to work to minimize that chance. Of course, it still happens occasionally and is never a big deal.

It's Sean's perception that concerns me. He said women have gone to extreme measures to arrange opportunities to be near him.

What if he thinks I orchestrated this three-week stay in his hotel, scheming to spend time with him? Hopefully, he thinks more of me than that. It's not my thing to latch onto a man for his money, power, or approval. I'm perfectly capable of taking care of myself.

I'm only going to Las Vegas to make sure Cassie's party is spectacular and to support her during the first week as the guest chef. I shouldn't care what Sean thinks.

Who am I kidding? What he thinks matters. He's not like previous guys I've dated. I could walk away from them, and we'd never see each other again. But Sean and I will be thrown together repeatedly if our best friends' relationship lasts. Even if he and I don't become close friends, it would be best if we're in a place of mutual respect, which won't happen if he wrongly thinks I'm chasing him.

Good grief. What is wrong with me? Sean has no reason to think I'm the mastermind behind Evan's last-minute party plans.

Get a grip!

Everyone's entitled to the occasional self-doubt, but there's no need to let others see it or let it take hold. Thank goodness no one can hear the thoughts running through my head. If they could, it would blow my image as a confident, skilled lawyer by day and self-assured, carefree woman the rest of the time.

You've got this.

As Evan pointed out, I'm the closest person Cassie has to family. She's like a sister to me. I'll never let her down. She's finally living her fairytale, which she deserves after everything she's been through. I'll be there to help her real-life royal prince make sure her story continues on its happily-ever-after path.

MY PLANE LANDS IN LAS VEGAS LESS THAN TWENTY-FOUR HOURS AFTER Evan's call. I couldn't manage three weeks of vacation. Instead, thanks to my law firm's remote-work policy, I rearranged my schedule to work from here instead of San Diego until after Cassie's restaurant opens.

Walking toward baggage claim, I'm pulling up a ride-sharing app when a guy blocks my path. He's holding an electronic tablet displaying my name and photo. "Ms. Upton, I'm Justin. Welcome. I'll help you with your luggage, and we'll be on our way."

With a quick stutter step, I narrowly avoid stumbling over Justin's bulky frame. "Thanks. I didn't know the hotel was sending a car for me."

"The VIP concierge made the arrangements. Please follow me. Your bags should arrive on carousel 5."

I'm stepping back into a different world—one filled with wealth, opulence, luxury, and *chance*. Hopefully, luck will be on my side when it comes to that last part.

After we collect my bags, Justin shepherds me into the back seat of a black limo, pops a cork, and hands me a glass of champagne before sliding into the driver's seat. My free hand caresses the buttery leather seat as my body sways to the music that's playing through the speakers surrounding me.

I could get used to this celebrity treatment.

As Justin whisks me to the hotel, the glitz of Las Vegas brings back memories of my visit five months ago.

I haven't forgotten a single moment of the steamy, passionate nights with Sean, not to mention a particularly satisfying ride in his private elevator.

We clicked in a way that was new for me. Not only did our bodies sizzle with every touch, but we also talked and laughed about random things. We even raided the kitchen in the middle of the night to refuel. Being with him felt strangely comfortable.

If my past hadn't taught me to avoid getting close to any man, I'd be tempted to reconsider a few more nights of mind-blowing sex with Sean.

That can't happen though. We both got what we needed, including a clean, no-questions-asked break at the end. We'll plan the party as though nothing happened between us. It'll be fun doing this for Cassie and Evan.

Justin interrupts my thoughts, saying, "We'll be pulling up to the VIP entrance in a few minutes."

"Thanks," I reply, looking out the window as the Grand Athena Resort and Casino comes into view. Spectacular white and blue buildings are the backdrop for a crystal blue lake that mimics the Aegean Sea. It's as if someone plucked the structures straight from the Greek islands. Fuchsia bougainvillea flowers drape over the lapis balconies. They create a breathtaking contrast with the bright white walls of the Mykonos Tower where Sean and I shared a long weekend of steamy nights in his penthouse apartment.

Now that I'm back, I can't help wondering what Vegas has in store for me this time.

Will there be magical moments, mysterious men, or more mayhem? It's time to find out.

3
LOWRI

The exterior of the Grand Athena is eye-catching, but it dims in comparison to the interior. Even though I've been here before, walking into the lobby still takes my breath away. I've magically stepped onto a Greek island. It's bright and airy with electric blue and dazzling white décor. Flowers cascade from every pillar surrounding the giant statue of Athena in the center of the lobby, and individual, white-washed reception desks dot the far side, watched over by statues of other Greek gods and goddesses.

Not to mention, the lobby is literally an indoor island. Yes, it's surrounded by water, and the glass wall behind the reception desks reveals an outdoor Greek-themed village with shops, cafes, and abundant flowers on the far side of the swimming pools. Small water taxis transport guests between the lobby and either the shops, the casino, or the Mykonos and Santorini guest towers. Other visitors hurry across walking bridges that connect all the areas.

As I'm heading toward the check-in line, a familiar man approaches, hand outstretched. "Ms. Upton, I don't know if you remember me. I'm Christian Laurent, the VIP concierge."

"Of course, I remember you. How are you doing?"

"Very well. Thank you for asking. Welcome back."

"I didn't expect to be back this soon, but there's a party to plan."

"That's what I'm told. Let me walk you to your room while I go over the schedule with you."

"Don't you need my credit card first?"

"That's not necessary. Your room and expenses have already been taken care of."

I squint in confusion. "What do you mean? Prince Evan is only paying for *part* of my stay. I'm still responsible for the rest."

"I don't know the details, but your room accommodations are set. Follow me this way. You're staying in the Lapis Suite in the Mykonos Tower. Your luggage has already been sent up. We'll make a quick stop to scan your palm print, so you can use it to open your door. Then we'll head upstairs."

"That's great. Wait a second. Did you say suite? I didn't reserve a suite."

"Due to security and other logistics, Mr. Cartwright and Prince Evan have made specific requests for your accommodations."

I follow him. "That makes sense, I guess. I keep forgetting the implications of my best friend dating a prince. Evan must always be worried about security."

"It's normal for us too. We have celebrities stay with us on a regular basis. Security is a constant concern."

"I can only imagine. What's next on the agenda?"

"Since the party is only three days away, Mr. Cartwright requests that you meet him in the Adonis Lounge at 6:00 p.m. tonight to work on the plans. Will that work for you? If so, I'll let him know."

"Yes. I'll be there. Do you know if the party invitations have gone out yet?"

"Given the extremely short notice, they went out by email and text today. At Prince Evan's request, we've invited the people he and Ms. Edwards met during their last visit, along with others Mr. Cartwright wanted to include."

After an express elevator ride, we arrive at double doors with a sign designating it as "The Lapis Suite." I start to ask a question, but when Christian swings the doors open, I lose my train of thought, gasping at the sight in front of me. This place is bigger than my condo in San Diego. We walk into an enormous living and dining room with glistening marble floors and white leather sofas covered in mounds of lapis, turquoise, and navy pillows. Glass and chrome tables, crystal chandeliers, and fuzzy blue and white rugs add to the suite's theme. My attention quickly turns to the twenty-foot width of frameless glass doors, opening onto a large balcony with a hot tub, overlooking the Las Vegas strip. Wow.

Christian says, "As you can see, you have a full bar to my left. It's stocked with drinks. The door at the left end of the bar leads to the bedroom. To our far right is a small kitchen where you will find various snacks. If you need anything else, Jenny will be at your service."

"Who's Jenny?" I ask.

"That would be me, Miss Upton," a fortyish woman wearing a black suit says as she emerges from the bedroom and bows slightly. "I'm your butler."

Doing a double take, I cover my shock with a cough, remembering Sean has a male butler, who interrupted us once during my last visit. His timing was unfortunate, to say the least. Oh well.

My job has taken me to a fair number of high-end hotels, but my own butler—really? What do I do with one? After an awkward silence, I say, "It's nice to meet you, Jenny. Forgive me, I've never had a butler before. I'm not sure what to expect."

Jenny smiles, saying, "All our VIP suites include them. We take care of your unpacking, laundry, pressing, mail, stocking your food and beverages, placing room service orders for you, and coordinating housekeeping service. In other words, whatever you need related to your room and clothing, I will see to it. I've already unpacked your bags. I've also laid out the clothes that Mr. Cartwright had delivered for you to wear tonight. The accompanying note is on the dresser."

Placing my hand over my mouth, I disguise my discomfort that she unpacked my lacey lingerie and *personal* electronics. I've never been shy, but she's a complete stranger. I'll have to ask Cassie how she's adapted to this life.

Not wanting to show my unease or appear unappreciative, I say, "Thanks for your help, Jenny." Fortunately, I've had years of experience masking my internal reactions.

"If you need anything else, such as reservations for dinner, shows, or transportation, my team will take care of it for you. Just give us a call," Christian says.

"Thanks," I reply, and he turns to leave.

Jenny is still here. As I'm wondering if she is a permanent fixture in my suite, she asks, "Will you need assistance dressing for the evening?"

Is she kidding? Did I walk onto a movie set? Hiding my amusement and trying to adjust to my new surroundings, I say, "No, thanks. I'd like to rest now. It'll be a late evening."

"Of course. If you need anything, please text me. My number is on your bedside table," she says as she opens the door to leave.

My shoulders drop as relief washes over me. A little privacy at last. Time for a shower and a quick nap before meeting Sean. Then it hits me, did Jenny say something about Sean sending me clothes for tonight? I run to the bedroom, anxious to see the surprise.

Does this mean Sean is reconsidering our ban on repeats too?

4

SEAN

A scotch in hand, I'm leaning against the bar in the Adonis lounge when I sense her presence. Turning toward the entrance, my eyes lock with the seductive, mint-green ones staring back at me. I raise my glass slightly in recognition as my gaze moves over the rest of her body in rapt appreciation. Damn, she looks hot in the low-cut, cobalt-blue minidress. It shows off her long, slender legs and mouthwatering cleavage to perfection.

Setting my drink down, I walk toward where she's already fending off others, who are practically salivating. There's something about her energy and magnetism that draws virtually everyone to her at first sight. Reaching Lowri, I pull her in for a hug, whispering in her ear, "You look magnificent."

"Thank you for the dress. I'm surprised you remembered my size," she comments with a playful glimmer in her eyes.

"I remember *everything*. It's unfortunate that tonight will be spent planning the party for Evan."

Chuckling softly, she says, "You're moving fast with the charm. You haven't even bought me a drink yet."

"Excellent point," I state, wrapping my arm around her waist and escorting her across the lounge to the sofa I've reserved in front of the small stage. As we sit, our dedicated server arrives with a bottle of Cristal, presenting it for my approval. "Lowri, is champagne acceptable?"

"Champagne is always acceptable." She smiles.

Raising my glass, I propose, "A toast to our love-blinded friends who, for better or worse, are heading down the relationship path." We clink glasses and drink.

"Better them than us, right? I wanted Cassie to have a little fun in Vegas. I never expected her to decide she was in love. As we talked about last time, I can't imagine being in a serious relationship at all. Who would have thought they would fall for each other so quickly? It's only been about five months."

"Their whirlwind romance caught me by surprise too. They appear happy, but their idea of bliss isn't ours. Like you said, settling down is definitely not for either of us."

"I couldn't agree more. Regardless, we're supposed to be planning this last-minute party. Christian said he handled the invitations. You and I are planning the entertainment and food. Is that correct?"

"Yes. In his email, Evan said that Cassie loves magic shows, so I've arranged for three magicians to audition for us tonight. We can select the best one for the party. How does that sound?"

"Entertainment and you for company will make for a perfect evening."

"That's only the beginning." I wink at her.

"Confident, aren't you?"

"Always."

"Have you forgotten our no-repeat agreement?"

"No, but let's not dwell on that now."

While we wait for the first act, we chat about changes I'm making to the hotel, her legal work, and Cassie and Evan's lightning-fast romance. She's starting to tell me about her plans for a cruise to Mexico when the lights dim further, and the emcee announces that the Night of Magic will begin with Seymour the Great.

I cringe, and Lowri whispers, "Why does that name sound like a magic cat?"

Wrapping my arm around her shoulders, I pull her closer, remarking, "I don't know. Based on the name, I doubt he's the next David Copperfield."

I'm not wrong. The act was trite. He pulls a rabbit out of a hat, makes a watch disappear, and levitates a playing card among other even less notable tricks. "Let's hope the next performer shows at least a modicum of originality," I say as we politely applaud.

"Fingers crossed," Lowri says as the server refills our glasses and leaves a small bowl of nuts on the coffee table in front of us.

We watch Edwin the Magnificent bend a spoon, "magically" reattach torn pieces of a newspaper, and pour water into a hat, making the liquid disappear. "You must be kidding," I murmur. "What was my entertainment director thinking when he chose these guys to audition for the prince's party? It would be generous to call them average." I groan, grabbing a handful of my favorite spicy cashews, crunching them in frustration.

"We still have one more. Let's see how he does," Lowri says as she squeezes my thigh, sending a ripple of warmth up my leg. Down boy. Not now.

Thankfully, the third performer impresses us.

As he leaves the stage, Lowri says, "He made the choice easy. What's our next task?"

"Picking the location for the party. We could have it here, but the Olympic Torch Bar is likely a better choice. They should have appetizers and signature drinks ready for us to sample."

"Let's go. I could use something to eat after all that champagne. My head's already buzzing."

I could use food too. I don't remember having anything for lunch.

With Lowri's arm hooked through mine, we exit the lounge, walk past the Sportsbook, which is the Athena's center for sports betting, and climb the Grand Staircase. Along the way, I enjoy the envious looks from onlookers wishing they were me.

We're immediately escorted through the dimly lit Olympic Torch Bar where flickering seashell candles at the cocktail tables give the guests a warm glow. The doors are open to the balcony, where they roped off a private area for our tasting tonight. Guiding Lowri to the glass wall, we lean on the rail, gazing at the Aegean and watching hordes of people walk up and down the Strip.

"We're here in time for the Olympic games. Have you seen the opening ceremony?" I ask.

"Not yet. You kept me busy with other activities the last time I was here." She winks.

"I don't remember any objections, but you can watch the show tonight."

Within seconds, trumpets blare, brightly colored lights flash, and the outdoor Olympic stage on the left side of the Aegean lights up. A toga-clad couple light the torch on top of the Olympic Tower at the end of the outdoor stage nearest us to kick off the show.

We watch the performers reenact ancient Olympic games, mesmerizing the cheering crowd. My gaze darts back to her. The wind blows her hair forward, hiding those gorgeous eyes. I've resisted as long as possible. Reaching up, I gently push a loose strand behind her ear, letting my finger softly trace the outer edge. I feel her shiver next to me as I'm pulling my hand away. My smile broadens at her reaction.

Not wanting to push too fast, I turn back to the show.

When a pair of wrestlers topple into the water, Lowri asks, "Was that supposed to happen? Are they ok?"

"It's all part of the act," I say as a server arrives with a scotch for me and a French martini for Lowri.

"They make it look incredibly real," Lowri says as we sink into the comfy swivel chairs at our table for two, sipping our drinks.

Our glasses are almost empty when Scott, the manager, approaches. His presence better mean that food is on its way because even I'm a little lightheaded at this point.

Scott says, "Welcome to the tasting. We have three signature beverages for you to sample, along with various appetizers for your approval.

"I can't wait to try them." Lowri beams giddily as a server approaches, depositing the first drink and appetizer onto the table.

"Let's get started," she says as she reaches for a cucumber cup filled with crab. Taking a bite, she moans, "Mmm. That is incredible. Cassie will love these."

I stare at her moist lips and listen to her sounds of pleasure, wishing we were upstairs in my apartment. Then she lifts one of the cucumber creations, urging me to try it. Nudging it into my mouth, she brushes her finger across my lips, sending a shock of electricity through me. Lowri pulls her finger away quickly, leaving me to catch the appetizer before it lands on my lap.

"Sorry. It slipped," she says, blushing slightly.

My guess is she felt the sizzle too but won't admit it—at least not yet. My goal is to abolish our ill-conceived no-repeat rule while she's here. We can reinstate the rule after she leaves. By then, we'll have each other out of our systems and be ready to move on.

"No worries. Those are great. We'll need plenty of them because I could eat a dozen by myself." More if she agrees to keep feeding them to me.

By the time the next drink and appetizer arrive, we're laughing, extremely happy, and slightly inebriated. We're not driving, so who cares?

When she tries to feed me this time, her aim is a little off. Sauce ends up coating my mouth and chin. No problem. She wipes it off with her index finger and uses her full, red lips to suck it clean.

Fuuuck.

Maybe another drink will quell my rapidly rising desire to fall to my knees and worship her with my tongue. Then again, there's no reason not to do that. Or is there? I'm not thinking straight. Wait a minute. We're in a restaurant. Am I getting drunk? No. I can hold my liquor. I never get drunk. Did I have breakfast today? Hmm. Better have another appetizer.

I scoot my chair closer to Lowri at the same time the server reappears. My sudden movement causes the new set of drinks and food to fly over the edge of the railing.

Scott hurries over, saying, "Don't worry, we'll replace those immediately. While you wait, we'll get you another drink."

"That's nice of him. I hope they hurry with the food. My head is starting to spin a little," Lowri muses, slightly slurring her words as she reaches to caress my hand.

"Here, drink some water. That should help," I say, handing her a glass.

She takes a long drink and clutches her throat. "That wasn't water. That's vodka."

Finally, I spot the server walking toward us with the last round of appetizers and drinks. I don't waste any time. The moment the plate is in front of me, I load my fork with a sizeable taste.

Shit.

The first bite was so spicy my eyes are watering. Lowri's not any better off. Her cheeks are bright red, and she's gasping. We simultaneously grab the nearest glasses and down the drinks.

When we can breathe again, Lowri rests her head against my shoulder. With each drink, we've relaxed even more. Her reaction to my touches and her closeness signal she also wants to pick up where we left off last time. Since we're both well past tipsy at this point, we may have to wait until tomorrow though.

"We still have one other venue that's a possibility for the party. Let's check it out now," I enunciate slowly, trying to avoid slurring my own words.

"Where is it?" she asks.

"It's a private part of the Omega, our rooftop nightclub."

"Okay. Let's go. I wouldn't mind a little dancing tonight." She teeters, losing her balance when she shimmies her hips as she tries to stand.

I groan as she tumbles into my chest. She's going to be the death of me, but man will it be fun.

5
SEAN

Scott insists we opt for the hidden elevator rather than navigating down the Grand Staircase. Reaching the casino level, we stumble and weave our way past the noisy Sportsbook on our right. Cheers of bettors rooting for their teams compete with dinging slot machines and raucous table games on our left.

"Does the constant … ummm … excitement of Vegas … ummm … ever get old?" Lowri asks.

The alcohol's getting to her now.

"Sure. That's when I head to one of my other homes in Maui or Paris," I say, speaking slowly, trying not to sound as drunk as I probably am.

"Wow. Ummm. That must be nice." She giggles.

"You could go with me next time," I say between hiccups.

She plants a big kiss on my cheek, and says, "That would be marvelous, darling."

I can't help laughing at her drunken imitation of an old movie star.

As we near the area with the Casino Stage, Lowri trips. Fortunately, she falls toward me, resting her palms against my chest to steady herself as she says, "Does all the clinking and dinging of the ... whatchamacallits ... make you happy? Does it remind you of the mooooneeeey you're maaaaking?" She laughs.

"You mean slot machines."

"Yeah, those."

"I grew up here. It's normal to me. Anything else would be boring."

"Your noooormal is straaaange. Hey, look over there. They're having fun," she says, tilting her head toward the exuberant crowd standing in front of the Casino Stage. They're dancing to the music blasting from nearby speakers.

"What's thaaaat above them?" she asks, pointing to the sign hanging over the elevated stage, which reads,

Couples Needed
Pose for Wedding Photos and Set a New World Record

I needed more food today. My head's spinning as I answer slowly, "I don't remember the details. It's something about setting a Guinness World Record. I think it's for the most photos at the same place on the same night," I say.

"There muuuust be two or three huuuundred couples. And look at their outfits. Feathers. Spandex, Weeeedding dresses. Tuxes. I loooove Vegas. You can beeee ... ummm ... any fantasy you waaaant. Noooo one ... umm ... will juuuudge you." She hiccups.

"Right. Weeee better hurry. Weeee don't ... want to beeee ... stuck in ... this crowd." Damn. I'm slurring my words now too.

"Waaaait. It looks fun. I've always waaaanted to ... ummm ... set a world record ... for something," she says as she tugs on my arm, pulling me toward the line of people near the registration table at the base of the stage.

"No way in hell am I waiting in that line for a photo." That's better. No slurring. I'm okay.

"Pleeeease. Do it for meeee." She pouts as she bats her lengthy eyelashes.

"What the hell. Follow me," I insist, leading her to the VIP area and bumping into a few obstacles along the way.

When the security guard recognizes me, he immediately escorts us to a registration desk with more privacy. It's one of the perks of owning the place.

Lowri asks the woman in charge a bunch of questions. I'm not sure they make sense, but I'm not paying attention. I tune back in when I hear her ask, "Can we ... ummm ... have our photo ... ummm ... taaaaken?"

The woman says, "Of course."

"Are the other couples married? They have flowers and ... ummm ... stuff. We're missing ... everything. Is that a problem?"

"No. We have what you need."

Lowri turns to me practically jumping with excitement. I barely keep her from falling over in her deadly high heels as she begs, "Let's do this. Pleeeease."

The last thing I want to do is dress up with props for fake photos, but why not, if it makes her happy. "Okay, if it's important to you." I cover my mouth with my suit sleeve, suppressing yet another hiccup, and turn to the woman, asking, "What's next?"

A server approaches, handing us flutes of champagne as the woman says, "Give me your IDs. Then you'll sign extra forms for the world record."

Handing over my driver's license, I say, "Deliver the photos to my apartment."

Recognition crosses her face as she looks at my ID. "Yes, of course, Mr. Cartwright. We'll have everything sent to you in the morning."

As we sip champagne, the woman takes care of the paperwork.

After that's done, she asks, "Lowri, which color bouquet would you prefer? We have roses in yellow, red, white, and pink."

Lowri stares at the flowers with a dreamy look in her mesmerizing eyes.

"Sean, wouldn't the whiiiite roses … ummm … look great with my blue dress?" Lowri asks, pointing a shaky finger to a small bouquet.

"Of course." I'm not sure why it matters, but Lowri being happy makes me happy.

The woman says, "Time to pick your rings. We have an assortment of styles and sizes for you to choose from."

"Do we need rings?" I ask between large sips of champagne. Why does another drink sound appealing right now?

Lowri pats my chest, laughing. "Of course, we do, silly. It's … ummm … part of the … wedding theme for … the … photos."

She steals my glass of champagne and finishes it off. Hers is already empty.

"Why not? Which one is your favorite?" I ask, struggling to control my speech.

"You should … umm … pick mine, and I'll … umm … pick yours."

"You neeeed the biggest one," I say pointing to a ring with a large pear-shaped crystal in the center and baguettes on each side. "How muuuuch is that one?" I'm slurring again. No more champagne.

"A hundred and fifty," the woman says smiling.

"A bargain. Weeee'll take it along with whichever ring Lowri picks for meeee."

When it's our turn, we hold the handrails to steady ourselves and climb the steps onto the stage. It's decorated with pedestals of white roses and greenery surrounding an arch in the center. Arriving at the rose-covered arch, we attempt to look happy but serious as we pose with an actor dressed as a minister. We're both fighting off snickers at this point.

The photographer says, "Smile for the camera," as the actor plays his role, asking, "Lowri, do you take this man to be your husband?"

"Yeeessss." She laughs.

"Sean, do you take this woman to be your wife?"

"Why not." I shrug, smiling for the photo.

The actor says, "Place the rings on each other's ring finger."

Between giggles and hiccups, we do as he instructs.

"Congratulations, you may kiss the bride now."

Finally, the good part. Leaning in, I pull her close and plant my lips on her warm, soft mouth. She throws her arms around my neck as she parts her lips, inviting my tongue to tangle with hers. A zap of electricity travels from my head to my toes as she moans. The world around us becomes fuzzy as we lose ourselves in each other. Grasping the back of her head, I pull her even closer, needing more.

A woman coughs and taps on Lowri's shoulder, breaking the moment and bringing our kiss to an end sooner than I wish. The woman announces, "It's time to throw the bouquet."

Lowri turns her back to the crowd on the casino floor and heaves the flowers over her shoulder.

As we leave with our souvenir rings, Lowri says, "That was soooo muuuuch fun. You knoooow what we should ... ummm ... doooo next?"

"I'm afraid to ask."

"Let's skip the Oooomeeeega and go straaaaight to the honey-mooooon. Okay?"

Thank fuuuck. Mission accomplished. She tossed our no-repeat rule out with the bouquet.

"Absolutely! Whatever my beautiful bride wants, she gets," I say, keeping the joke going and moving the evening toward my bedroom.

What could be better than a honeymoon without having to actually get married?

First, we'll sober up over a late dinner. Otherwise, we'll be too drunk to enjoy our fake wedding night.

6

SEAN

We detour to one of my restaurants and take our time sharing a steak-and-lobster dinner for two with tons of water. When we finally arrive at my apartment, we've sobered up enough that we're only a little tipsy rather than flat-out drunk.

"Aren't you supposed to carry me over the threshold?" Lowri chastises, refusing to leave the private elevator that opens directly into my penthouse apartment.

I grin, happy that she's still in the *honeymoon* mood.

"That would be tradition, wouldn't it?" Rather than pick her up in my arms, I throw her over my shoulder and playfully smack her ass, hauling her straight to my bedroom.

She drums my back with her fists, laughing as she says, "You're doing it wrong. Put me down."

"This isn't a *real* marriage. There is no right way. Besides, you owe me," I say, depositing her onto my oversized bed.

"Why do I owe you?"

"I didn't get a bachelor party."

"You poor, poor man. That was certainly unfair, wasn't it? I'll remedy that," she offers in a sultry, raspy voice as she slowly rises from the bed.

She gently runs her thumb across my lips and lets her fingers trail down my chin and neck until they're grasping my necktie. With a gentle tug and a come-hither glance, she leads me to the straight chair near the window.

Damn. Playful Lowri is hot as hell.

She trails a hand across my chest and around my shoulders as she seductively moves behind me. "You won't be needing this," she whispers, peeling my jacket down my shoulders and tossing it aside.

Beyonce's *Dance for You* begins playing as Lowri circles back in front of me and places the phone she found in my pocket on a nearby table.

With a hand on each shoulder, she nudges me down onto the chair, instructing, "Lean back and relax. I'll take care of *everything*. I have a special treat for the groom."

"Whatever you say, my naughty girl."

If this fake bachelor party is headed where it seems, I wouldn't mind getting fake married more often.

She bends forward, her glorious cleavage only inches from my mouth, making me swallow hard to avoid drooling like a teenager. She removes my tie and unbuttons my shirt, letting her long red nails tickle my chest as she draws them toward the waist of my trousers. As I reach for her, she pulls back, wagging her index finger. "Uh-uh, no touching."

Stretching the tie in front of her, she says, "You won't be needing this, but *I* will," she teases as she moves behind me again. "Hands behind the chair, my bad boy."

Trusting Lowri in a way I wouldn't others, I comply and feel the tie loosely bind my wrists together. She reappears in front of me, asking, "Are you going to behave now?"

"Is that what you really want? I thought you like it when I'm bad." I smirk.

Without answering, she lip-syncs to the song, mouthing words of adoration and love while she sways to the beat. Tossing her head back, she crosses her arms over her chest, hugging herself. Slowly, Lowri slides her hands down, uncrossing her arms as her fingers move across the soft fabric encasing her ample breasts. Her thumbs caress her nipples through the fabric. I watch as they harden to stiff points, pressing against her dress. Splaying her fingers, her hands roam farther down her dress as her eyes close and her tongue moistens her lips.

Even though we're playacting tonight, for a second, in my semi-inebriated state, I wonder if we could be an actual couple. It'll be hard to let her go. This vixen ignites a fire in me and brings out a possessiveness I've never felt before. That's just the alcohol talking. Shaking off those thoughts, I concentrate on the swaying of her hips and bobbing of those delicious breasts.

Her body is undulating in waves as she turns her back to me and lifts the hem of her dress, bending forward to reveal a black lace thong between her tight cheeks. With painful slowness, she places her thumbs under the waistband and inch by inch lowers the thong to her ankles, giving me a full view.

Damn.

As the song describes what she wants to do to me, she backs closer to my lap and pulses her sweet ass up and down within inches of the rock-hard bulge in my trousers, making me ache for release.

When I think this dance can't get hotter, she flips around and straddles me. She reaches for the back of her dress, unclasping the hooks of its halter top. The shimmery fabric falls forward baring her luscious breasts for me. With her left hand, she laces her fingers in my hair and pulls my head into her chest. No longer able to resist, I suck one of her nipples into my mouth, giving it a nip with my teeth. As I'm moving to the other one, I feel Lowri's right hand unfastening my belt and lowering my zipper.

She's killing me.

Freeing my cock, she sinks down onto it. Wrapping her long,

stiletto-clad legs around the back of the chair, she begins pulsing up and down to the music.

"*Fuuuck.* I'm not going to last long if you keep doing that."

Mercifully, neither is she. Her core tightens around me, and she throws her head back, shouting, "Sean! Yes! Yes! Yes!"

Any modicum of control I had left disappears, and I tumble over the edge with her, experiencing the best orgasm of my life.

We collapse against each other, breathing heavily, not saying anything.

When our heart rates eventually slow, Lowri breaks the silence, asking, "How long before you're ready for round two?"

I laugh. "What do you have in mind?"

"Well, I never had a bachelorette party. How are you going to make that up to *me?*"

"Untie me, sit on the edge of bed, and I'll show you."

She follows my instructions.

I stand in front of her and take my time giving her my best impression of a more hands-on, or should I say *cock-in*, version of the Australian male revue that's popular for bachelorette parties in Vegas. After all, I wouldn't want Lowri to miss out.

7

LOWRI

Knock, knock, knock. "Noooo," I moan. Why is someone jackhammering inside my head? Stretching, my leg collides with a wall—a heated wall. Huh?

Hearing a groan, it dawns on me. I'm in Sean's bed, and it's his muscular leg that's hot as fire. As memories of last night flood in, the bedroom door flies open.

Like last time, Sean's butler, Walter, is bursting in on us. Sean groans. "Lowri, give me a couple of minutes, and we can go again."

"Sean, wake up. Walter's here," I mutter, reaching for the sheets to cover myself. Unfortunately, Sean and I are tangled in the mass of fabric, leaving my breasts on full display.

"Walter, turn away this instant!" I demand, wincing at the loudness of my voice. Walter's clearly accustomed to walking in on Sean and his flavor of the night, but that's not okay with me.

He swivels, placing his back to us. "My apologies, Ms. Upton. I didn't realize you were here."

"Don't tell me that my arrival eluded your stellar radar," I say softly, feigning surprise.

"I retired early last night," he explains.

I couldn't resist letting Walter know it's not that easy to fool me. I don't believe him for a minute given he's holding a tray with two glasses of water and two medicine bottles, which hopefully contain something to ease my throbbing headache. While nothing about Sean's apartment or its guests escapes Walter's notice, at least he has the decency to pretend otherwise.

Finally freeing myself from the sheets, I find a robe as Sean moans, "Ugh. Walter, go away. We're trying to sleep."

Coughing, Walter says, "My apologies for interrupting. You received a delivery. They said you insisted it be delivered directly to your apartment. Presumably, it's important."

Rolling onto his back and rubbing the sleep from his eyes, Sean pushes his bare torso up, securing the sheet at his waist as I tie the belt on my robe. "Fine. Turn around and give it to me," he growls.

Handing a thick manila envelope to Sean, Walter asks, "Will there be anything else, sir?" as he places a glass of water and pain relievers on each of our bedside tables.

"We'll need breakfast and tons of coffee. Pronto."

"Of course, sir," he says. As he exits the bedroom, I straighten the sheets on my side of the bed and crawl back under the covers.

"What's so important that Walter had to wake us up?" I ask.

"I have no freaking idea. I'm not expecting any documents this morning," he says.

As he tears open the envelope, a memory from last night panics me. I reach for Sean's arm, saying, "We didn't use condoms last night. Should I be concerned?"

"*Shit.* Lowri, please tell me you're on birth control?"

"Yes, and I'm clean. What about you?"

"I'm clean. I haven't forgotten condoms in the last decade."

"Whew. That's a relief."

"No kidding. Last night could have been a disaster," he says as he extracts a pile of papers from the envelope.

After a quick glance, he hands the stack to me, saying, "Oh, it's the photos from our fake wedding last night."

"The woman did say she would have them delivered this morning." I chuckle as I thumb through the photos, amused at our inebriated expressions. After the last photo, there's a stack of documents, which causes my smile to evaporate. Confusion takes over as I scan a bill from a jewelry store for $160,000 plus tax. I hand it to Sean, asking, "What's this?"

He reads, "One woman's ring with a four and a half carat, pear-shaped center diamond and baguettes on each side, totaling one and a half carats, set in platinum. $150,000." He turns toward me. I frown, staring at the glimmering ring on my third finger, left hand. Without saying anything else, he continues, "One men's platinum ring with basket weave design. $10,000." We both look at his left hand, which is sporting the ring as described.

Eying my ring again, I ask, "Do you think it's real? I remember them saying the ring was one hundred and fifty. I thought they meant dollars, not one hundred and fifty thousand dollars. There must be a mistake. If it's real, there was a misunderstanding. We can return it. Let's see what else is in the stack of papers. Look. Here's a certificate congratulating us for being part of a world record attempt for the most wedding photos of different couples in one night."

"You can keep that as a souvenir," he says.

I laugh until I see the next document, pausing to read it. In shock, I read it again more carefully. "Take a look at this" I say, tossing it onto his lap. "How the hell did we get married?"

"What are you talking about?" he asks as he picks up the paper and reads, "State of Nevada Marriage Certificate. They took the fake wedding photos to an extreme. This looks almost real."

Straining to reign in my panic, my voice is tight and my body shudders as I say, "Sean, I believe it's real. Here's a copy of our marriage license. All these documents indicate it was a real wedding."

"No fucking way!"

"Yes fucking way!" I shout, losing my last thread of control. "Look at all the discounts they've included for newly married couples to take advantage of. You said it was a stunt for photos of couples to set a record—not a real wedding! This is all your fault." I'm angry enough to cry, and I don't cry in front of others.

"What do you mean it's all my fault? You're the one who wanted photos."

"All I wanted was fun photos pretending to get married. Not a real wedding! Didn't you read the papers you signed?"

"You're the lawyer! Why didn't you read them?" he retorts, a look of pure scorn on his face.

"It's your hotel—your event. You should have known they were setting a record for real marriages. I trusted you."

"Do you know how many thousands of events we have here every year? I don't keep track of all of them. And I certainly didn't marry *you* on purpose," he grumbles.

He didn't want to marry *me*. I'm too stunned to respond at first. Why does it bother me that he made his declaration personal? I shake it off and softly admit, "I didn't want to get married either. You better fix this. Now." I rarely cry, but a single tear softly flows down my cheeks as my emotions rise and fall with each breath. I've never planned or wanted to marry. It's still sad to know the only wedding I'll likely ever have was fake. Even worse, it's specifically *me* that the groom didn't want to marry.

I feel a warm arm wrap around my shoulders and pull me close. All the harshness is gone when he says, "Don't cry, Lowri. It's not a big deal. My lawyer will have the marriage annulled."

More tears escape. "We slept together. We consummated the marriage. How can you have it annulled?" I ask.

He chuckles. "You're not thinking clearly. We slept together a few months ago too. It doesn't matter. We were drunk and didn't realize we were getting married. That's a legitimate reason for an annulment. It'll be as if it never happened." He grins, squeezing my arm.

"Great. What a cliché. I got drunk and got married in Las Vegas. We can probably buy T-shirts with that phrase in the gift shop," I moan.

My heart aches. Then another horror dawns on me. "Cassie doesn't know we hooked up when I was here before. She suspected there was chemistry between you and me. I sidestepped confirming it though. I don't want her to know about my alcohol-induced wedding vows. This situation is extreme even for the party girl in me."

"Don't worry. I won't be sharing this. Evan would never let me live down a fake wedding that turned out to be real."

"That's a relief. Can you also do me a favor?"

"Depends. What do you need?"

"I know this isn't a real marriage but promise you won't sleep with anyone else before the annulment."

"As long as you're in my bed, why would I need anyone else?" he jokes.

"I'm serious. It's important to me. I can't handle cheating, even by a temporary husband. I'm sure the annulment will only take a week or two. Please do this for me."

I don't share that my dad cheated on my mom and eventually left my family for his secretary. I always swore I wouldn't put myself in a position to trust someone as completely as my mom had trusted my dad. My solution was to never have a husband. I've blown that part now, but I won't tolerate cheating.

He turns and kisses me. "No problem. On a lighter note, why is your ring fifteen times more expensive than mine?" he teases.

I playfully punch him in the arm. "Very funny. I'm keeping the ring until our marriage is annulled. I want you motivated to clean up this mess quickly."

Sean attempts to comfort me, placating, "Quit worrying. It'll all be over soon."

My mood darkens. While I don't want all that a marriage entails, why does thinking of the annulment make me feel cold and alone? It doesn't make sense.

Before I can delve into further self-analysis, I hear another knock at the door. "Breakfast, sir," Walter announces. At least I'm dressed for his second intrusion.

8

LOWRI

"Let me show you something," Sean says as we finish breakfast.

"What is it?" I ask, following him. He doesn't say anything until we reach a door in the hallway near his bedroom.

"Place your right hand against the panel." He points to the wall.

Curiosity has me speculating as to what secret lies behind the door. I'm not sure if I'm nervous or excited as I place my palm flat against the five-by-eight-inch, black acrylic panel mounted on the wall. A second or two later, there's a click.

In a deep, gravelly voice, Sean says, "Open the door."

I turn the handle as my imagination runs wild. Is he revealing a naughty playground? Other than in my mental fantasies, this party girl has her limits. Does he expect more than I'm ready to give? If it's his version of *Fifty Shades of Something*, should I run or stay?

Opening the door slowly reveals something entirely unexpected, and I'm not sure if I'm disappointed or relieved. "Huh? It's an elevator," I say, turning to him with a mystified gaze.

"It is. It will take you to your suite, which is directly below mine. Your handprint opens the door, allowing you to easily travel between your suite and my apartment without having to use the hallways. This way you can leave most of your clothes in your room. If Cassie drops by, she won't suspect you're staying with me." He grins.

"Does *everyone* who stays in my suite have direct access to yours?"

"Of course, not. We disable the elevator unless I've reserved the suite."

"That's why you upgraded my room. Wait a minute though. How often do you *reserve* the suite? You said you rarely have women stay over. What's up with that?" Without meaning to, I let my emotions show. I woke up accidentally married, but I'm not ready for my temporary husband to be a liar too.

"My friends use it a lot. My *male* friends. It makes it easier to handle security and access to my floor if they stay in the suite below. Am I detecting a little jealousy in my new wife?"

"Don't flatter yourself. I merely wanted to know if you'd been truthful with me about avoiding relationships, even short ones. It was presumptuous of you to assume that I'd be interested in hooking up again, particularly after we agreed we wouldn't."

He smirks. "I didn't hear any complaints last night. I've also had security give you access to the Maze, which means you can move around the hotel quickly while we finish planning the party. I'll have my assistant, Emily, give you a tour of our underground tunnel system and an app for your phone so you won't get lost."

"That sounds great. What else do we need to do for the party?"

"Finalize the food and beverage order, select the décor, and approve the room layout. Also, Evan wants to meet with the magician ahead of time. I can book him. I'm hoping you can oversee the rest. Emily set up a meeting with the event coordinator for 11:00 a.m. this morning. She'll text you the info. Unfortunately, I'm stuck in business meetings most of the day."

"No problem. My schedule has a little flexibility while I'm here. I can take care of the remaining details for the party. Don't forget to call your lawyer. We need *unwed* as quickly as possible. Unfortunately, my law license doesn't allow me to appear in court in Nevada, or I'd take care of it myself. I'm only licensed in California."

"I promise to take care of our misadventure. Don't give it another thought. Let's meet on my balcony for drinks at 7:00 p.m. to share updates," he suggests, kissing me quickly on the forehead as I step into the elevator.

Less than a minute later, the doors open. I find myself in the walk-in closet in my suite's bedroom. Hmm. I can't help wondering how many women have taken that ride. Rather than dwell on that thought, I find the bathroom and indulge in a long, hot shower before readying myself to meet with the event planner.

After applying makeup, I start putting on my earrings and bracelet when my eyes catch the flashy wedding ring on the bathroom vanity. I debate what to do with it. It doesn't feel proper to wear it on my finger even though I told Sean that I'm keeping the ring until our marriage is annulled. Instead, I put it on my gold neck chain with the heart pendant from my mom and tuck it into the neck of my shirt for safekeeping.

Grabbing my phone, I hurry to the lobby.

A couple of minutes after arriving, I recognize Emily as she approaches. She's an unassuming woman who I'd guess is somewhere in her late twenties or early thirties. She's wearing a light-gray suit and dark-rimmed glasses. Her hair is pulled back in a tight bun, reminding me of a librarian. It's clear she's quite attractive despite her attempt to look nondescript, which makes me wonder why she's hiding her beauty. It's none of my business, so I squash my curiosity when she extends her hand.

"Hello. Welcome back, Lowri. I don't know if you remember me. I'm Emily."

"Emily, it's nice to see you again. Thanks for helping me today."

"It's my pleasure. We're excited that Prince Evan and Ms. Edwards will be back in a couple of days. Isn't it romantic that he wants to throw a party for her?" She sighs.

"Definitely. Cassie will love the party if we can pull it together in time."

I barely notice, but a longing and sadness pass across Emily's face that's quickly replaced with her perfunctory smile. Did she lose a love, or does she merely wish for one? Either way, that's another reason I'm not interested in relationships. One way or another, they result in pain and heartache. No thanks.

Emily says, "We'll work fast. Our team is fantastic and will make it happen. Let's start with a quick tour of the Maze, and then I'll take you to the Olympic Torch Bar to introduce you to the event planner for the party. Will that work?"

"That's perfect. I've heard about the Maze from Cassie. I'd love to see it."

"Follow me, and I'll show you. It's an extensive network of tunnels, rooms, and storage facilities underneath the hotel and casino. It saves time moving between various parts of the property by avoiding the crowds. It'll be particularly helpful when Mr. Cartwright is with you because people often try to stop him when he attempts to move through the casino," Emily says.

"Cassie said the Maze reminded her of a small-scale subway system that never sleeps."

"That's an excellent analogy. They have the lighting set to mimic around-the-clock daylight. And rather than trains, golf carts zip along the tunnels, moving people from place to place. If you walk through the Maze, watch out for speeders." She laughs.

When we stop in front of a bigger-than-life-size bronze sculpture of a Greek goddess with widespread wings, Emily asks for my phone to load the MazeApp. While she works on that, I admire the statue. The goddess stares at the wreath that her left hand extends skyward. She's majestic.

Who is she? Roaming my eyes over the nearby wall and the sculpture, I finally spot a discreet engraving on the base, declaring she's *Nike, Goddess of Victory*. Wow. If I'd paid more attention when we studied mythology, I would've remembered that Nike was a woman. Gotta love powerful, kickass women.

Handing my phone back, Emily says, "Here you go. Now place your palm against the inside of Nike's right hand."

Following her instructions, I hear a familiar click, and a door snaps open. This time I know to expect an elevator like in Sean's apartment. I'm surprised again. A stairwell is hidden behind the sculpture.

As we descend into a brightly lit tunnel, Emily says, "The Maze is fairly easy to navigate using the color-coded, neon emblems and arrows painted on the walls." Then she has me pull up the app and gives me a quick tutorial on how to find my current location, program a destination, and follow a navigation route. She even shows me how to summon a golf cart. "You can go between any two places in under 10 minutes in a cart. The palm scanners only allow approved personnel into the Maze. It's the most secure path to take around the property," she explains.

After the tour, I meet with Amy, the event planner, and bury myself in preparations for Cassie's party. As we're working, the cold diamond in the wedding ring tickles my cleavage. I'm reminded of my bizarre situation.

Sean said he'll fix it, but counting on a man is the ultimate challenge for me. I prefer to be the one in control. Unfortunately, Vegas is his turf, not mine. That means he's the one with connections to quietly undo our accidental trip to the altar.

9
LOWRI

As Amy and I are finishing the party plans, my phone dings.

Sean: Would my wife join me at Athena's
new acrobatic show tonight?

Me: Didn't you rid me of the "wife" title
today?

Sean: Working on it. What about the show?

Me: Would love to see the show. What time?

Sean: It starts at 9:30. Meet me in my suite
at 8 for drinks first. We can grab a late dinner
after the show.

Me: Perfect. See you then.

With the party plans set, it's time to return to my suite and take care of the legal work for our firm's client. I've only been here a day, and I'm already behind. My boss, Noah, is impatiently waiting for my analysis on whether our client's former employee is faking his work-related injury. If so, Noah wants to know how we can prove it. Thank goodness I'm not meeting Sean until 8:00 p.m. It'll take every minute to catch up.

THANKS TO THE ALARM ON MY PHONE, AT 8:00 P.M. ON THE DOT, I'M ready. Pressing my palm on the black panel at the back of my closet, I summon the elevator for my secret ride to Sean's place. On the way up, I smooth my silky, red cocktail dress and reapply my lipstick. There's something about having my makeup in place that bolsters my outward confidence.

When the doors open, Walter is waiting for me.

"Good evening, Mrs. Cartwright. Mr. Cartwright is waiting for you on the balcony."

I stare daggers through him as I grit out, "I'm *not* Mrs. Cartwright."

"Forgive me. Mr. Cartwright informed me that you are now his wife. I apologize if I misunderstood." He smirks.

"It's temporary, and regardless, I'm keeping my maiden name."

"As you wish then, Ms. Upton. Please follow me."

Walter waves me onto the patio where Sean is leaning on the balcony. At the sound of my heels clicking on the tile, he turns and his eyes light up, making me feel warm and tingly.

Meeting me by the sofa, smiling broadly, Sean leans forward, kissing me on the cheek. "You look fantastic as always. Have a seat. I'll pour you a glass of prosecco."

"Thanks, I could use one. Why the hell did Walter call me Mrs. Cartwright?"

"Sorry about that. I had to share the news about our marriage with him. He can be trusted not to mention it to anyone. I suspect he was having fun with you. I'll talk with him. It won't happen again."

"It's not funny. It's ... it's horrifying." I'm not ready to share the details. But after what my mom went through with my dad, marriage is not for me. I can take care of myself.

"I know that I'm not husband material, but that's a little harsh, don't you think?" He laughs.

"I didn't mean *you* are horrifying. I was referring to the idea of marriage."

"We can agree on that," he says, handing me a glass of sparkling liquid. "Help yourself to the bruschetta. In case you have allergies, the chef insisted I tell you that the ones on the left have crispy prosciutto, ricotta, and a balsamic glaze, and the others have a mixture of shrimp, tomatoes, and basil."

"No allergies, but that was thoughtful of your chef. It looks delicious. After last evening, my plan is to eat more and drink less tonight to ensure my judgment is better."

"We've already done one outrageous thing. I'm not sure we could top it."

"Let's not find out. Speaking of our misadventure last night, it's annoying the heck out of me that I can't handle the annulment myself. I can work for a company here, at least temporarily, but as a California attorney, I cannot go to court in Nevada without teaming up with a local attorney."

"I'd be frustrated too, but my lawyer will fix it."

"What's the status? Do you have annulment papers ready for me to sign?

"Not yet. I left a message for him and sent over copies of the marriage license. We should hear something within a day or two."

"I'm surprised you didn't hear back today. Didn't you tell him how urgent this is?" I ask, trying to mask my annoyance.

"I made it extremely clear that we want this resolved quickly. Don't worry. He'll take care of it. In the meantime, let's enjoy tonight. How did the party planning go today? Did you meet with Amy?"

If he's not worried, I can let it go—or at least try—for one night. It's not a complicated legal process given that we didn't intend to marry, and both want it annulled. It should be straightened out in a couple of weeks.

Returning to Sean's questions about the party, I answer, "Amy is terrific. She had everything organized. We finalized the orders for food, beverages, décor, and setup. The party will be fantastic. Did you confirm the magician?"

"The magician will be there. Now we wait for Evan and Cassie's arrival."

"How are we going to hide our accidental marriage from them? I don't want them to know about our *mistake*. It's embarrassing."

"Excellent point. There's no real reason to hide our connection though. Let's admit to hanging out together when you were here before and say we're catching up again now. We enjoy each other's company. What's the harm in them knowing we're hooking up? It's no big deal. We just won't mention the marriage."

"That could work, assuming your staff doesn't let anything slip about the wedding. Who else knows we tied the knot?"

"The ones working the event plus Walter and Emily. Emily has already contacted the staff from last night and instructed them not to mention it to anyone. She also made sure all our photos were pulled from the digital monitors around the casino."

"A lot of people saw us on the stage though."

"The majority of those people wouldn't recognize me from that distance. Don't worry about them. We've done all we can do. In the end, it may come out. Hopefully, the annulment will happen first. No one will care then, and we won't comment on it."

"You're probably right." I shrug, reaching for an appetizer.

"To keep the party a surprise, you should come up with a reason for why you're here earlier than Cassie expects you. Have you given that any thought?"

"Fortunately, that's easy now. Cassie left a voicemail today, asking me to come to Vegas tomorrow instead of later. She wants us to catch up before she's immersed in the restaurant opening. I texted her that I'd try. I suspect Evan prodded her to issue the invitation."

"I'm sure he did," Sean says as he looks at his phone. "The show will start soon. When we finish our drinks, we should leave for the theater."

10

SEAN

Three million dollars over budget, our new *Pyrobatics Treasure Hunt* show finally received safety approval from our stage manager and opened two nights ago. Unfortunately, Emily couldn't fit it into my schedule until tonight. It'll be more enjoyable having Lowri with me anyway.

Hmm. That's an unexpected thought.

If Lowri weren't here, another pretty face would be with me. I've never had trouble attracting a desirable companion who's thrilled to enjoy a show with me. Lowri isn't one of those random women though. We have more in common than my typical hookups. She's Cassie's best friend, and we shared a long weekend together about five months ago. So, it shouldn't surprise me that I'm especially looking forward to spending time with her tonight.

That's all it is. No worries, there's not a chance either one of us will fall for each other. That's not who we are.

With that reassurance, I guide Lowri down the theater steps to our row.

"Wow. These are the best seats in the house," she says.

"They are."

"Then why are there empty seats all around us?"

"When the theater first opened, my father permanently reserved this row of ten seats and the row behind us. He insisted on seats centered in front of the stage and at eye-level with the performers."

"Why not the front-row seats?"

"He preferred these to the front row because he couldn't stand staring up at the stage all night to watch a show. He said it killed his neck, and he was happy to leave those 'horrid seats,' as he called them, for others willing to pay extra for the painful experience. He also made sure there was a walkway and low guardrail in front of these seats. Dad didn't want anyone blocking his view."

"Your Dad was not only practical, but he also knew what he was doing."

"He did. He taught me a lot."

"You still didn't explain why the other seats in this row and the one behind us are empty. Didn't anyone want them?"

"We usually give our unused seats to ultra-VIPs. I asked Emily to make sure we had these rows to ourselves tonight. I don't want strangers eavesdropping on us. It would be fodder for social media tomorrow."

"That would be a problem. You said the show is called *Pyrobatics Treasure Hunt*. What are *pyrobatics*?"

"It's a combination of the latest technology for pyrotechnics, which is effectively indoor fireworks, combined with death-defying acrobatics and music that tell a story."

"Acrobats always amaze me, and I could watch fireworks every night. The story must relate to a treasure hunt, right?"

"It does. The characters face various challenges while searching for treasure. As you'll see, the plot has a comedic element to keep it lighthearted and appropriate for audiences of all ages."

"How fun. I can't wait for it to start."

A server delivers our drinks as the lights dim. Perfect timing.

Enveloped in darkness, a deep voice booms from the speakers, "Welcome to the Grand Athena's *Pyrobatics Treasure Hunt*. The fireworks on stage are real and dangerous. Therefore, you must remain seated throughout the performance for your safety and that of those around you. Enjoy as the performers risk their lives battling obstacles while searching for lost treasure. In the end, one of you may hold the key to their dreams."

The curtain rises, and the voice fades, replaced by the rumbling thump, thump, thump of music synced to the footsteps of scantily clad performers running onto the stage. We watch as dancers grasp silks and soar into the air while acrobats build human structures and hurl themselves through rings of fire in their search for treasure that's hidden deep in a forest.

Sparklers and steam randomly pop up, causing the performers to jump, tumble, and dance around the pyrotechnic obstacles. When a performer slips from one of the silks and limps to the back of the stage, Lowri asks softly, "Is that part of the show?"

"Not sure. I'm told they have built-in missteps to show the difficulty of fortune hunting. But that guy's limp looks real," I whisper.

The show continues as performers walk on steamy hot coals, cross river rapids, and build human pyramids to climb over a stone ledge to reach the forest of fortune.

Not having seen a dress rehearsal, I was holding my breath that the show would meet my high expectations. Thankfully, it has so far. The sets and props are impressive, and the scene changes are extremely smooth, which is expected. The acrobats and fireworks are spectacular—the best I've seen. Hopefully, Dad would be proud.

As the music grows louder and ominous, a tired and bedraggled bunch of treasure-hunting adventurers traipse through a dense forest carrying bags of tools. They finally reach a windowless cabin with a padlocked steel door and unsuccessfully attempt to break it down. Losing hope, one of the performers shouts, "If only we had dynamite, we could blow open the door."

Suddenly, a spotlight shines on a woman holding a microphone. She's standing next to a man in the front row. He yells, "I have explosives," holding up red sticks marked DYNAMITE in giant letters.

The audience laughs in unison.

Leaning toward Lowri, I whisper, "This is where the audience member saves the day."

"That's what the announcer meant when he said one of us may be the key to their dreams. Is that guy part of the show?"

"No, they talk with the person sitting in a specific seat in the front row before the show starts and clue them in on their role. It's usually a VIP who wants a chance to be in the spotlight."

We watch as the woman ushers the audience member onto the stage.

"He doesn't look like a VIP. He's a little disheveled. His tie's so loose, the knot is hitting him mid-chest."

"You'd be surprised how much the VIPs let their hair down when they're here. Remember, what happens in Vegas stays in Vegas." He chuckles.

"I'm counting on it."

"Touché."

"But do you think he's been drinking a little too much?"

"He's walking fine. It shouldn't be an issue."

Once on stage, the man hands the sticks of dynamite to one of the performers who connects a fuse and sets the sticks in front of the cabin door. Everyone scurries to hide behind trees, while the guy from the audience drags the long fuse with him as he walks toward a huge tree in the middle of the stage. There must be hidden stairs on the back side because his head is gradually rising higher and higher until he reaches a platform wedged at the base of the three main branches. The platform sits ten or fifteen feet above the stage. Standing on the platform, he grasps the smaller, leaf-covered branches that form a fence around the platform to steady himself.

We see him reach forward, pulling back on an oversized lever built into one of the branches. Within seconds, an explosion of fireworks rocks the theater and smoke fills the stage.

The music soars louder and turns from ominous to jubilant as the smoke clears, revealing gold coins pouring from the cabin. The treasure hunters fill bags with their riches and, hearing the clop-clop of horses' hooves and gunshots, one shouts, "Someone's coming. Quick. Hide in the trees." They grasp dangling vines that raise them to the treetops as the curtain drops.

We join the rest of the audience in a standing ovation. I'm expecting a curtain call for the performers to take a bow. It never happens. Instead, a couple of minutes later, the lights turn on, signaling it's time for the audience to leave.

Before we have time to plan our exit, one of Athena's security team catches my eye as he approaches.

In a quiet voice, he says, "Mr. Cartwright, could you accompany me backstage? There's been an accident."

"It looked like one of the performers twisted his ankle. How can *I* help? Wouldn't it be better to call the doctor?"

"Umm, this accident is on the serious side. The stage manager insisted that we notify you," he says.

"I see. Give me a second."

Turning to Lowri, I say, "They need me backstage. Someone has been hurt."

"Oh, it must be the guy who fell from the vine," she says.

"That's my assumption. You can wait for me in your suite or my apartment. This shouldn't take long."

"If you don't mind, I'd love to come with you to see what happens backstage at one of these major productions."

"Okay. Let's find out what happened, and then I'll show you around."

11

SEAN

The month I spent working on one of the Athena's productions was one of the most enjoyable rotations Dad ever assigned me to as part of what he referred to as *my training to become him*. The enthusiasm and energy are palpable before a performance.

Even after a show, there's usually a buzz of excitement while costumes are collected, sets and props are stored, performers hustle to change into street clothes, and the various cast and crew offer their congratulations on a successful performance. It's also when VIPs holding backstage passes can meet the performers and experience a behind-the-scenes look firsthand.

Tonight is different.

Backstage, the atmosphere is sedate. It doesn't make sense. The audience enjoyed the show and laughed at the correct times. Other than a hobbling acrobat, it went off without issue. Why is everyone glum?

Reaching the stage manager, who's engrossed in a conversation with three others, I ask, "Ron, what's going on?"

When he turns to face me, his face is stricken, and he's mopping sweat off his forehead. What the hell?

"Mr. Cartwright, can we talk in private?"

Stepping away from his group, I signal for Lowri to stay close.

Noticing Ron's hesitation, I say, "Go ahead. You can say anything in front of her."

"Umm. If you're sure, sir."

"Get on with it. I don't have all night."

"I don't know how to tell you, but there's been a terrible accident."

"We saw the acrobat fall and twist his ankle. Give him the time he needs to recover and call in a backup for the show. Won't that work?"

"Yes, sir. We can use a backup for Reese. That's not the accident I meant. The audience member fell. And … and he's … umm … dead," he whispers, staring at his shoes.

A quiet gasp escapes Lowri's lips. I reach for her hand, giving it a squeeze, as I sternly ask, "What do you mean, he's dead? How could that have happened?"

"The platform he was standing on collapsed when he pulled the lever to start the fireworks. As he fell down the hole, his necktie caught on the hooked end of the lever and strangled him."

"How the hell could that happen?"

"We don't know, sir. No one heard anything. The fireworks and music were too loud. When it was time for the curtain call, the performer assigned to escort the audience member backstage couldn't find him. That's when we discovered him … umm … hanging in the trunk of the tree."

"What's his name? Where is the man now?"

"His name is Owen Brentwood. The hotel doctor came. He had us move the man and attempted to revive him."

"Did you call the police?"

"Not yet. We waited for you."

"Damn. Call them now. No one leaves or moves until they arrive. Do you hear me?" I grit out.

"Yes, sir." Ron turns to spread the word, and I hear the security guard phoning the police.

I reach my arm around Lowri's shoulder. Pulling her closer, I ask, "Are you okay?"

She nods, and with a serious tone I've never heard from her, she says, "Someone better get photos of the scene quickly. You need proof that the Athena wasn't negligent in the set design. Can we look at the tree before the police arrive?"

That's when I remember that she's a lawyer.

"We can. Are you sure you're okay seeing where the victim died?"

"This will be our only chance for a close look. After the police arrive, they won't let us anywhere near it tonight. You need to know what you're facing so your attorneys can protect you. A guest was mortally wounded on your stage. Whether you like it or not, someone will expect to be compensated. Let's go. I can handle it if you can."

"I've never seen this serious side of you."

"When it comes to legal issues, you better believe I'm serious. That's how I keep my clients out of hot water. They know they can count on me. Let's hurry. Have Ron find two pairs of plastic gloves and meet us at the tree. We need a witness to confirm we didn't tamper with anything."

My cock shouldn't be twitching now. Damn, tough Lowri is hot as hell.

12

LOWRI

Sean is pissed off that the stage manager and his team let this happen. He's ready to chop their heads off for signing off on the safety of the elevated platform wedged at the base of the three main branches of the tree. If it wasn't sturdy enough for one average-size man, then no one should have been allowed to stand on the platform.

As we walk toward the tree at the center of the stage, I quietly caution him to keep those concerns to himself until he can talk with his lawyer under the protection of attorney-client privilege. Anyone else he speaks with could be forced to share what he said if there's a lawsuit. He needs to be careful not to assume the Athena has done anything wrong until after the investigation.

He's not happy but knows his attorney would give him the same advice. He asks, "Then I shouldn't be talking to you. You're not my attorney."

"Technically, I'm not *your* attorney. There's no attorney-client privilege." Then it hits me, and I slowly say, "However, I *am* your wife. Anything we say to each other while married is privileged."

"Excellent. That's a useful twist."

"Let's get started. While we wait for Ron, we can walk around the outside of the tree. If you see anything out of the ordinary, point it out and take a photo. It could be evidence of tampering or faulty construction."

"Understood."

After making two full circuits around the tree, nothing is obvious.

"There's Ron," Sean says.

"Here are the gloves you wanted."

"Thanks. We're going to look inside. We want you to witness that we are only looking around. We're not going to move anything," I explain.

"Okay." Ron nods.

Sean and I don the plastic gloves and peer through the open doorway on the back side of the tree prop.

Despite my bravado, my stomach churns, knowing a man just died here. Closing my eyes and taking a deep breath, I muster my courage and focus on determining why the platform collapsed.

Analyzing the interior of the tree, we see that the trunk consists of a small, hollow room supported by vertical metal posts.

Turning to Ron, I ask, "What is this space used for?"

"It was designed for someone to be inside the tree when it's rolled onto the stage. That person would use an interior ladder to climb up to the platform when it was time for them to appear for an acrobatic scene. They were going to swing from the tree."

"No one was inside the tree trunk tonight, were they?" I ask.

"That's correct. We aren't using this space now. After the prop was designed, the show's producer eliminated that acrobatic scene. He replaced it with the scene where the audience member climbs an exterior ladder and sets off the final fireworks from the platform."

"How did Mr. Brentwood fall?"

"There's a trap door in the center of the platform to allow a person in the tree trunk to climb up. For some reason, the door fell open, and he dropped into the trunk.

"Where's the trap door now?" Sean asks.

"It's hanging on its hinges," Ron says, pointing to a square piece of wood dangling inside the tree.

"Why wasn't the door secured shut?" I ask.

"It was secured from below. I don't understand how this happened," Ron says.

"Could Mr. Brentwood have opened the trap door from the top of the platform?" Sean asks.

"No way. When we're using the external stairs, we secure the latch underneath. When that latch is locked, it cannot be opened from above."

"Does that mean the latch failed?" Sean asks.

"We don't know yet. We moved Mr. Brentwood, but we haven't touched anything in there."

"Sean, can you shine the flashlight from your phone up there? On the door latches," I say.

When the light hits the wood, four empty holes are visible.

I turn and whisper into Sean's ear, "Take a photo without Ron noticing. Also, take a photo of the interior floor of the tree trunk. I'll explain later."

Stepping away from the opening in the trunk, I place my hand on Ron's back, turning him toward the side of the stage as I say, "We're finished here. Ron, can you show me where the tree was kept before it was brought to the center of the stage."

By the time Sean rejoins us, the police and EMTs have arrived and taken over. Two hours later, we finally return to Sean's apartment and collapse onto the bed.

Stressed, exhausted, and sad, we lie next to each other, staring silently at the ceiling.

Eventually, sleep consumes us.

13

SEAN

"Prince Evan and Cassie—oh, I'm sorry, I mean Ms. Edwards —have arrived. Christian escorted them to the Monarch Suite five minutes ago," Emily says as she walks into my office.

Standing up, I grab my suit jacket and tuck my phone into the inside pocket. "Excellent. Time to set the rest of tonight's plan in motion."

Ten minutes later, I greet Evan with our standard brotherly hug and back slap. "Man, it's been forever. Can't you text occasionally?" I lay it on a little thick, implying we haven't talked or emailed lately. We don't want Cassie to suspect we've been planning a party.

As I'm pulling Cassie in for a welcoming embrace, Evan says, "We've been busy with my family. I'm sure you saw the news that my brother married after a dramatic set of events."

"Who didn't hear about it? Hopefully, you'll fill me in on the details that weren't in the news."

"Join us for a late breakfast while we talk. I can't wait any longer for one of the Athena's famous apricot-pecan croissants," Cassie says.

"I wouldn't mind one. They're my favorite."

Between bites, we chat about the bizarre events surrounding Evan's brother's wedding. It could be the plot for a movie where rom-com meets thriller, but they assure me it happened in real life.

"Enough about my family. What's going on here? Is it true that a guest died during a show yesterday?" Evan asks.

"I don't know how you heard about it already. Unfortunately, it is true. It was a horrendous accident." I grimace, recalling the images from last night.

"How did it happen?" Cassie asks.

"We're not sure yet. The police and the stage manager, who's in charge of safety, are investigating. The lawyers in my life don't want me talking about it at this point."

"I'm sure they don't," Cassie says.

"On a happier note, I have a surprise for you. Kai's here today and invited you to meet him this afternoon if you're available. He wants to show you around the kitchen you'll be using."

"I'd love to catch up with him and tour the kitchen. I haven't seen Kia in person since the cooking competition. We've been talking and emailing about the restaurant renovation though. He's excited about becoming your permanent chef after my month as the guest chef. Evan, would you mind if I spend the afternoon with Kai?"

"Of course not."

"Evan, if you don't have other plans, we could hit my gym while Cassie hangs out with Kai. I upgraded the equipment recently."

It's true we're going to my gym. We won't be working out though. Evan wants to speak with the magician before tonight, so we're meeting at my gym while Kai distracts Cassie.

"That would be great. What time?" Evan asks.

"Kai's expecting Cassie at 2:00 p.m. Let's meet at my apartment then."

"Perfect."

My phone buzzes.

"Unfortunately, I have a meeting now. Keep your seats and enjoy the rest of your breakfast," I say, standing.

As I'm walking to the door, I casually turn and say, "I forgot. There's a new magic show at the Olympic Torch Bar tonight. You should join me."

"I love magic. That would be fantastic, but Evan may have made other plans." Cassie stares at Evan expectantly.

"I'd made dinner reservations, but we can change them. As long as the drinks are plentiful, I'm not opposed to a magic show," Evan says, covering his mouth to hide his grin from Cassie.

"Don't worry, Athena's staff won't leave you thirsty. I'll meet you here at 7:30 p.m. tonight. We can take the Maze to avoid the crowds."

"By the way, my friend Lowri may be arriving today. Do you remember her? She was here for the dinner in the wine cave earlier this year," Cassie says.

Biting my lip, I'm not sure how much to share at this point. Deciding to keep it simple, I say, "Of course, I remember your best friend."

"If she arrives in time, is there room for her to join us at the magic show?" Cassie asks.

"Absolutely. I'll have Christian let her know about the show when she checks in."

"Thanks so much." Cassie beams.

Mission accomplished.

14
SEAN

Cassie's expecting me at their suite in ten minutes, but that was never the *real* plan. Instead, Christian will meet them, explaining that I'm running late and will see them at the magic show. That gives Lowri and me time here at the Olympic Torch Bar to oversee the last-minute party arrangements.

I'm jaded from growing up under the neon lights of Las Vegas and Dad's tendency toward perfection. However, the décor vastly exceeds even my expectations. Despite little advance warning, they've turned this place into a miniature version of the Magic Castle, an exclusive, private magic club in Los Angeles. It's dark and mysterious while still welcoming. There's even a magic word required to enter. And the lounge is buzzing with people ready to welcome Cassie back to Vegas for her month as guest chef of the Grand Athena's Pinot & Pie restaurant.

As Lowri and I do a final walk through the venue, I ask, "Have we missed anything?"

"I don't think so. Amy did an excellent job."

"You did an outstanding job too. You're the one who selected everything. Evan will be happy that it's refined and elegant. I suspect he wanted your help for fear I'd plan something less appropriate."

"He did say not to let you turn it into a frat party like you guys had in college." She laughs.

"He forgets that I'm no longer a twenty-one-year-old, but I'm not complaining that Evan arranged for you to arrive early. You've been a tremendous *partner* this week," I tease.

She playfully punches my upper arm, saying, "I'm sure you wouldn't have spent the week alone. It has been fun though, except for the end of the show last night. And of course, the marriage part. Get that fixed."

"It's under control. Emily scheduled a call with my lawyer for tomorrow morning. It will be resolved soon. There's no reason to worry."

"I know. I'm just kicking myself for not reading the forms we signed. Can you imagine the crap I'd get at my law firm for that? God, I hope they never find out."

"I doubt they will. On a lighter note, do you think Cassie will be surprised?"

"Absolutely. She'll also be a little overwhelmed that Evan did something this extravagant for her. She hasn't had a man in her life who put her first and made her feel special in a long time."

I almost miss the fleeting look of longing that passes over her face. It's swiftly replaced with her normal, cheery smile.

Amy approaches as my phone dings.

> Christian: I'm at the Monarch Suite now.
> We'll be there in less than 15 minutes.

> Me: Got it.

"They're on their way. Does everyone know what to do?" I ask.

Amy nods. "We have a lookout watching the Grand Staircase to alert us when they arrive. We're ready."

"Surprise!" we shout in unison as Cassie and Evan enter the lounge.

Cassie scrunches her eyes in the dim light, looking mystified. Evan whispers in her ear. She turns quickly, wrapping her arms around him as reality dawns that the party is in her honor.

By the time she pulls away, Lowri and I are standing in front of them. I notice Evan, giving me an odd look. That's when it hits me that my arm's wrapped tightly around Lowri's waist. It's become unconscious. When we're this close, I can't help touching her.

Cassie gasps, throwing her arms around her best friend and pulling Lowri out of my grasp.

"Lowri, you're here! I didn't know if you got my invitation to join us this weekend. Wait a minute. Were you in on this?" Cassie asks.

"This was all Evan's idea. Sean and I merely helped with the details."

Cassie met most of the party guests on her last visit to the Grand Athena. They take turns greeting her as the servers meander through the crowd handing out drinks and appetizers. We kept the group reasonably small, but there are still forty to fifty people here between the film crew, hotel staff, cooking competition judges, and even the police detective who played a role in the events that brought Evan and Cassie together.

Between the upbeat background music and chatter among the guests, the party is a success.

We've all been eating, drinking, and talking for about twenty minutes when the music grows softer, and our attention shifts to the stage where a spotlight illuminates Amy. She steps up to the microphone, saying, "Everyone, thank you for being here to celebrate Cassandra Upton's debut as guest chef of the Grand Athena's Pinot & Pie restaurant. Let's give her a big round of applause."

The crowd cheers and claps loudly.

Amy continues, "Now, it's time for tonight's entertainment. Please take your seats. The magic show starts in five minutes."

"You mean, there really is a magic show? It wasn't a ruse to get me to the party?" Cassie asks.

"Of course there's a magic show. Evan insisted on one," I say, grabbing Lowri's hand and guiding our foursome to the reserved table near the small, slightly elevated stage.

The Virtuoso of Magic doesn't disappoint. He even levitates a server while she balances a tray of drinks.

When the server is safely back on the ground and the applause tapers off, the magician says, "I'm going to need a little help from the audience for my next trick. I understand that our guest of honor tonight is Chef Cassie. Where are you?"

Lowri quickly points to Cassie, calling out, "She's here."

"Excellent. Cassie, would you be willing to assist me with the next illusion?"

She doesn't immediately react, so he says to the audience, "Let's give her a little encouragement."

Clapping and chants of "Cassie, Cassie, Cassie," follow as Evan stands to help her up.

When she reaches the stage, the magician pulls a long-stemmed, red rose from behind his back, offering it to her. "A rose for the lovely lady."

"Thank you," she replies, smiling as she sniffs the petals.

"You know, this trick will be easier with a second person. Can we talk your date into helping us out? Can you point him out to me?"

"He's over there," she says, pointing to where Evan is sitting at our table.

"Sir, would you mind joining us on the stage?"

Evan shrugs. "Why not?" He stands and walks to the stage as the crowd claps.

"Please stand facing each other about two feet apart," the magician says, and they comply.

"Evan, please hold your left arm out, palm up."

"Like this?"

"Exactly. Cassie, hold the rose in front of you in your right hand,

and please keep your eyes on Evan's left hand while everyone counts to three. Are you ready?"

"I'm ready," Cassie says, smiling with anticipation.

"Everyone, I'll need your help with counting down from three. After we reach one, we'll all shout the password you used to enter tonight. Are you ready?"

The audience murmurs a soft "Yes."

"You can do better than that. ARE YOU READY?"

A resounding "Yes!" erupts in response.

"That's more like it. Here we go. THREE! ... TWO! ... ONE! ... Shazam!"

A puff of white smoke instantly covers Evan's left palm. When it dissipates, he's holding a small, purple, velvet pillow with a large ring perched on top. In a single fluid motion, he sinks to one knee.

The audience gasps in unison.

You've got to be kidding!

My bachelor friend is proposing.

"Cassandra, when we met here about five months ago, you were unexpected. You mesmerized me and enchanted me from the first time we crossed paths. I had come here looking for something to give real meaning to my life. I didn't know if I'd find it, but I did. It's you. You fill me with love, purpose, and a path forward that I can't imagine taking without you. Will you marry me and be my princess?" Evan asks.

Cassie says, "Yes. Yes. A million times yes," as she stares at him with a look of shock, awe, and adoration.

Evan stands, sliding the ring onto her finger and pulling her in for a long kiss.

I'm still processing this totally unexpected development when the magician says, "Please join me in congratulating Prince Evan and the soon-to-be Princess Cassandra of Catalinius. Turning a lovely lady into a real princess. How's that for a little magic? I can't top that trick, so that concludes the show for tonight. Thank you for being here. I'm told a round of champagne is being delivered to everyone compliments of His Royal Highness. Enjoy the rest of your evening!"

With a big puff of smoke, The Virtuoso of Magic disappears.

Why the hell does Evan want to get married? Hell, I don't even understand why he wants to be in a relationship. That's not for me. No. Never.

Then it hits me.

Shit. I already did. I'm married to Lowri.

That doesn't count. I didn't do it on purpose.

15
LOWRI

When I run toward Cassie, a burly security guy steps between us.

"Get out of my way, you dumbass. You know damn well who I am. My best friend doesn't need protection from me. Now, move it," I demand, putting my palm on the chest of the black-suited giant, pushing him to the side and clearing my path to Cassie.

We hug and she whispers, "Pinch me. I'm not sure this is real."

"It's real. I'm incredibly happy for you. Let me see that rock he put on your hand. That's the largest, most amazing emerald I've ever seen. And those diamonds surrounding it are sparkling like mini fireworks."

"I can't believe it. It's the ring that caught my attention when Evan gave me a tour of the Royal Jewel vault. I had no idea he was planning to propose, much less this soon. I can't believe you knew and didn't give me a clue."

"Wait a minute. I didn't know. Evan only asked us to plan a party with a magician to celebrate you being guest chef here. He never even hinted that he planned to propose. I'm glad he didn't tell me. It was hard enough to keep the party a secret. I'm certain that Sean didn't know either."

"Evan is a clever one. I'm also starting to understand why his parents insisted that we travel with security. They must have been guarding this ring."

"I hate to tell you this. It's not only the ring they're guarding but also their next princess."

"That's impossible to wrap my head around."

"I have no doubt that you'll quickly adapt to your new role. You're living a well-deserved fairytale. Enjoy it."

"It's your turn next. You'll be marrying your prince before you know it."

That catches me off guard, triggering a coughing fit.

"Are you okay?" Cassie asks.

"Swallowed wrong."

Thankfully, Sean redirects everyone's attention when he joins us on stage and grabs the nearby microphone, announcing, "Everyone, raise your glasses to the newly engaged couple. May happiness always follow you. Cheers!"

When our champagne glasses are nearly empty, Evan asks, "We would love it if you two would join us for a drink in our suite. The four of us can catch up."

"Are you sure you want company now?" I turn toward Cassie with raised eyebrows.

"Come up for one drink and tell me how you planned all of this. Don't worry. Evan and I will have plenty of time to celebrate."

Sean says, "Okay, one drink. We can take a golf cart through the Maze to avoid the crowds."

Followed by the two hulky security guys, we sneak out of the party. Before we reach the hidden door to the Maze, a man I vaguely remember walks up to Sean. "Could I have a minute of your time?" he asks with a slight Southern drawl.

"Of course, Detective Fielder. What can I do for you?"

I'm close enough to overhear the detective whisper, "I wanted to give you a heads-up. While we initially believed the death last night was an accident, there were a few things that didn't make sense. We're investigating further."

"Thanks for letting me know. Keep me posted on what you learn. It's difficult to believe it was anything other than an accident though."

"We still need to tie up the loose ends to be certain."

Hmm. Something about the accident is bothering me too. I can't put my finger on it, but the police will figure it out. It's none of my business anyway.

Or is it? I'm married to the owner.

Why the hell did that thought run through my head? I'm not *really* married to Sean.

16

LOWRI

Cassie and I agreed to meet at the spa today. As much as I'm looking forward to girl time with my bestie, it's going to be awkward keeping my marital status a secret. We don't usually hold back important life events. I know—I didn't tell her about the party, but that's different.

I'm hiding my situation from Cassie for a couple of reasons. I look like a hypocrite. Marriage has always been on my never-ever list, and now here I am—married and looking foolish. It's embarrassing. She's also a lawyer. Whether she says anything or not, she'll know I should have read the papers before signing them.

All I can hope is that Cassie will be focused on her engagement instead of my love life.

Stepping into the spa's circular reception area, the peaceful indoor garden setting immediately starts to alleviate my worries. Soothing music plays in the background, interrupted only by the sound of trickling water from a cherub-topped, multi-tier fountain in the center of the room. As my eyes follow the fountain upward, they land on a domed skylight, surrounded by hand-painted clouds and birds. Green ivy trails over the edges and down the sides of each tier, and orange roses float in the water, filling the air with their fragrance. They must have trouble convincing people to leave this sanctuary.

"Good morning!" Cassie chimes from behind me.

"You're looking more rested than I would have expected after last night," I tease.

"It was an exciting evening. I still can't believe Evan proposed," she says, admiring the sparkling green ring on her left hand.

"Where's your security guard?" I ask.

"Standing outside. I tried to leave him behind completely but failed. The compromise is that he'll stay outside. I mean, how can we talk if he's listening?"

"Exactly. Now let's get our fingers and toes done."

An attendant shows us to the women's locker room and an adjacent relaxation room where we stretch out on cushy lounge chairs while we wait.

Between sips of cucumber-infused water, I ask, "Does the engagement change your plans to be the guest chef here?"

"Of course not. Why would it?"

"I'm not up on royal protocol."

"It doesn't matter. I won't do anything to embarrass the royal family, but Evan and I aren't married yet. I'm not giving up the opportunity to fulfill a lifelong dream. Thankfully, Evan doesn't expect me to."

"That's a relief. Do you know when the wedding will be?"

"We'll talk with his parents about the timing. I'm hoping you'll be my maid of honor."

"Of course, I will. Is the wedding going to be in Catalinius or San Diego?" I don't mention that if the wedding is in the next few weeks, I'll technically be her *matron* of honor. That's unlikely, I think, as I absentmindedly press my fingers against the fabric hiding the wedding ring that's hanging on the chain around my neck.

"The wedding will be in Catalinius. Princes must marry at the royal church."

"This is all extraordinary."

"It's still unreal to me too. Talking about unexpected surprises, what's going on between you and Sean? You were pretty cozy last night."

"What are you talking about?"

"I knew it."

"Knew what?"

"You're pulling on your earlobe. You only do that when you're trying to hide something from me. Spill. Now."

"It's nothing. We hooked up when I was here earlier this year. It was nothing more than a fun weekend."

"Uh-huh. You're hooking up again now, aren't you?

"Maybe."

"There's no *maybe* about it. I need details."

"We're having a little fun. I've been here a couple of days. We worked together planning your party. One thing led to another, and we decided to enjoy each other's company while I'm in town. It ends when I leave. No strings."

"If you let him see the serious side of you, it may turn into more."

"You know I'm not looking for more. Guys I date only get the fun-loving version of me. The serious side is left for work."

I've already fucked that up. Not only did I marry Sean, but also, I let him see the serious me. When we found out Mr. Brentwood was dead, I instinctively went into protective mode to look after Sean's business. Why did I do that? I've never been protective of other guys I've hooked up with.

"I know, you don't mix business and pleasure. No one sees both sides, except me."

"You know me better than anyone. We've helped each other through tough times during and after law school."

"Maybe it's time to let people, or at least Sean, know you're more than a fun-loving party girl. Not all men are your dad."

"Even if that's true, it's not worth the risk. Dad completely broke

Mom's spirit when he abandoned us. She never recovered emotionally. It destroyed her ability to love anyone."

"I know. That doesn't mean the same will happen to you. Remember, I wasn't looking for love, but it still found me."

"It did, and I'm super happy for you. So, let's concentrate on the amazing changes in your life. The next one is your restaurant opening. What type of food will be on the menu?"

"As you know, the restaurant will be called Pinot & Pie because wine and dessert are two stress relievers for me. Therefore, I was planning a wine bar vibe with upscale comfort food and fabulous desserts. But after spending time in Catalinius with Evan, I've decided to incorporate more fresh fish and vegetables into the menu for a lighter and fresher version of comfort food. Of course, we'll still have outstanding wines and scrumptious desserts. I can't wait for you to try everything. Please promise me you'll stay for the opening."

"Wouldn't miss it. I've already arranged to work from here for the next two and a half weeks. And I'm available to taste test, particularly if it involves desserts."

"Deal. By the way, you should use your influence to convince Sean to serve something other than this foul-tasting water. Does anyone actually like cucumber-flavored water? Yuck." She grimaces, shaking her head.

"Not me." I laugh.

There's yet another reason we're best friends. We don't automatically follow trends. We form our own opinions.

17
SEAN

Gabe Santini will be here in five minutes. We've been loyal friends since childhood. In those early days, we managed to get into plenty of mischief together. If one of us was caught, we never ratted out the other though. As a result, we built a strong bond of trust that's never been broken. That's the reason Gabe's my lawyer. He's the only one who I'm certain will be completely discreet in delicate personal matters, such as my accidental marriage. He'll minimize who else at his law firm knows about my situation, which adds a degree of comfort that's worth his premium billing rate.

Before the five minutes are up, Emily shows Gabe into my office. He's prompt—another plus.

"Gabe, thanks for meeting me here today. This is a matter that I'd rather not discuss at your place."

"No problem. I welcome an excuse to get out of my office."

"We should grab drinks soon. But you're charging me by the minute today, so let's get down to business. How soon will my marriage be annulled?"

"Slow down, Sean. First, tell me how you came to be married and why you want an annulment."

"Why the hell does that matter? Lowri and I want the marriage annulled."

"There are forms to fill out to justify an annulment. I can only help you if you give me the required info. Start by telling me the circumstances that led to you being married."

After sighing heavily, I go through the drunken details of the escapade with Lowri that led to us exchanging unintended vows. To Gabe's credit, he tries not to laugh. He doesn't completely succeed.

Finishing the story, I say, "My understanding is that being intoxicated is grounds for an annulment."

"That's correct. If one or both of you were intoxicated, then the marriage lacked consent and can be voided. It's not automatic. A judge must approve the annulment."

"We were both intoxicated. That should make it even easier. File the forms today."

"I don't recommend doing that."

"Why the hell not?"

"I'm sure you remember that the Grand Athena is in a trust, and you are the trustee."

"Yes. What does that have to do with annulling my marriage to Lowri?"

"When you turn 40, the ownership of the Athena will transfer to you personally, and the trust agreement will be dissolved."

"Understood, but why are we discussing the hotel's ownership? That's not why you're here."

"The ownership of the Athena will only transfer to you if you have complied with all the terms of the trust agreement. One of those terms relates to your marital status. The trust document requires that if you marry before age 40, you must remain married and live with your wife for a minimum time period before an annulment or divorce."

"You're joking, right?"

"I'm dead serious."

"What happens if I ignore that provision of the trust agreement?"

"You lose control of the Grand Athena. It will remain in trust for perpetuity. A board of directors will be formed, and the board will decide who runs the hotel going forward. That could be you or anyone else of their choosing."

"Why the hell was the trust set up that way? Why didn't I know about this part?"

"My father drew up the trust. I checked with him. He said you were given a copy of the trust document when your dad died. My father tried to explain the various terms to you. You shut him down when he brought up marriage because you never planned to tie the knot. Dad said he insisted that you still read the agreement in its entirety, specifically the marriage clause.

"I'm guessing you didn't read it because if you had, you would know about this provision. If you ever decided to marry, my father assumed you would reach out to us to prepare a prenup before taking the plunge. He would have gone over the terms with you then."

"I wasn't planning to marry. Of course I didn't read the whole damn document. It's an inch thick. I skimmed it to understand the key terms. This one must have been buried somewhere. Back to my previous question: Why include this restriction at all?"

My father said it was your dad who insisted on this term. He took marriage extraordinarily seriously and loved your mother deeply. He wanted you to find that same happiness. He didn't want you to take marriage lightly, and if you got married before 40, he wanted you to give it a real chance. Your dad wanted to require you to stay married for a year. My father talked him into a tiered, age-based scheme instead. The younger you married, the longer the marriage had to last. Since you're past 35, it's only three months. You owe my dad for that."

"Damn it. You know my dad was never the same after Mom died.

He couldn't have been thinking straight. No one in their right mind would include such a draconian requirement. You're not telling me it's enforceable, are you?"

"Actually, I am. My father's an extremely talented lawyer. It's airtight."

"Shit. So, you're saying you can't get the marriage annulled?"

"No. I'm saying that unless you're willing to lose the Athena, you'll stay married, living with Lowri, for three months. After that, we can file for an annulment. There's also something else you should know. Nevada is a community property state. That means Lowri could own half of all the assets you acquire while you two are married, unless the marriage is eventually annulled."

"Are you freaking out of your mind? We didn't even intend to get married. It was an accident," I say in shock.

"That's the law. You need to follow the rules of the trust and then get the annulment. It will be as though the marriage never happened."

"How the hell am I going to convince her to move to Las Vegas for three months?"

Gabe shrugs, saying, "The usual way. Give her something she wants. You'll come up with something. Give me a call if you need my help. Until then, I need to return to my office."

Fuck.

I've always avoided letting women get their hooks into me, and now I've not only been hooked but also been nailed to the wall. My entire future depends on convincing Lowri to help me keep my inheritance.

Wait! Does she need to know? What if I hired her as my lawyer for the lawsuits that Mr. Brentwood's family are certain to file? She said she could temporarily represent a client in Nevada.

With the help of my management team, we can insist that she work from Las Vegas until the matter is settled. She was there when the accident happened. No lawyer is better positioned to know the facts and look after the Athena's interests. It would only make sense that she stays with me while she's here. That would satisfy the term requiring us to live together. With excuses about delayed paperwork for the annulment, we can stay married for the necessary three months.

There's a problem though. If she ever finds out, she'll never forgive me for tricking her into staying married longer than necessary.

I'll tell her. Eventually. I'll just wait for the right moment.

The next step is to inform my management team that we'll be engaging Lowri's legal services.

On the one hand, I'm relieved that telling Lowri about the trust terms can wait a day or so. On the other hand, my shoulders feel the brutal weight of what's at stake. The consequences of this accidental marriage are potentially devastating.

Based on my experience, most people would think they had won the lottery if they were in Lowri's situation. Luckily, she doesn't seem the type to take advantage of me. Let's hope I'm right because otherwise, with the control that she holds over me, it will be astronomically expensive.

Shit.

18
SEAN

Gabe left me sitting here in stunned silence.

I'm in deep shit. I still can't believe that Lowri would own half of all the assets I acquire while we're married if something goes wrong with the annulment.

I better call my yacht broker and postpone my purchase until after this marriage is undone. Otherwise, I could be gifting Lowri millions with a single signature on that contract. Don't get me wrong, I like her considerably, but I wouldn't give my best friend half a yacht.

What's wrong with me? She wants the annulment as much as I do. It's all going to work out. I'll get through the next three months. If I make it easy for Lowri to stay, she should be okay with it. The plan Gabe laid out is sound. Time to execute.

> Me: How about dinner at Prime Claw
> tonight?

> Lowri: Are we celebrating the annulment?

Me: Not yet. Making progress. I'm in the
mood for seafood. Does 8 work?

Lowri: Can we make it 8:30? I have a memo
to write for work first. You can give me an
update on the progress over dinner.

Me: Deal. Meet me at the restaurant.

Lowri: Okay.

What the hell am I going to tell her about the "progress"?

The even bigger question is, what am I going to do with a wife for the next three months?

19
LOWRI

My memo is finished and emailed to the team, but I'm regretting agreeing to a fancy dinner tonight. The stress of work and the events of the last couple of days are getting to me. A pint of pralines and cream, a comfy tank top, and sleep sound much better. If I shared that guilty pleasure with Sean, it would ruin my party-girl reputation. Those nights are reserved for when I'm by myself, which is more often than most would believe.

That's fine with me. I'm alone by choice, which is far better than ending up bitter like Mom.

I could feign a headache and bow out of dinner. That would mean waiting another day to hear about Sean's meeting with the lawyer. That's not going to happen, so I splash cold water onto my face, apply my makeup, slip on a little black dress, and hurry to the restaurant.

SEAN IS WAITING FOR ME. PULLING ME INTO A GENTLE HUG, HE WHISPERS IN my ear, "You're a goddess. I can't wait to worship you later tonight."

Had anyone else said that, I'd be laughing. But he says it with such heat and sincerity that chills run down my spine.

"That's an invitation I can't resist, but food first. I'm starving."

"We'll take care of that," he says, turning to the host. "Amber, is our table ready?"

"Yes, sir. Right this way, please."

Seated in a corner booth for two, the low lights, velvety leather, and dark wood create a warm and cozy atmosphere.

"Did you and Cassie catch up with each other today?"

"We did. We went to the spa, which is out of this world, except for one thing. Cassie made me promise to tell you that we hate the cucumber water they serve."

"Why? Isn't that a spa standard?"

"It is, but we both agree it shouldn't be. They should change it to something that tastes better—perhaps orange or strawberry water."

"I'll pass that along. What did you do for the rest of the day?"

"Buried myself in work in my suite. It's a case where we're certain the former employee is faking a back injury. We're having trouble proving it though."

"What makes you think the injury isn't real?"

"This is the third company he's worked for where he claims to have been injured during the first month on the job. The coincidences are becoming too frequent to believe, and he can't point to a specific accident where it happened. That makes it suspicious. If he's in pain, he deserves compensation. If not, it's fraud."

Why am I sharing work-related stuff with Sean? I don't do that. Business and pleasure are meant to be kept separate in my world. Time to change the subject.

"Let's not talk about work. What are we having for dinner?" I ask.

"The chef is preparing a tasting menu for us. He'll be out to explain it in a minute. While we're waiting, can I ask a favor?"

"What's that?"

"I'd like to hire you as the Athena's attorney to handle any legal issues related to Mr. Brentwood's accident. Will that work?"

"What? Why me? You have a whole stable of lawyers on call."

"This is different." He shrugs.

"How could this possibly be different?" He's not making any sense.

"You were there, which means you have firsthand knowledge of the accident scene. Your instincts to investigate and protect my business kicked in automatically. You were impressive. I trust you to look after my best interests."

"I see." I turn my head, staring into space, considering whether I'd be allowed to take on the case. Even though I'm his wife, it should be fine. I don't know if it would be wise though.

The tap, tap, tap of Sean's finger against the table interrupts my thoughts. Is he nervous about my answer? Does he feel obligated to ask me to help but hopes I'll turn him down?

After a couple of minutes, I meet his eyes, shaking my head. "I can't do it. You should find someone else."

"What do you mean? Of course you can do it. I assumed you would jump at the chance to have the Athena as a client."

"I didn't mean that I'm not qualified to do it. I don't have time. My work for other clients is already keeping me ridiculously busy."

"Your firm has an abundance of attorneys who can help with that work. Bringing in the Grand Athena as a client would be great for your career. It would certainly impress the partners at your law firm. Teaming up would be a win-win for both of us."

I pause before conceding, "It could be."

Why does Sean look relieved?

20
SEAN

This doesn't make sense. There's no reason for her to be hesitant.

Regardless, it's time to seal this deal, so I press forward. "Please, do this for me. There's no question it will be beneficial for both of us." If she only knew what's at stake for me. Ironically, I'm leery of her finding out.

"It *is* within my area of expertise. Plus, you're correct that bringing in the Athena's work would grab the law partners' attention. There's one problem. I'm still not sure we should entangle our lives further, but if you sincerely want me to, I'll do it."

She agreed, so I'm not going to worry about what's going through her head. There *is* one more condition to weave into the deal.

"I do. Thank you. It's a relief to know that you've got my back on this. Having you here will make it much easier to deal with the repercussions of the accident."

Her head whips around. "You expect me to stay in Las Vegas while I work on this?"

"It makes sense. The witnesses are all here. The accident took place at the Athena, and the prop that caused the accident is on our stage. Also, any lawsuit will be filed in Las Vegas. This is where settlement negotiations will take place."

"I can't argue with those points, but there's no need for me to stay here full time. I can fly over for settlement negotiations or court dates."

"For now, it will be simpler for you to be on site. You already have a place to stay. It'll be convenient for both of us. You won't be here long if Mr. Brentwood's family is reasonable. My preference is to reach a settlement as soon as possible. I'd rather not rack up enormous attorneys' fees for the next year or two when it appears the Athena needs to compensate Brentwood's estate for the accident."

"Agreed. I could stay a little longer to interview everyone, take another look at the tree, and reach out to the family to offer a settlement. Who knows, we may wrap this up quickly."

"Let's hope so."

Just not too quickly. Three months will be perfect.

"I'd like to tour the stage again and interview some of the performers."

"I'll have Emily take care of everything. She'll contact you to coordinate."

"There's one more thing. I don't mix business and pleasure," Lowri says with a look of determination.

"Understood. Neither do I typically. From here on, when we meet with anyone relating to the accident, we'll keep it completely professional. No PDA."

"I meant that I separate business and pleasure completely. We'll need to quit spending our nights together."

Shit! I didn't see that coming. That won't work. The trust requires us to live together.

Concealing my panic, I calmly ask, "Why?"

"When I'm working, I become extremely serious. I'm not the all-smiles, fun-loving woman you've been spending time with. I can't rapidly switch between those states of mind when dealing with you.

Besides, clients expect their attorneys to be serious all the time, so I've made it a point never to date anyone involved in my work. Our play time together is ending anyway. This is the perfect time to make that break."

The glimpses she's shown me of her so-called serious side are actually rather hot but sharing that won't help. We're not in a real relationship.

Taking my time before answering, I question whether to play the card I'm holding. It's my best option, so I proceed.

"I understand. Of course, you won't always be in fun mode. I want you to focus on my work when necessary. However, when we're not working, let's enjoy each other until our marriage is properly annulled. At your request, we *did* agree to be monogamous."

I wouldn't break my promise not to cheat regardless. The problem is that my father handcuffed me with a brutal trust provision. That requires pulling out all the weapons to ensure she lives with me for the next three months—even if it means reminding Lowri of her request.

"You spoke to the lawyer today. How long did he estimate it would take?"

"It's a straightforward process. He's starting the paperwork. A judge must sign off on it, and he doesn't know exactly when that will happen. It should be soon."

Three months will fly by, won't it?

"Did he think getting a judge's approval will be difficult?" she asks.

"He said it shouldn't be. Can we agree to continue sharing our nights while we wait? It will be easier on both of us."

"We could take care of ourselves. Are you saying that's not an option?"

"Not exactly. We already agreed to stay together until the annulment goes through. It'll be enjoyable for both of us. Besides, it's not for long. Why not?"

"I won't argue that it would be more pleasurable, and we are technically married. Okay. We can keep our arrangements the same while we're married."

"Deal. The chef's headed our way. Let's see what he has on the menu for us tonight," I say, lifting my glass for a long swig of Macallan to disguise my relief.

Damn. That plan almost backfired.

21

SEAN

Emily knocks on my office door, distracting me from thoughts of Lowri. I'm thankful for the interruption because it's time to get my head back into the game rather than dwelling on what I'd rather be doing with her.

"Sean, Detective Fielder is here. He insists on speaking with you."

"What's he doing here?"

"He wouldn't say. I can ask again."

"Never mind. Send him in," I sigh.

Just what I needed today—a visit from a homicide detective. That can't be good.

"Detective, come in and have a seat. I'm surprised to see you. How can I help you today?"

"Mr. Cartwright, thank you for meeting with me. I'm sorry to bother you unannounced, but our investigators have been looking into Mr. Brentwood's death. They've asked me to take over."

"What exactly does that mean?"

"As you know, his death may not have been an accident."

"That's not what I was hoping to hear," I say.

"The evidence requires further investigation. You see, there's a latch that locks the hatch door in the tree platform in place, but the latch failed.

"That sounds like an accident to me."

"The problem is that all four screws securing the latch fell out at the same time. We found them lying on the floor of the tree. That's suspicious. It may be nothing, but we're looking into it."

"Were the holes for the screws stripped, or were the screws too small? Or was Mr. Brentwood too heavy for the platform?"

"We don't think it was any of those issues. The holes for the screws were fine. In fact, when they put the screws back in, they held. The investigators even had an officer much larger than Mr. Brentwood stand directly on top of the platform's hatch. No problem. The hatch held his weight."

"Then why did the hatch drop open during the performance?"

"We've come up with two theories. Someone may have forgotten to put the screws in the latch to begin with or didn't tighten them enough. The hatch door fit snuggly in the opening. If no one stood on it, the door would stay in place regardless of whether the screws were securely in place. The other theory is that someone purposefully removed the screws. If that happened, we could be looking at carelessness or murder, depending on why the screws were removed."

"It's still probable that it was an accident, don't you agree?" I blow out a sigh of relief.

"Yes, but we're concerned that so many people on the show have been injured. We wouldn't expect that many accidents."

"Accidents? I'm not aware of any except for the performer who sprained his ankle."

"Yes, we interviewed that guy. His name is Reese. He complained about the production being unsafe. He said his ankle and the death were part of a lengthy list of accidents."

"What the hell? Why haven't I heard about them."

"Prior to the death, the accidents were likely minor and didn't merit your attention."

"Recurring problems should always be brought to my attention," I say, turning my head to stare out the window as my fists clench.

What is wrong with my employees? They never would have let down Dad like this. I may be young, but I'm not merely a trust-fund figurehead. I've worked a rotation in every damn department in this business. Dad made sure I learned the ropes firsthand to be ready to take over. Will our staff ever show me the respect and loyalty they showed Dad?

I'm not merely frustrated. I'm furious. If the production isn't safe, I should have been informed, and the show should never have opened. I can't believe my trusted stage manager would put people at risk. Not securing the hatch door with screws is beyond careless. On the other hand, if someone intentionally removed the screws to work on the hatch, did they forget to put them back? Or was it malicious?

One way or another, I'll find out what happened.

As I'm about to ask a question, my head of security, Daniel, pops his head into my doorway. "Mr. Cartwright, do you have a minute? Oh, I'm sorry. I didn't know the detective was here. Do you need my help with anything?" he asks Detective Fielder.

"Not now. I was updating Mr. Cartwright on the investigation into Mr. Brentwood's death. If you run across any new evidence though, be sure to contact me."

"Will do."

"Daniel, are you here to give me an update on your side of the investigation?"

"No. I wanted to let you know that the guys who were monitoring security footage caught something unusual on one of the video screens. I can come back later if you prefer."

"That's okay. Let's deal with it now. What did they see?"

"A couple of the Rossi family's guys were talking to an Athena employee outside a back entrance near the parking garage. It didn't look like a friendly conversation."

"How do you know it was an employee?"

"He was carrying a blue keycard. Those are only issued to employees."

Damn. Just what I need—the Vegas mafia involved with someone who works for the Athena. The Rossi family should know better than to mess with me. Our families have had a standing agreement for forever. Why break it now—particularly when my college friend, Paxton Rossi, has taken over as head of the family?

"Have you spoken with the employee?" I ask.

"No. That's the problem. We don't know who it is yet."

"What do you mean? You have him on video," I say through gritted teeth.

"The man had his back to the camera, and after they finished talking, he walked away. He didn't enter the building or the parking garage, so we can't see his face. The only way we know he's an employee is that we got a quick glance at the blue keycard in his hand. Those color video cameras we installed are paying off."

My anger is rising higher as I bark, "Find out who it is. Now! I won't have the mafia anywhere near my business. Do you hear me?"

"Loud and clear, boss. Don't worry. We'll find out who he is and kick him out the door," Daniel says, saluting me as he walks away.

"The organized crime guys can check it out for you," Fielder offers.

"Let's hold off on that option for now. "We'll figure out who the guy is and fire him. He'll be banned from ever setting foot on this property again. That should take care of it. If not, I'll let you know."

"Okay. I'll keep you posted on what we find out in the Brentwood matter."

"Thanks. My attorney is also looking into the accident. Her name's Lowri Upton. She's Cassie's friend. You met her earlier this year at the Guest Chef Competition dinner."

"I remember her. She's quite attractive. I didn't realize she was your lawyer."

"She wasn't then. We recently hired her to represent us in the legal issues surrounding Mr. Brentwood's accident."

"I see. If she's going to be around for a while, I wouldn't mind asking her out. Could you put me in touch with her?"

"She's not available," I declare, staring holes through him for even having that thought.

Hands up in surrender, he says, "Sorry, man. I didn't know you were involved with her."

"It's not like that. She's ... never mind. Just leave her alone."

He chuckles. "No problem. Message received. I promise to stay away unless we're talking about the investigation, okay?" he asks as he's leaving.

"Sure," I grumble.

I'll be around for those talks. Lowri doesn't need his attention.

Feeling a little possessive, are we? Shit. What's happening to me?

"Emily, get in here," I yell.

"Yes, sir. What do you need?"

"Set up a meeting for me with Paxton Rossi. ASAP."

Her eyes go wide, shoulders tense, and the writing pad she's holding drops to the floor with a thud.

"Are you alright?" I ask in a calmer voice, watching her retrieve the notepad.

Without looking at me, she says, "I never expected that name to be spoken here."

"I gather you're familiar with the Rossis?"

"Isn't everyone who's spent time working in Vegas?"

"That's true. Don't panic though. I'm not in business with him in any way. Among other things, I want to remind him to keep his employees away from the Athena. Do you know how to get in touch with his assistant?"

"I can figure it out. Where are you meeting?"

"Somewhere neutral."

Strangely, her shoulders relax, and she lets out a sigh, saying, "I'll take care of it now."

As she walks out the door, I wonder why she had such a strong reaction to the Rossi name. Perhaps learning that her boss is meeting with the head of a mafia family shocks her.

Emily's reaction is the least of my concerns, considering my unintended marriage, a dead guest, a series of unexplained accidents, and now the mafia on my doorstep. I'm afraid to think what's next.

22

LOWRI

Emily sent a security guard to escort me this morning. I'm thankful for the company when we walk into the desolate theater. Alone, it would be spooky.

The darkness is broken by spotlights softly illuminating the row of seats where Sean and I sat during the show. We decided that would be the perfect location to hold the individual meetings, so he had Emily arrange for lighting.

Leaving the guard near the entrance, I weave my way to the lighted row. Facing the dimly lit stage, I replay the mesmerizing performance in my head. My body shivers, remembering the moment we learned about the tragic accident.

With the show temporarily closed, the managers and crew have time to address safety concerns. They also cancelled rehearsals until the investigation is complete. That means only a handful of people are working in the theater today. Fortunately, Emily arranged for the ones on my list to be here.

My first meeting is with the lead female performer, Amelia.

"Ms. Upton, is that you?" a woman's voice asks from behind me.

Turning, I say, "Yes, I'm Lowri. You must be Amelia. Please join me and have a seat."

"Okay. They said you wanted to ask me questions about the other night."

"Yes. I'm one of the attorneys for the Athena. I'm investigating Mr. Brentwood's death."

"I didn't see what happened."

"Understood. Will you answer a few questions anyway?"

"Sure."

"Do you mind if I record our conversation? I'll use it to make notes later." Technically, I don't have to ask in Nevada. Unlike California, if one person consents—namely me—that makes it okay. I want Amelia to be comfortable though.

"No. That's fine."

"Did you notice anything different during that performance compared to the first two nights of the show or the rehearsals?"

"Everything went as usual, except it was the first time we used the tree to set off the fireworks."

"What do you mean? I understood that the show had opened two nights before?"

"It had, but the tree wasn't ready. During the earlier performances, the audience member stood on stage with the performers and pretended to light a fuse with a match."

"I see. Why couldn't you use the tree?"

"We'd had a few mishaps during rehearsals. The prop guys were unwilling to use the tree until they were certain it was safe. I heard Ron pressuring them to make sure it was onstage the night Mr. Brentwood died."

"Why that night?"

"Because Mr. Cartwright would be attending."

"Oh. Do you think they cut corners, and the tree still wasn't ready?"

"I don't know what to think. Clearly, there was a problem with the tree that night, but it wasn't what we thought was broken. We thought the control lever for setting off the fireworks wasn't working. We hadn't heard about any problems with the hatch door in the platform. We've had so many mishaps that I'm starting to believe the show is jinxed."

"What other mishaps?"

"The first accident was when the fireworks went off at the wrong time, burning the leg of one of the dancers. Another day, a dancer slipped on an oily spot on the stage and hurt her shoulder when she fell. Those are the only accidents that I witnessed firsthand. I've heard about others."

"What else did you hear about?"

"I heard that the fake rock wall fell, and a bunch of performers landed on top of each other. The makeup crew said they spent forever covering up the resulting bruises. Then Reese messed up his ankle the same night that Mr. Brentwood died. He said the silk that he was supposed to climb gave way, causing him to fall."

"Is it common to have this many *issues* in a show?"

"There are always a few snags but not like this, particularly when it's a high-end show."

"Do you think they were all accidents, or do you suspect someone has been trying to sabotage the show?"

"Before the last one, each accident seemed minor. Together, they start to add up, particularly given what happened to Mr. Brentwood."

"Right. Has anything else happened that you considered out of the ordinary?"

"No. Oh, wait a minute. There was one odd thing. During a dress rehearsal, one of my costumes was filled with pins that left me with pricks all over."

"Ouch! Were the pins left in after alterations?"

"That's what was strange. The woman who does our fittings swore she hadn't done any alterations because the costume was perfect the last time that I tried it. That incident gave me nightmares. I woke up the next morning in a sweat having dreamed I was a voodoo doll, and someone was repeatedly poking me with pins. Remembering it makes me cringe," she says, wrapping her arms around herself in a hug.

"That's horrible," I say as chills run down my spine.

With a nervous laugh, she says, "No kidding. I didn't sign up for costume acupuncture or the nightmare." Looking down to check her smartwatch, she says, "I have to leave for another appointment. Is there anything else I can help with before I go?"

"That's all for now. I appreciate your time. Hopefully, the show will be up and running again soon. Where can I find the person in charge of props?"

"That would be Kenny. He's our prop master. Follow me, and we'll find him."

Amelia shows me around backstage as we search for Kenny. After a few minutes, we spot him on the catwalk high above the stage.

"Hey, Kenny. Do you have a minute? Can you come down? The hotel's attorney needs to ask you some questions," Amelia shouts.

He calls down, "Sure. Be there in a minute."

"Good luck figuring out what happened. The show needs to reopen soon, or else a bunch of people will be out of work," Amelia says, a frown darkening her face.

"We're doing our best. Before the show starts up again, Mr. Cartwright needs to make sure it's safe." That means figuring out why there have been so many mishaps, including the ultimate tragedy that befell poor Mr. Brentwood.

The prop master arrives as Amelia exits the stage, waving a quick goodbye.

"Kenny, I'm Lowri. Is there somewhere we can talk?" I ask as we shake hands.

"Sure. Let's go to my office."

As I'm following him across the stage, we walk around a cart with several long sashes and various hardware. I stop, asking, "Kenny, are these the sashes the acrobats use?"

He returns to the cart, saying, "They're called aerial silks. And yes, those are for the acrobatics."

"Mr. Cartwright and I noticed one of the performers hurt his ankle during the show. What happened? Was there a problem with his aerial silk?"

"That was Reese. He messed up his ankle when his silk tore. He was furious."

"What happened?"

"He's over there. You should ask him. Hey, Reese, come here for a minute."

"What's up, Kenny?"

"This is Lowri Upton. She's an attorney investigating the accidents we've had. She wants to ask you questions about when the silk ripped during the last show."

"Okay," he says skeptically.

"Nice to meet you, Reese. Where did the silk tear? At the top?"

"No. For that scene, the silk is rigged with a loop at the bottom where I put my foot. The loop ripped open. It caught me off guard. I tried to hold on with my hands, but I slipped before my grip took hold."

"How did it tear?"

"I don't know. The rigging specialist inspects the silks before each show. Originally, I assumed the silk caught on something sharp, but no one has found anything that could have snagged it. I wonder if someone messed with the silk on purpose."

"Kenny, is that what you think?"

"Of course not. The silk likely had a weak spot or tiny tear that the rigging specialists missed."

Fisting his hands at his side, Reese says in a slightly raised voice, "They are professionals. They wouldn't miss anything that important. Besides, it's my life on the line, so I double-check my equipment. It was fine before the performance."

"From a distance, your silk looked like a vine. Was it one of these?"

"Vines were intertwined with a silk for that scene," Reese explains.

"I see. Could the leaves have hidden a weakness?"

"No. If you don't have any other questions for me, I'll get back to work. I'm rechecking all my silks," Reese says.

"That's all. Thanks for your time," I say.

"Kenny, how can you prevent accidents in the future?"

"I'll have a second rigging specialist double-check every silk during the rigging. It'll slow down the setup, but I can't afford another fall. Reese was lucky he only dropped about two or three feet. It would have been much worse if he'd been higher when the silk tore," Kenny says.

I shiver at how close we came to two dead men that night. That brings me back to the main reason I'm here. "Is the tree still backstage, or did the police take it as evidence?"

"It was too large for them to haul away, so they wrapped it in crime scene tape."

"That's too bad. I hoped you could demonstrate exactly how it was supposed to work."

"I can point out the general idea from the outside. Follow me."

"Thanks. Why didn't you use the tree during the first two nights of the show? Was there a problem with the hatch door or the platform where the audience member was supposed to stand?"

"No, that wasn't the issue. There was a wiring issue that prevented the lever from setting off the fireworks. We gave up on troubleshooting it and completely rewired it the morning of the show you saw. That fixed it."

"Had you tested the platform?"

"Of course. We had been on and off the platform several times that day. There wasn't anything wrong with the platform."

"Then how did the trap door in the platform fall open when Mr. Brentwood stood on it?"

"I have no idea. I've been racking my brain trying to figure it out."

"Have you inspected the interior of the tree? The night of the accident I saw several screws on the inside floor of the tree trunk. Could they have fallen out under Mr. Brentwood's weight?"

"No. The platform was built to withstand several times his weight."

"Is it possible that not all of the screws were installed in the first place?"

Kenny's demeanor turns from friendly to gruff in an instant. "How dare you accuse me of running a shoddy operation here. I'll have you know my crew and these props are top-notch. We take safety seriously. The door in the platform was properly installed and secured," he growls.

"I didn't mean to question the professionalism of you or your crew. We're all human, and sometimes people forget things or make mistakes."

"We don't make that kind of mistake. People's lives are at risk here. I'd swear on my grandmother's grave that there was nothing wrong with the tree when we inspected it that afternoon."

"Are you saying that someone sabotaged it?"

"I'm saying it wasn't me or my crew. You can draw your own conclusions. I need to go now."

That was an adamant denial of fault. What about all the other mishaps Amelia mentioned? Are they all random accidents rather than safety failures? Or is sabotage to blame?

Hopefully, the stage manager can shed more light on the situation.

Nope. Twenty minutes later, I still don't know much more. Ron was understandably upset about what happened and had trouble discussing it. He blames himself for Mr. Brentwood's death because it occurred during one of his productions. He's beating himself up over it.

I'd hoped Ron would have an explanation for all the injuries and issues during rehearsals. Instead, he chalked them up to bad luck, carelessness by performers, and snags in perfecting a complicated production. As for the tree prop, he's convinced the latch was defective and wants to sue the manufacturer. When pushed for his reasoning, he didn't have any support. His theory is pure speculation.

Bottom line: I know more than before the interviews. However, my list of unanswered questions is longer. Most importantly, why are so many performers suffering unexplained injuries?

I'll listen to the recordings on my phone and type up notes. Then I'll talk to Sean.

23
SEAN

Finally escaping my office around 7:00 p.m., I expect to find Lowri in my apartment. Instead, I'm met with silence. While that was my comfortable, pre-Lowri norm, today it's unsettling. I've quickly become accustomed to her cheerful presence. Extracting my phone from the inner pocket of my jacket, I quickly send a text.

Me: Where are you?

Lowri: In my suite typing notes from my interviews.

Me: Come on up. Let's talk about what you learned. I have new info to share too.

Lowri: Sounds good. Do you have any snacks? I'm starving.

Me: I have plenty to fill you up.

Lowri: You're such a comedian tonight. I need actual food.

> Me: Couldn't resist. Don't worry. I'll order snacks. We can't have you losing your strength this early in the evening.

> Lowri: You're too much. Give me 10 minutes.

I was only half-joking. She'll need her strength for the evening I've planned. Food is easy though. One of the advantages of living in a high-end hotel is the twenty-four-hour room service.

Order placed, I change into khakis. As I'm pulling on a knit shirt, I hear the elevator from Lowri's suite open.

"Sean, where are you?" she asks as the doorbell rings.

"Lowri, that should be the food. Walter has the night off. Can you let them in? I'll be out in a second."

"No problem."

When I emerge from my bedroom a couple of minutes later, Lowri is already moaning over a mouthful of truffle macaroni and cheese. She didn't even bother to sit down. I knew she would enjoy comfort food.

Wrapping my arms around her waist and pulling her back against me, I joke, "I'm the only one who should elicit those sounds from you."

"You're on a roll tonight with the teasing." She laughs.

"I can't help it when I'm around you. My mind wanders elsewhere."

"So do your hands. Is it your mind or your cock that's in charge?"

"Both. But I'll be good and let you take in a little nourishment while we share what we've learned today. Then I have a surprise for you."

"If I've seen it before, is it really a surprise?"

"Very funny. I'm referring to a real surprise. Now let's talk about your interviews. How did they go?"

With the tragedy, we've quickly fallen into the "Tell me about your day" marriage routine. Surprisingly, my stress level is lower after talking with Lowri—never expected that.

After summarizing her meetings with Amelia, Kenny, Reese, and Ron, she asks, "How was your day?"

"Infuriating. Detective Fielder stopped by to tell me they aren't sure Mr. Brentwood's death was an accident. Then as an aside, he mentioned that there had been several unexplained *accidents* during rehearsals for the show. Unbelievably, that was the first time I'd heard about them. My staff hadn't mentioned a single one. Do you know how embarrassing that was, not to mention upsetting? Hell, you just said the performers discussed the accidents with you today. Why hadn't one of my employees brought the incidents to my attention?"

"You should have been told. I could understand not mentioning one or two minor incidents. However, if someone is burned on the stage, that should escalate to your level."

"I'd expect to hear about that the day it happened."

"Exactly. Do you remember the guy who limped off stage during the performance?"

"Yes. It looked like he sprained his ankle. Regrettably, dancers are always pulling muscles and twisting joints. I don't expect to hear about those injuries unless it's serious."

"That's not what happened to Reese. His aerial silk tore, causing him to fall."

"No way. The rigging specialists are extremely diligent about inspecting the silks. The performers' lives depend on them."

"He swears the silk was fine when it was rigged."

"You spoke with him?"

"Yes. He didn't say it explicitly, but it's clear he suspects sabotage."

"We've never had these problems in prior shows. We have to figure out what's happening."

"What's going on with the police investigation? Why do they think it wasn't an accident?"

I share what Fielder told me and add, "Even in light of that conversation, it appears more likely than not that Mr. Brentwood's death was unintentional."

"True, but something still seems off to me."

"What's bothering you?"

"It's a nagging feeling that I'm not connecting some facts together. Do you know if there is video from the night Mr. Brentwood died?"

"They usually record the shows, and the theater is filled with security cameras. What are you looking for?"

"I'm not sure. I'd like to watch the portions leading up to the two incidents to see if anything looks out of place."

"I'll let Daniel know tomorrow. He can set up the replays for you."

"Would the cameras have recorded the accidents that occurred during rehearsals? If so, I'd like to see those as well. Those videos could help solve the mystery behind the injuries."

"During a rehearsal, people are constantly moving, which would trigger the motion-activated cameras. We have some on stage and backstage that would have been recording during rehearsals. It depends on when the accidents happened as to whether we still have those video files. The IT team deletes them regularly to save disk space. If Rob can pinpoint when the incidents occurred, Daniel can have his team check."

"Can you ask Rob now? Unless the police made IT save the videos, the files could be deleted at any time."

"I'll text him."

"Also, I've been wondering how the audience member was selected. You said something about it being the person in a particular seat, didn't you?"

"That's correct."

"Is it always the same seat? If so, is that seat available for anyone to purchase, or is it given to VIPs?"

"I'm sure that it depends on the night. Why?"

"I'm wondering whether Mr. Brentwood selected the seat not knowing he'd be invited on stage or was he given the ticket because he's a VIP?"

"He's not a VIP. I already checked. I don't know how he ended up in that seat. I'll look into that tomorrow. Now, it's time for that surprise I promised. Should we walk or ride?"

"How far is it?"

"A block or two down the Strip."

"Definitely walk. I've been cooped up forever. Breathing fresh air would be heavenly. First, I'll pop downstairs to my room and change into lower-heeled shoes."

"I didn't know you owned any."

"Don't worry. They still have red soles."

"I should have known. You're always the pillar of fashion."

"Look who's talking. I rarely see you wearing anything other than a suit with French cuffs, perfectly arranged."

"There's nothing wrong with dressing for success. Let's go find your walking shoes. Tomorrow you should have Jenny move the rest of your clothes up here."

"We'll see. By the way, is there any news on our annulment?"

"Apparently, Nevada treats annulments seriously. While you can get married easily, there are more hoops to jump through to untie the knot, but don't worry. My attorney will get it done. Let's give him a little time. The judges' calendars are likely full, and annulments aren't their top priority. Who knows, it's possible the judges take their time hoping couples will change their mind."

"No way. I know the process for marrying is faster than that for an annulment. This is still slow. I should talk to this attorney myself. Are you sure he knows what he's doing?"

"I'm certain he's got this under control. He knows we both want the marriage to end. He'll take care of it. We need to be patient a little longer."

"I swear if he doesn't give us an update showing progress by next week, we're both going to meet with him."

"We'll deal with that another day. Tonight let's find you that fresh air and have fun. Does that work for you?"

"Absolutely."

What was I thinking? I never walk down the Strip for security reasons. As the owner of the Athena, the possibility of being kidnapped is a real threat. But there's no turning back now. I loved the smile on Lowri's face when I offered a walk. Grabbing my phone, I text security. They can assign someone to follow us.

It will be fine.

24
LOWRI

Nothing compares to the electric vibe of the Las Vegas Strip at street level. At night it's beyond spectacular. Tourists from around the world fill the sidewalks as we pass from city to city and country to country. Where else can you find Paris across the street from New York City, Monte Carlo, and Italy?

It's like we're all actors on a movie set where anything can happen. My point is proven as we approach a small crowd. I do a double take to make sure my eyes aren't deceiving me. Everyone is watching a woman in a skintight, black leather bodysuit using a crop to spank a bent-over middle-aged man. His wife, laughing uncontrollably, is filming it with her phone while encouraging the woman with chants of "More, more, more."

"*What happens here stays here* probably doesn't apply given all the phone cameras aimed in his direction," I whisper to Sean.

"Vegas is still a place where your fantasies can come true without being judged. Everyone needs a little of that. I suspect that couple will have a great evening."

"I agree. We all need a little fantasy in our lives, but next time I'll try not to get married," I joke.

"Marriage hasn't been that bad, has it? I'm enjoying it so far."

My head jerks to face him. "You're not suggesting we stay married?" I gasp.

"Of course not. It was a compliment. I always thought that having someone around for an extended time would be suffocating, but it's been the opposite with you. We're having fun and you've had my back during the catastrophe with the show. Don't get me wrong. We both know this is temporary, which is the way we want it. But it'll be strange when you go. I'll miss you."

Wow. The way he's staring directly into my eyes, it's clear he's being sincere.

I've been extremely careful not to share this much of my life with any man before. It's too risky. He's right though. Our *whatever-it-is* has been comfortable, and it's been heaven waking up next to him each morning, spooned against his warm body.

After a moment of silence, I say, "We've both acclimated to the unforeseen circumstances better than expected. I'm enjoying our *short* time together."

Ouch. I didn't mean for my words to sound that formal and stilted. His comments caught me off guard. I'm not used to a man divulging warm and fuzzy feelings. I didn't know what to say, so instinctively, my protective walls went up. Too late now.

A brief sadness haunts his eyes. It disappears quickly as he says, "Good. I'm glad we're on the same page. We better hurry if we're going to make it to your surprise in time."

With his arm on my back, Sean and I fall into sync with the parade of people.

"Let's weave our way toward the outer edge of the sidewalk so we can cross the street up ahead. That will also give you a better view of the hotels across the street," he says.

I nod and edge to the right, snaking between the tourists.

Reaching the crosswalk, the light turns red, so we stop. I close my eyes, taking a deep breath and exhaling slowly. Whew. The fresh air is invigorating.

Leaning into Sean and wrapping my left hand around his upper arm, I say "It's wonderful to be outdoors. The all-encompassing indoor life in Vegas captured me. Days passed without me seeing the real sun or night sky, much less inhaling any natural air."

"With the exhaust fumes on the Strip, I'm not sure how *natural* the air is, but you're correct. People are drawn to stay indoors. That's the goal. We prefer that the guests remain inside the hotels and casinos, spending money and having fun."

"That's fine if you're only here for two or three days, but *you* live here. Don't you crave time outdoors?"

"You make it sound like I'm a prisoner in my own hotel. I promise that's not the case. Take tonight for instance—we're not trapped inside." He laughs.

Whoosh!

"Ouch!" I scream as my arm is yanked forward. I try to pull back. I'm not strong enough.

Sean yells, "Let go of your purse," as he pulls me away from the street and into his arms.

My eyes follow a guy on a moped, zigzagging his way between cars. A big guy with an Athena baseball cap runs after the moped. The maneuverability of the two-wheeled vehicle allows the thief to disappear quickly, and my purse vanishes with him.

"Sweetheart, you're shaking. Are you hurt?" he asks, holding me tight against his chest.

At his voice, I tilt my head upward. Between gasps for breath, I whisper, "My arm hurts."

"Let me look at it," he says, trying to pull away. I clutch his shirt as if my life depends on having his warmth.

"No. Please hold me."

Returning one hand to my back, he strokes my hair with the other as I tuck my head under his chin, nestling closer, if that's even possible.

I softly say, "That was scary. He could have pulled me into traffic. I could have been run over." My whole body shivers at the thought, and a tear runs down my cheek. Why am I crying in front of Sean again? I'm better at controlling my feelings than this.

"I've got you. You're okay. I wouldn't have let that happen."

"Who was the Good Samaritan who tried to chase the thief down?"

"That was Max. He's on my security team. That may not be true much longer though. His only job was to make sure we were safe."

"You had someone following us?"

"It's a standard precaution when I'm in crowds. It's usually not an issue. Tonight was the exception. Max should have stayed closer. I shouldn't have let you stand next to the street. I'm sorry, sweetheart."

"Sean, none of this is your fault." I wrap my arms around him, closing my eyes.

As Sean continues stroking my hair and tenderly kissing the top of my head, my pulse rate starts to slow. A calmness begins to settle over me.

At the sound of heavy breathing next to us, my eyes fly open and my body tenses, sensing danger.

Relief floods through me when I see that it's Max returning from chasing the thief.

"Max, you were supposed to be protecting us. What the hell?" Sean asks.

Trying to catch his breath, Max says, "I'm sorry, Mr. Cartwright. The moped came out of nowhere, and the rider grabbed her purse while speeding by. There wasn't time to stop him."

"Did you get the number on the license plate?" Sean asks.

"No, sir. The plate was missing."

"Great. Just great. Get us out of here."

"I've already called for backup. Let's step to the side. A car will be here shortly."

"Don't be mad at Max. No one could have stopped that guy," I whisper to Sean.

"He didn't protect you. That's not acceptable."

"I'll be okay. You don't need to yell at Max."

"Security never let anyone harm my parents," he says under his breath.

About ten minutes later, Sean whispers in my ear, "Our ride's here. I'm going to help you into the back seat."

That's my clue to ease the bear hug hold on him.

Safely cocooned in the limo, Sean instructs the driver, "Take us back to the Athena."

"Wait a minute, what about my surprise?"

"We'll reschedule it for another night."

Regaining my composure, I shake my head. "No. That criminal is not going to ruin the rest of our evening too. I was frightened, but I'm okay now, thanks to you. Please take me to my surprise."

"Let me look at your arm first. Is it still hurting?"

With a tender gentleness, he inspects my arm. An ugly bruise has already taken shape where the shoulder strap temporarily caught as the thief yanked my purse off my arm. Otherwise, I'm still intact, at least physically.

"Nothing appears broken. Let's put ice on your arm to prevent swelling. We should go back to the Athena and let you rest. You also need to report the theft to the police."

"We can contact the police tomorrow. The probability of them catching the thief and recovering my purse is miniscule. I'll be fine. I want to enjoy the rest of our evening."

"Are you sure?"

"I'm positive."

"Change of plans. Take us to the High Roller and close the partition," Sean says to the driver.

"Will do, sir," the driver says.

The glass rises, providing us with privacy from him and Max, who's in the front passenger seat.

25
SEAN

Feeling Lowri shaking in my arms crushed me. She was vulnerable and scared. It was my fault. I didn't protect her. That won't happen again. I'll take better care of her while she's here.

Despite insisting we move on with the evening, Lowri's body signals she's still shaken, which is not surprising. She's twisting and untwisting her neck chain tightly around her finger. If I don't distract her, it's going to break.

I'll start by trying to ease the pain in her arm. We have ice. There has to be something that will serve as a makeshift ice pack. You'd think we'd have a plastic bag somewhere. Lacking a better solution, I pick the best option at my disposal.

"Lowri, I'm sorry we don't have any plastic bags. Try holding this glass of ice on your bruise while I fix you a drink," I say.

"You can pour something in this glass. I'll alternate between sipping and icing my arm. Don't waste another glass."

Pouring my favorite Scotch for both of us, I say, "This should calm the nerves."

I could use something calming as well. She's not the only one who had visions of a much more disastrous outcome. At first, I thought someone was trying to take Lowri rather than her purse. I grabbed her left arm so tightly she probably has a bruise on it too.

Settling back onto the seat, I wrap one arm around her shoulder and pull her against me, leaning down to kiss her cheek. "It's okay now."

"Except that my phone, credit card, and ID were in my purse. They're all gone. Until I can get a replacement credit card, I can't buy a new phone or pay for anything. Without a phone, I don't have a way to get a replacement credit card. I stored all my info in the damn phone. It's a major mess to deal with."

Her spunk is coming back. That's a good sign.

"All that matters is that you're okay. Everything else is replaceable."

"The recordings of the interviews at the theater are gone too."

"Are the interviews backed up in the cloud or on your laptop?"

"I'm not thinking straight. That didn't occur to me. They should be. I synced my phone with my laptop while I typed up notes for the interviews."

"No one would be thinking clearly after being mugged. The interviews are probably backed up. Regardless, you have your notes. I'll help you figure out the credit card situation. We can look up the main number for your credit card company on my phone and give them a call now. I'm sure they can figure out your account based on all those dumb security questions they always ask." I chuckle.

"You mean questions like 'Who was your first boyfriend's second favorite teacher?'"

"Exactly. Now, which credit card company do you use?"

"American Express."

"Excellent. That's even easier. We'll call the service number for my Black card. That should expedite the process."

She lets out a huge laugh. "You may be surprised to learn that not everyone has a Black Amex card. I'm a mere mortal. Mine is a plain green one. *Your* special hotline won't help me."

"Sweetheart, have you already forgotten that you're my wife? Of course they will help you."

"I'm not used to being married. I should have known my temporary, billionaire husband has instant access to shortcuts around bureaucracy and red tape."

Five minutes later, her replacement card was on its way to me. The woman even apologized as if it was her fault Lowri was mugged.

"There are perks to our marriage. Your Black card will arrive tomorrow morning," he says, smiling.

"Black card? You mean my replacement green card, don't you?"

"No. I upgraded it when you gave the phone back to me."

"I can't afford one of those. Call them back. Now!"

"Calm down. It won't cost you anything extra. I took care of it. The woman asked if she should give you a card like mine and whether I wanted to charge the upgrade fee to my account. I said yes. Consider it a wedding gift or an annulment gift if you prefer. It's no big deal. Now, let's enjoy the rest of the evening."

"You really do live on another planet. I'll let it go *for now* because I want to enjoy the surprise you promised."

She keeps pointing out how different my life is from the norm. It's funny though. As long as we're married, it's her life too. Unlike Lowri, most women would be taking advantage of their newly found position.

Hmm. Yet another attribute that sets her apart.

26

LOWRI

"What's the High Roller? Are you taking me to an exclusive gambling club?" I ask.

"No. Your guess is way off. We're headed to the LINQ Promenade. You'll see."

"Oh! You mean the big Ferris wheel? Is it called the High Roller?"

"It's not exactly a Ferris wheel, but yes, that's where we're going. It has one of the best views of the Strip."

"I can't wait. This is going to be amazing!"

"The cheerful Lowri returns. It's incredible how quickly you bounce back from adversity."

If he only knew. Unfortunately, I had practice at an earlier age.

I need to refresh my lipstick. Damn—no purse, no lipstick.

Minutes later, our limo pulls into the driveway beneath the High Roller. We hop out and take a quick elevator ride to the boarding deck where we're greeted by our host.

"Mr. Cartwright, thank you for joining us tonight. Your private cabin with a bar is ready. Our senior bartender, Lucas, will take care of you this evening."

"Thank you. We'd prefer to be alone. We can pour our own drinks," Sean says.

"Of course, sir. Right this way. Your cabin will be arriving shortly."

"Thank you."

We follow the host to our designated boarding spot and wait as cabins slowly slide by. Embarking passengers swiftly replace those exiting. It's a well-orchestrated operation.

"Mr. Cartwright. You will be boarding the next one," our host says.

As the cabin approaches, the door opens and a man says, "Welcome aboard."

We step in as our host says, "Have a lovely evening. Lucas, please step out. Your services will not be required."

I watch as Sean deftly palms a few bills into Lucas's hand, drawing an appreciative smile and nod. It's reassuring to see that Lucas didn't lose his tip merely because we want privacy. Not all billionaires would give a second thought to Lucas. The fact he did is important to me.

I just wish he would tone down his attitude with the Athena employees when they don't live up to his exacting standards. He doesn't show that level of frustration with others, so I'm not sure what's causing him to take that approach to managing his staff.

That said, he's welcome to bring his alpha-ness to the bedroom. He's sexy when he's growly. Who am I kidding? He's always sexy regardless of whether he's the one in control.

"Here we go. Are you ready to see Vegas from a new vantage point?" Sean asks.

Without stopping, the cabin moves forward and the door closes, leaving us sealed in our own little world.

Turning toward him, I nod.

Sean pulls me in for a kiss. As he deepens it, my heart rate rapidly rises and the earlier events of the evening melt away. I'm completely lost in the moment.

A deep voice interrupts, saying, "Welcome to the High Roller." I jerk away.

"Who's that? I thought we were alone."

"We are. It's the recorded program."

"Of course. I'm still a little skittish."

"Understandable," Sean says, pulling me close again.

The voice proclaims, "Tonight you'll soar 550 feet into the air on the largest observation wheel in North America. As you circle above the Las Vegas Strip, you will have a breathtaking, 360-degree view of the world-famous Las Vegas Strip. Your journey tonight will last thirty minutes. Enjoy!"

"Do you want a drink or a snack?" Sean asks.

"I'd like to take in the view. Thirty minutes will go by quickly."

"That works for me."

The cabin itself is impressive. Monitors mounted around the top edge display various facts and statistics about the High Roller and Las Vegas. Bench seats near the center offer a place to rest as you sip a drink and watch the neon lights of the Strip. Those not frightened by heights can stand against a railing within inches of the glass walls and take in the sights as if floating in the air above the hotels, casinos, and people, who appear like specks moving along the sidewalks below.

While I'm not comfortable with heights, that won't stop me from appreciating the amazing sights. I slowly walk toward the full-height window and gaze out onto the Strip with all its extravagant lights illuminating the dark night sky. Warm arms slip around my waist, pulling my back into Sean's hard chest. I sigh.

A soft kiss lands on the top of my head. Then his lips caress my earlobe, and a puff of breath sends tingles down my spine.

"Are you feeling up to a little more fun?" he asks.

"It depends. What do you have in mind?" I whisper.

"Don't be coy with me. You know exactly what I have in mind."

"We can't do that here. There are cameras."

"That makes it a challenge. We'll be creative. Are you game?"

"I'm game if it won't end up on the internet."

The lawyers at my firm wouldn't understand. I'd lose my job.

"I promise that won't happen. I've got you covered. Literally. Lean forward. Support yourself against the glass and arch your back. I want that gorgeous ass in the air."

He keeps his arms around my waist as I follow his instructions, resting my hands on the clear wall.

His hand reaches under my skirt, migrating slowly up my inner thigh.

"You bad, bad girl. You should have told me earlier that you were bare. Why were you hiding that from me?"

"I didn't have time to put on underwear."

"You should always be like this," he mumbles into my shoulder as his fingers trace circles around my swollen clit.

"That feels amazing, but it may not work. My nerves are still frazzled from being mugged. I don't know if I can relax."

He stops circling my nub, leaving his finger pressed against it.

"That's why my beautiful girl needs this. Close your eyes. You don't need to do anything. Let me make you feel better. Will you let me do that?"

"I'll try."

His finger resumes the circles, first one way and then the other. I moan as he increases the pressure.

His other hand moves to my breast, squeezing gently. My nipple pebbles under the fabric. He rolls it between his thumb and forefinger, causing sensations to run through me.

He nibbles on my ear and softly blows behind it. As chills run down my neck, he chases them, dotting soft kisses from my earlobe to my shoulder. His teeth graze my shoulder just hard enough, I know he's leaving a mark.

I groan as he moves his hand to my other breast and removes his other hand from my swollen clit. "No, don't stop."

"Patience, my dear."

With his freed hand, he moves my hair to the side and peppers kisses along the back of my neck and up to my other ear.

As his fingers toy with my nipple and give it a gentle twist, his other hand roams down my front and finds its way between my legs.

"Oh my god, yes," I moan as he slips a finger into my core and circles my bud with his thumb.

"If you keep doing that, I'm not going to last long," I add.

"That's the idea. Come for me, sweetheart," he says, thrusting a second finger into me. I go over the edge instantly, squeezing tighter and tighter until the pulsing finally slows.

"Oh my, that was soooo good."

The deep, recorded voice startles me again, saying, "You are one-third of the way through this journey."

"That felt like we were all the way." I laugh.

"We're only getting started," Sean growls.

I feel him reach between us to unfasten his belt. The sound of his zipper opening has me panting in anticipation. He's making good on his promise for more. With one hand pulling me into him, his other hand slides the back of my skirt up. Then his steel cock slips between my cheeks and down where I crave it. With a commanding thrust, he fills me and begins moving slowly at first.

"More. I need more. Please," I beg.

"Whatever you want," he says, entwining both his arms around me and holding us close as he gives me everything I could want.

"I'm close—so close. Don't stop. Yes. That's it. Yes. Yes. Yes!" I scream as he takes me over the top again and joins me in his release as the deep voice interrupts us again.

"You have now reached the peak. We hope this is the highlight of your evening."

We both burst into laughter as Sean carefully extracts himself, smooths my skirt, and discreetly deals with the condom he had somehow managed to don.

"You don't think they saw us, do you?" I ask.

"No, I promise no one saw anything. I kept my back to the

camera, and you were safely hidden in front of me. And as an extra precaution, my IT people are friends with their IT people. The cameras were set to have a little glitch for the last 30 minutes."

"You bad boy! Why didn't you tell me that to start with?"

"It wouldn't have been as much fun."

"True."

"Their prerecorded message was timely though. That was definitely the highlight of my evening so far."

"Mine too. Can I have that drink while we watch the view on the ride back down?"

"Absolutely."

27
LOWRI

Thanks to Sean, last night ended significantly better than it started. We soared on the High Roller, literally and figuratively. Then Sean whisked me to a romantic Italian dinner at an upscale restaurant named after a Las Vegas icon: Sinatra.

Satiated and fed, exhaustion followed. We returned to the Athena and crashed in Sean's oversized king bed, each claiming our respective sides for once. We needed to catch up on sleep rather than be tempted to go another round.

A loud knock on the door startles me from my slumber, and I sense daylight seeping in. I'd have sworn my body didn't budge all night given how hard I slept. I would have been wrong. Sean and I still managed to meld our bodies together during the night. Somehow our arms and legs are intertwined, and my head is resting on Sean's warm chest. I sigh. He *is* yummy.

Untangling, I stretch my arms over my head as I yawn. It's no wonder I had sweet dreams. Who wouldn't, cuddled up to that man?

As my mind starts functioning, it also hits me that there's another benefit to being *married* to Sean. Walter no longer barges in on us. I'm not sure if Sean had a talk with him or if it's a respect thing on Walter's part. Either way, I appreciate the added privacy.

Regardless, it's still annoying to be awakened this early given our late night. According to the bedside clock, it's barely 7:00 a.m. We didn't need to wake up until 8:00 a.m. Why is Walter so early?

"Sir, madam, may I come in? You have a visitor," he calls through the door.

"At this hour of the morning? No way," I murmur groggily to Sean.

Sean looks my way and pulls a sheet over my upper body before answering, "Come in."

"Sorry to bother you earlier than expected. Ms. Upton, a woman is here with a new phone for you. She's waiting to set it up and restore your data from the cloud."

"I didn't order a replacement phone yet. How would the company know to send one, much less have someone deliver it here?" I ask.

Rubbing the sleep from his eyes, Sean says, "I forgot to tell you that I texted Emily last night. She arranged for delivery of one this morning. It didn't occur to me it would be this early though."

"Walter, please offer the woman coffee and breakfast. We won't be long, but we need a few minutes to wake up and dress," Sean instructs.

"Of course, sir," Walter replies, closing the door on his way out.

"You ordered a new phone for me. That wasn't necessary but thank you. I didn't know there was a personal service that delivers replacement phones though."

"It's common for businesses. We have people breaking screens and losing phones all the time. We can't afford to pay employees to sit at a phone store half a day waiting for a new one. The delivery service saves us money in the end."

"I wouldn't have minded another hour or two of sleep. At least this time Walter's morning surprise was a welcome one, unlike the day he delivered the marriage certificate," I mumble.

Sean laughs. "True. Let's grab a quick shower together and throw on clothes. Then you can get your new phone."

"We better shower separately. I'm not sure she wants to wait as long as our joint showers last."

"I *did* tell Walter to feed her breakfast. That should entertain her for a while."

Playfully punching him in the arm, I laugh. "I don't want Walter coming back to hurry us up when we're in the shower. Based on his past behavior, he might walk straight into the bathroom."

"He knows better now, but okay. You go first. I'll deal with my emails while you get ready."

A mere thirty minutes later, the world is right again. The woman from the phone store worked her magic and restored my life—*I mean, my phone*—from the cloud.

Whew! She saved me a ton of time. It's such a relief being reconnected to work and everything else. It's just in time too. As the front door is closing on her way out, my phone dings with an incoming text from Cassie.

> Cassie: Want to join me for lunch at Pinot & Pie? I could use your input on a couple of new menu items that I'm testing today.

> Me: Absolutely. I'm always up for taste testing, especially if it includes one of your fabulous desserts. Hint. Hint.

> Cassie: Dessert is always included. Does noon work?

> Me: Sure. I assume the restaurant is locked up until opening night. Is there a secret code or will my palm print let me in? LOL.

> Cassie: The doors are unlocked. We have loads of people coming in and out, working on finishing touches to the décor and various last-minute projects.

Me: Okay. See you soon.

Hearing footsteps, I look up as Sean emerges from the bedroom, sporting one of his many bespoke, dark-navy suits, a merlot tie, and ornate cufflinks.

"You're looking hot, bad boy. Can I convince you to skip work today?" I ask while he adjusts his cuffs.

"Unfortunately, no. My calendar is full. I'm scheduled for one-on-one meetings with my department heads. I'm also trying to find out why Rossi's guys showed up here and which employee is involved with them. I'm sure additional fires will pop up as the day progresses. They always do. What about you?"

"This morning I'll catch up on work for one of my clients. Then I'm meeting Cassie for lunch at Pinot & Pie. She wants me to see the restaurant's new décor and try a couple of the recipes that she's putting on the menu."

"The design looked impressive on paper. I haven't had time to stop by yet. Let me know what you think."

"Okay."

"If you're finished by 2:30 p.m., stop by my office. Ron's going to explain how he's addressing the safety problems on the show. I plan to make him go through every accident we've learned about. It would be helpful if you could sit in on that meeting," he says, giving me a goodbye peck on the cheek as he heads downstairs to his office.

"I'll be there," I reply.

"See you later."

As the door clicks shut, I head to my makeshift office: Sean's dining table.

Jenny moved most of my clothes and work-related stuff to Sean's apartment. It saves time—no need for a trip to my suite each morning.

Walter quickly adjusted to my routine as well. A steaming mug of coffee with a small pitcher of cream and a bowl of oatmeal sprinkled with crunchy granola and fresh berries are waiting for me.

Given how much I value freedom and spontaneity, it surprises me how easily I've fallen into this comfortable groove with Sean and his life here. My normal self would be happy this is ending soon so my life can return to its two distinct worlds: the serious work one and the fun, no-strings, social one. Instead, I'm inexplicably sad about the inevitable conclusion to my time here.

Huh.

I don't have time to dwell on my emotions though. A client expects me to send them a draft settlement agreement today. They finally reached an amicable resolution with an injured employee and want me to quickly finalize the agreement. That's my priority.

Shoot. My laptop's downstairs. After the interviews yesterday, I worked in my suite instead of returning here. Oh well, I'm not as settled into this life as I thought.

"Walter, please keep my coffee warm. I'll be right back. I'm going to grab my laptop from downstairs."

"Of course, ma'am."

THE PRIVATE ELEVATOR MAKES FOR A SHORT RIDE TO MY SUITE. EXITING, I abruptly freeze.

Noooo! This can't be happening to me. What did I do to piss off the universe?

Staring in shock, I take in the shambles. The bed linens are strewn across the floor, the mattress is askew, the lamps are smashed, and the drawers are open—the few sets of underwear I'd left here are spilling over the edges.

Shit. I've been robbed—again.

<h1 style="text-align:center">28</h1>

SEAN

Rushing into Lowri's suite, I'm out of breath. My eyes scan the room searching for her among the security personnel and housekeeping staff who have taken over the messy scene. Panic begins to set in when I don't see her.

"Where's my wife? I mean, where's Lowri?" I call out loudly enough to cause everyone to stop what they're doing and stare at me.

Daniel, my head of security, walks over. "Mr. Cartwright, she's in the bathroom collecting herself. This was quite a shock for her."

"After I check on Lowri, I want a full report. There are too many unexplained incidents happening at the Athena."

Not waiting for his reply, I quickly stride into the bedroom. Soft sobs are coming from behind the closed bathroom door. My heart sinks. First, she was mugged, and now this.

"Lowri, may I come in?"

The door opens slowly. I slide inside, kicking it closed behind me for privacy.

"Did they hurt you?"

"What?" she asks.

I do a quick perusal of her from head to toe. Her eyes are red and swollen, and streaks of black mascara are running down her cheeks. At least her clothes are intact, and there's no sign of bruising other than from the mugging.

Pulling her into my arms, I softly ask again, "Are you hurt?"

"I'm upset, but why would I be hurt?"

"Daniel called Emily, and Emily found me. She said you had been attacked."

"My room was attacked. Thankfully, I wasn't here."

"Thank fuck. I panicked, thinking you'd been assaulted."

"I'll be okay. Sorry I'm such a mess. It was a massive shock to walk in and find that someone had ransacked my suite. They threw all my clothes, including my underwear, onto the floor. My laptop and work papers are gone."

"Stop apologizing. Anyone would be upset. Do you know if anything else is missing?"

"I'm not sure. I'd already moved my jewelry and a bunch of my clothes upstairs. If I had worked in your apartment after the interviews yesterday, my laptop would have been there instead of here. This is a disaster."

"We'll figure out who did this. Until then, a guard is going to stay near you when I can't be."

"How many rooms were robbed?"

"I don't know the extent of the thefts yet. Daniel is going to brief me in a minute."

"I'm going to be in mega trouble with my law firm for losing the laptop."

"All that matters is that you're not hurt. Jenny will move the rest of your stuff up to my apartment and coordinate with Walter. I don't want you returning to this suite again. Security will disable the elevator as an extra precaution. As for your laptop, we can replace it."

"I feel violated. I've never been the victim of theft before and within twenty-four hours, I've been robbed twice. It's unsettling and creepy to know a stranger invaded my space. They touched my underwear and went through all my personal items. It's too much."

"Let's get you out of here. We'll make use of the elevator one last time to access my apartment. Then it will be locked off."

"Okay. Let me wipe my face first. Could you give me a minute?"

"Sure. I'll tell Daniel to meet us upstairs when he's through with his investigation here."

29
LOWRI

Sean wanted me to cancel my lunch appointment with Cassie, particularly after we learned no other rooms were robbed and *only* my laptop and work papers were stolen. He's worried that I'm being targeted for some unknown reason.

Despite Sean's concerns, I insisted on going forward with my plans. It's been several hours since I discovered the robbery, and without a laptop, I can't work. There's no reason not to enjoy lunch with my bestie.

This day needs a restart, so I freshen my makeup, pull my casual burgundy dress out of the closet, and find my matching lace bra and panties. There's something about sprucing up my makeup and pulling on luxury underwear that gives my confidence a boost.

With a guard in tow at Sean's insistence, I go to meet Cassie. Normally, I would have fought Sean about the security guy but not this time. Considering the events of the last twenty-four hours and the potential threats, I'll admit my fear level has risen several notches. Sean would prefer to lock me safely inside his apartment, but that's a no-go for me. I won't cower in a corner.

Besides, catching up with Cassie and taste testing her new recipes will greatly improve my day.

Climbing the Grand Staircase on the far side of the casino, we walk past the Olympic Torch Bar and find the door to Pinot & Pie. It's the restaurant Cassie will call her own for the next month. This has been her secret dream for as long as I can remember, and it's finally coming true.

Testing the door, it's unlocked as promised. I wander inside and gasp in awe.

My eyes are drawn upward. The ceiling is at least three stories high. Letting my eyes scan the rest of the space, I continue to be wowed. The décor is stunning. Floor-to-ceiling gray slate tiles with vertical, charcoal striations create accent walls, and contemporary, crystal light globes dangle from the ceiling at various heights throughout the room.

Modern designs can feel cold, but not here. Deep-purple drapes hang between the full-height windows overlooking the Aegean Sea. Dark carpeting with cream accents covers the floor, and soft violet spotlights focus on each table. Together with the overall dim lighting, these features give this marvelous space a warm and welcoming vibe that draws me further into the room.

Looking around, I don't see Cassie. Workers are busily installing various finishing touches, so I ask one of the men where the chef is. He points to a frosted glass partition on the far-right side of the room.

Stepping around the partition, I find double swinging doors. Aha! Of course, the chef is in the kitchen. I can't help giggling. It's funny to think of Cassie as the *chef*. We've always been either law students or lawyers, stressing over clients and deadlines. Now she's delving into her creative side and conjuring up delicious and artful food for the rich and famous.

Pushing one of the doors open, I call out, "Cassie, are you in here?"

"Lowri, come in. I'll be there in a minute," she shouts from somewhere to my left.

Following instructions, I enter the giant kitchen and walk toward a long stainless steel table covered with chopped carrots, celery, and onions.

As I turn my head, Cassie is hurrying toward me. "Are you okay? I got your text and rushed to your room. The guards wouldn't let me in. What happened?"

"I'm fine now. My purse was stolen yesterday, and today my room was ransacked. It's been a traumatic morning. Luckily, I was with Sean last night, and I wasn't in my room when the thief broke in this morning."

"Yeah, we're going to talk about you and Sean in a minute. First, what was stolen? Anything valuable?"

"They took my laptop and work papers. It's strange, they left behind two hundred dollars in extra cash that I'd hidden in a dresser drawer under my lingerie."

"They probably didn't have time to search the drawers."

"That's what's strange. The dresser drawers were pulled open. The cash was in plain sight after they rummaged through the top drawer."

"That is odd."

"I've been helping Sean with the investigation into the accident that killed Mr. Brentwood during the pyrobatics show. The fact that my work papers were taken makes Sean and me suspect someone didn't want a record of what I learned from interviewing the various performers. We're also questioning whether my purse was specifically targeted last night because someone wanted my cell phone with the recorded interviews.

"That sounds like the plot of a suspense movie. Events like that don't usually happen in real life. The two thefts probably aren't even related."

"I know, but we haven't come up with another explanation for why they took my work papers."

"If they were on top of your laptop, they probably grabbed the papers with your computer and will toss them into the trash. Do you have backups?"

"Yes. My laptop is backed up to the cloud, and Sean had a replacement phone in my hands early this morning. I can recover everything."

I ignore Cassie's raised eyebrows. She's wondering why Sean purchased a new phone for me. I'll skip the explanation. My thoughts are elsewhere anyway.

If there was a sinister, orchestrated plan behind the thefts, the thief wouldn't know I had backups. They would assume the thefts eliminated the proof of what the witnesses said to me. Not knowing that, will the thief intimidate the witnesses into not speaking up again? Will they come after me for what I remember? I shudder at the thought, but that's masked by the rumbling of my stomach.

"I heard that. We better feed you quickly. You must be starving."

"I am."

"Then you're in the best possible place. You won't be hungry after what we've planned for the tasting."

"I can't believe this is happening. You look so professional in your fancy, black chef's coat. It even has your name on it. But why does it say Cassandra instead of Cassie?"

"Because Evan had the coats made for me, and he always uses my full name. I'm lucky he didn't put Princess-to-be Cassandra on it as he threatened. He wants to tell the world about our upcoming wedding." She laughs.

"That's hilarious. I can't believe how much your life has changed this year. It started with us both working our asses off as lawyers in San Diego. Then you finally took a chance and entered the guest chef competition thanks to a little prodding by me."

"I know what you mean. Now I'm chef here for a month, and a real prince swept me off my feet and proposed. It's too much to process."

"You're living your fairytale."

"I know. Evan pinches me daily to remind me this is all real," she says looking upward, arms sweeping around the kitchen.

"Are you sure that's the only reason Evan pinches you?" I joke.

"Very funny. Let's go out to the dining room. I'll show you around while the team finishes the tasting dishes."

"Okay."

I'm thankful Cassie's been in my life since law school. She's the sister I always needed. Nothing against my brother, but there are certain things only another woman understands.

With those thoughts, emotions wash over me. I'm not sure how much longer we'll have each other with all the drastic changes in Cassie's future. It hadn't occurred to me before. Our lives are diverging quickly. The thought of not having Cassie to turn to, when times are tough or something exciting happens, leaves me with an unsettling emptiness. Reining in my selfishness, I promise myself that I won't rain on her well-deserved happiness. So, biting my lip, I quash the sense of looming loss, at least for now, and force a smile.

Excitement in her voice, Cassie points out the off-white chairs and purple, upholstered booths. "I can't believe they made all the changes so quickly. What do you think? Do you like it?" she asks.

"It's spectacular. What did it look like before?" I ask as she guides me to sit on a bench seat in one of the booths while she sits in a chair across from me.

"It was an outdated theme and far from ideal for a new opening."

"Sean must have spent a fortune redoing this for you."

"Not exactly for me. Kai takes over as the permanent chef soon after my month ends. Sean promised to renovate before then. Kai asked if it was possible to finish the remodeling in time for my opening instead. That way we could work out any kinks ahead of his debut. When I agreed to Kai's plan, Sean arranged for this magical transformation to take place a few weeks earlier than originally scheduled. And Kai was kind enough to ask for my input on the redesign."

"Isn't it odd that another chef would be okay with you using his remodeled kitchen and restaurant first?"

"We met during the guest chef competition and got along great. Kai's ego isn't as big as those of the chefs on cooking shows. Besides, I'm helping him out. He'll be guaranteed a smooth opening. We've had fun working together on the theme too. It didn't take long to decide that purple should be the main color, and the restaurant should have a modern, comfortable feel. We told the designers and let them work their magic. The result was this magnificent design."

"Wow. They nailed it," I say.

"They did. The designers are incredibly talented. I wasn't sure about the wood and glass trim on the booths at first. Then they brought in this brown walnut with the dark chocolate streaks and swirls, and it was a perfect contrast to the purples, grays, and whites," she says, reaching up to stroke the highly polished trim.

"I'm no designer, but I wouldn't change a thing," I say, glancing around the room once again.

"Thanks. Sorry for talking a mile a minute. My excitement level is at the moon. Not to mention, my to-do list feels like it would circle the globe at least once. I'm working at warp speed to get everything done."

"If we talk fast, maybe we can catch up on everything. With you in Catalinius all summer and me taking on extra work at the law firm, we're way behind."

"I know. It's been out of control."

"By the way, the wine room behind that glass wall is impressive. It must be thirty feet high. What's up with those white and lavender sashes hanging from the ceiling in there? They look like the aerial silks that acrobats use."

"They are aerial silks. When someone orders a bottle of wine, the acrobats use the silks to climb up the tower of wine, grab the bottle, and slide down. If the bottle is high enough, the acrobats even do flips and turns on the way down. It's quite a show."

"I can't wait to watch. Do you have a list of the bottles near the top?" I ask.

"That's exactly what I asked when I first saw the wine tower. The more expensive the bottle, the higher its slot. The goal is to entice customers to purchase a pricey bottle to watch the server climb to the top."

"Great marketing strategy."

"That's what I said. So, if you want a bottle from the top, my suggestion is to let Sean order it for you."

"Why would Sean be ordering expensive wine for me?"

"Because of your relationship." Cassie smiles knowingly.

"It's not a relationship. I'm helping him with the legal issues related to the accidental death at the show. He hired me to handle the settlement with the man's family."

"Uh-huh. That's why Sean always has his hand on your back or arm when Evan and I have seen you together. You can't fool me. There's more to it."

"I've already told you we're having a little fun along the way, but he did hire me."

Her head tilts, and she looks down as she moves and twists the mini orchid plant at the center of our table. It's as if she's arguing with herself about something. I know I'm right when she says, "I'm not sure I should question what's going on with you and Sean because you seem particularly happy, and dare I say, *content.* But it is out of character for you to mix business and pleasure. What led to this exception?"

I do my own little dance to buy time as I remove the white napkin from the matching tablecloth, being careful not to disturb the tiny candles or the beautiful silverware. Slowly unfolding the fabric and rearranging it to my liking, I finally lay the napkin on my lap and reach for my water glass.

Taking a long sip, I wonder how much to share with my best friend. It's such a strange question to be asking myself when we've always confided in each other. I want to tell Cassie about my temporary marriage and the fact that I love waking up next to Sean for the time being, but I can't. I promised Sean not to tell anyone, especially if it would make it to Evan's ears.

I say, "Consider it a lapse in judgment that will be remedied when I leave Vegas. We enjoyed being together while we were planning your party. Then when the accident happened and Sean needed help, he insisted that I was the perfect lawyer because I had first-hand knowledge of the event. I was there. It made sense. Besides, who would turn down the Athena as a client?"

My answer to Cassie was a compromise, which we lawyers are trained to do when it comes to negotiating what will work and keep us within the rules. I stuck with the truth for my best friend, albeit with a couple of omissions. That allowed me to keep my promise to Sean. I smile, proud of myself.

"Be careful. I don't want you to get hurt. Are you sure you have this under control?"

Why couldn't she leave it alone? Because I wouldn't have either.

Fidgeting with my knife, I avoid her eyes. "Of course. Sean and I spend time together in the evenings. It's nothing serious. It's just convenient for both of us. We figured with you and Evan here, we'll all be spending time together anyway. It works out for now. Sean and I are both on the same page—no strings."

Well, no permanent strings.

"I'm torn between leaving this alone and wanting to make sure you're okay. I've tried to convince myself you must have a good reason for what you're doing. But if something is wrong, I'll never forgive myself for not having your back. So, I need to ask you something. When I arrived at your room this morning, the guards wouldn't let me in. I would have made a bigger scene and insisted on seeing you, but Sean had just arrived. I'd swear that I heard him ask where his *wife* was. Is it true? Are you two married?"

"Shit. No one is supposed to know. It was an accident. Like I said, when I leave Vegas, it will be over. We're getting an annulment."

"Are you saying you accidentally married Sean?"

"We were drunk."

"Why didn't you tell me? Did Sean tell Evan?"

"No. We were embarrassed and didn't want anyone to know. There are also complications with the annulment."

I explain our situation in detail, relieved to finally be talking this over with my best friend.

"Wow. I don't know what to say, except I'm here for you if you need my help getting out of this mess. It's an extremely *convenient* arrangement though. You work together during the day and play together during the night." She laughs.

Changing the subject, I say, "You're one to talk. Weren't you completely avoiding relationships too? I knew you and Evan had a strong connection. To be honest, I assumed it would be a summer fling on an island with a prince, and the attraction would fade after the shine of dating a prince wore off. Instead, you're engaged. What changed your mind about giving your heart to a guy?"

"It's hard to explain. It feels right, and I'd be crushed if he wasn't in my life. We make each other better. I never expected to find this connection. Hopefully, it will happen for you too. Sean could be the one," she says.

Fortunately, we're interrupted by servers bearing small plates, and I'm saved from further discussion of me and my arrangement with Sean.

The first server says, "Chef, we have your main course tastings for you."

"Excellent. Thank you." Turning to me, Cassie continues, "Lowri, I'm excited for you to try these. We have three tasting portions. Let me know which one you like best."

Placing a forkful of the short ribs and polenta into my mouth, I'm in heaven. It's out of this world. "Yum! This is a winner. It's delicious and comforting. What's the red sauce? It gives it a little kick."

"It's a spicy red pepper puree. Do you like it?"

"Love it. What's this next dish?"

"It's chicken and orzo with seasonal veggies. I should've had you taste it before the beef because it's a lighter dish without the spice. Your palate is overpowered at this point but try it anyway."

We both taste it.

"It needs more lemon, don't you think?" Cassie asks, making notes on a small pad of paper she extracts from her pocket. She's a perfectionist.

"If you think so. It tastes fine to me."

"Definitely more lemon. The tilapia tacos are the last savory tasting. They are going to be on our bar menu. Let me know if the Cajun crust competes too much with the salsa verde or whether the sliced avocados pull it together. I can't decide."

"You're the expert, but I'll give you my opinion."

"Thanks. I've tasted so many samples in the last few weeks that I'm starting to second-guess myself. Evan's no help. He says he likes everything I make. It's up to you to give me an honest opinion."

"I'm with Evan. Everything you make is fabulous."

"Thanks, but feel free to nitpick. I want everything to be perfect. Oh, I have other news too. I forgot to tell you that I officially resigned from the law firm yesterday. Can you believe it?"

Thank goodness I hadn't taken a bite of the taco yet because I would've choked on it.

"Are you serious? You completely quit. You're not working remotely or part time for a while?"

"Yes, I'm serious, and no, I'm not working remotely. I'm completely free of that life. It feels amazing."

"I'm shocked, but I shouldn't be. You've been burned out for quite a while, but this guest chef gig only lasts a month. What will you do afterward? Won't you be bored sitting around all day in princess dresses?" I say, half-teasingly.

My mind races with worries for her. Cassie gets bored easily. She's always been driven and busy. What if the engagement falls through? How will she pay her bills? It's nearly impossible to return to a big law firm after leaving. Will this opportunity as a chef at the Athena be enough to open another door for her if she needs it?

"Quit squinting. You do that when you're worried. There's no reason to be concerned about me being bored. Evan and I will be incredibly busy with the new charities we're working on. I'll put my legal background to use with them and will be contributing to the community in a much better way than I ever could at the law firm. My life will be busier, and I suspect more fulfilling than ever. I couldn't be happier about it."

"I'm glad you two have thought this through, and I *am* thrilled for you. Forgive me for worrying. You know me. I instinctively protect my friends, and you're at the top of that list." Before I say more, heavy footsteps are growing louder. Turning my head, I say, "Look who's walking toward us."

Cassie jumps up at the sight of Evan. He wraps her in a hug, kissing her thoroughly. Not what I expect of royalty in public, but it's only us and twenty or thirty workers. Is it considered the public?

"You're in time to join Lowri and me for dessert. We're tasting my recipe for pumpkin pie cheesecake."

"I won't pass up a bite of pudding if you two don't mind me joining you for a bit," Evan says.

"Didn't you say we're having pie or cheesecake?" I ask.

"We are. To Evan, desserts are called pudding. I'm slowly acclimating to his version of English." Cassie laughs.

An attentive server quickly sets another place next to Cassie, and we're presented with slices of what looks like a thick pumpkin pie with a graham cracker crust and topped with whipped cream. The first bite has the tang and creaminess of cheesecake with the fall flavors of pumpkin. "Mmm. I'm in love with this. Can I get a whole pie to take with me?" I ask.

"I agree. This pudding is delightful," Evan says, leaning over to give Cassie a quick peck on the lips.

"I'm glad you both like it. Even though the temperatures outside are still warm here, I want my menu to reflect the current season. Nothing signals fall better than pumpkin."

"Your twist makes it special. But please don't add a pumpkin coffee to the menu. That's been way overdone," I say.

"No worries. You know I don't drink coffee. My special after-dinner drinks will go in a different direction."

"The offer of food distracted me. I stopped by with news," Evan says.

"What is it?" Cassie asks.

"Bri's been invited to a Las Vegas charity gala and tennis tournament in a couple of weeks. She's trying to arrange her schedule to arrive early to be here for your opening night. Wouldn't that be brilliant?" Evan asks.

"It would be fantastic to have your little sister here," Cassie gushes.

Turning to me, she says, "Lowri, you're going to love Bri. I can't wait for you to meet her. She's full of sunshine and fun."

Evan chuckles. "She is a ball of energy and makes us all smile. Then when she's in tennis mode, she's quite serious. It's rather amusing watching her transform into the tennis professional when she steps onto a court."

"Can we watch her play? Lowri and Sean could come too," Cassie says.

"If you'd like, Bri should be able to secure tickets for us. I'll ask."

Taking a quick look at my phone, I'm surprised at how late it is.

"Sorry to leave this party. It's time for me to get back to work. I'm running late for an appointment," I say.

"My to-do list is waiting. This has been fun. Are you stuck working for the rest of the day?" Cassie asks.

"Sean and I are interviewing Ron. He's the stage manager for the *Pyrobatics Treasure Hunt*. We're following up on several unexplained accidents in the days leading up to Mr. Brentwood's fall."

"I'm off too. Dad expects me on a video meeting in twenty minutes. Lowri, I'll walk you out," Evan says standing up.

Cassie leaps up and gives him a quick kiss. "I'll be finished here by 8:00 p.m. tonight. Can we grab dinner then?"

"I'll make reservations," he says.

I give Cassie a hug. With a quick wave, Evan and I hurry out.

As we're about to part ways, Evan says, "Thank you for all the hard work on the party for Cassie. I'm incredibly grateful for your help. Forgive me for not sharing that it was an engagement party. It was important to me that Cassandra was the first to know. That is other than my parents. Catalinius law required that I ask their permission."

"There's nothing to forgive. It would have been difficult to keep the secret. It's better you didn't tell me. I'm thrilled the party turned out the way you wanted."

"It was perfect. Good luck with your inquiries this afternoon," he says and, with long, quick strides, disappears into the crowded casino.

He truly is smitten with Cassie, and she with him. Watching those two together, I can't help being a tad envious of the love they share.

I've never been loved that deeply by a man. Hell, my father didn't love me. Why do I think another man would? Dad only cared about my brother, Jerry. He had no use for a daughter who didn't play sports.

When Dad cheated on Mom and eventually left her for his young assistant at work, I vowed never to give my heart to a man. No way would I allow someone to treat me the way he treated her.

I sent Dad an invitation to my law school graduation, hoping it would make him proud. He didn't even acknowledge the accomplishment. By then, he had a new family with his second wife. He'd moved on from my family and didn't look back. I've never contacted him again and never will.

Based on my experience, men suck when it comes to relationships.

Then I see Cassie and Evan together. He was there for her when she needed consoling and support during the guest chef competition, and he's quick to hug her and cheer her successes. They're perfect for each other.

But that's not my life. After college, I learned the only way to deal with men was to join them in their game. At work I'm serious and play hardball; outside of work, I play. All I've wanted was to have fun and enjoy sex—just like men—with no strings attached.

So why am I standing here, wishing for a chance at what Cassie and Evan have? I'm torn between preserving the protective shell I've created and hanging onto a smidgen of hope that maybe there's a special man for me too.

My dream guy is someone like Sean. He respects my legal advice, cuddles me after I've been mugged, replaces my stolen items, and rocks my universe in bed. Sean even agreed to monogamy when we got married, which would be a requirement for being Mr. Perfect.

Of course, Sean's not my forever guy. We're on the same page. No relationships.

30
SEAN

Right on time, Emily shows Ron into my office.

"Ron, take a seat. We have a lot to discuss today," I say.

Turning to Emily as she grabs the doorknob on her way out, I add, "Emily, please bring Ms. Upton in as soon as she arrives."

"She's getting off the elevator now, sir."

The rapid click-clacking of Lowri's signature high heels confirms her arrival.

"Hello, everyone. I hope I'm not late. I'm still learning how much time to allow for moving around the Athena," Lowri says.

"You're right on time, please come in," I say.

"Ron, you remember Ms. Upton. I've asked her to join us this afternoon. I believe you've already met."

"It's good to see you again. We met briefly when she interviewed me after the accident," Ron says, turning toward Lowri.

"Let's start by discussing the accidents that occurred before the night Mr. Brentwood died," I say.

"What do you mean?" Ron asks.

"Come now. Are you saying that you were unaware that a dancer suffered burns from the fireworks, another dancer slipped on an oily patch onstage and hurt her shoulder, or that a group of performers sustained significant bruises when a wall fell?" Lowri asks.

"Those were minor mishaps. They were nothing out of the ordinary for a large stage production."

Raising my voice a notch, I say, "Don't mess with us, Ron. You and I both know that pyrotechnics misfiring and burning someone is uncommon and unacceptable. How did these incidents happen, and why wasn't I informed about them?"

"Umm. You see, it ... Ah ... Umm ..."

Ron's stammering and stalling is interrupted by the ringing of my office phone.

"Emily, what do you need?" I ask.

Her response is surprising. I hide my shock, calmly saying, "Really? That's unusual."

She offers to handle the situation for me, but I'll take care of this myself.

"No, show them to a conference room and serve them something to drink. Ms. Upton and I will join them shortly," I say.

Disconnecting the call, I turn back to Ron. "There's an urgent matter that can't wait, but this conversation is far from over. We'll finish it later. By then, you better be ready to give us straight answers as to the cause of the accidents and what you're doing to remedy the safety failures. Do you understand me?" I manage to say without exploding.

"Yes, sir."

Ron leaves in a hurry, clearly glad for the reprieve. As the door clicks shut, I let out a sigh.

"What's going on?" Lowri asks, staring at me questioningly.

"This day is not getting better. You'll never guess who is waiting for us in a conference room."

"Who?"

"Mr. Brentwood's heir and his attorney."

"What? They showed up without an appointment?"

"Yep. Anyone else arriving unannounced would be sent away. Given their loss, I won't do that to them."

"No, you can't, but I wanted Ron's answers before we had to meet with any heirs. My advice is to offer your sincere condolences and listen to what they say. It's too soon to make any promises or decisions. We need time to investigate and figure out what happened."

"Agreed," I say, rubbing my stiff neck.

Lowri steps behind me and starts massaging the knots forming in my shoulders, whispering, "Close your eyes and relax. Tell me what you're thinking."

I'm not usually one to open up about feelings, but I decide to share anyway. "It's crushing me that a man died at my show. It never should have happened."

"I know. I'd be worried if you weren't upset. Do you think the accident was Ron's fault? Is that why you raised your voice to him?"

"I don't know what to think. I keep wondering if my employees would be doing their jobs better if Dad were still in charge. He brought out the best in everyone. I'm not my dad."

"You're not supposed to be your dad. You're doing a fantastic job, but don't assume your employees aren't doing their best for you too. Sometimes things go wrong, and it's better to work on the solution than find someone to blame."

"You're right. I always knew responsibility for the Athena would fall on my shoulders, and I looked forward to managing it one day. That day came about twenty years sooner than expected, so many of the employees knew me as a young boy. That's how they still see me. It's hard to change that image."

"I get it. It's only been a couple of years, but you've already shown that the Athena is thriving under your leadership. I'm not saying you should never be angry with anyone, but showing your frustration too often may undermine your desire for them to see you as Sean-the-man rather than the boy. Be patient with those who respected your dad. You'll earn their respect too. Just a thought."

"You've got a point, but I won't lower my expectations."

"Nor should you, but right now, the most important thing to remember is that Mr. Brentwood's death wasn't your fault. You're going to help his family and make sure no one else is hurt. That's all you can do. We've got this."

Lowri's voice is soothing, and her hands send a warmth through me.

I haven't felt supported in a long time—not since losing my parents.

Subconsciously, I twist the cufflinks that belonged to Dad. If he could handle this place, so can I, particularly with Lowri on my team.

31
LOWRI

Emily signals that our unexpected visitors are waiting in the conference room.

As Sean and I walk down the hall, butterflies flutter rampantly in my stomach. Why is this happening? It's normal to be slightly anxious before meetings with people who want something from my clients. This time I'm outright nervous.

Then it hits me. It's because this feels personal. I witnessed the accident, and Sean is a friend and *technically* also my husband. My job is to protect him. I don't want to let him down. What if I'm not experienced enough? In situations like this, clients always want a law firm partner, not a mere associate like me.

Why am I second-guessing myself? My experience is more than sufficient, and Sean insisted he wants me as his attorney. He trusts me.

Deep breath. Slow exhale.

It's time for my professional side to shine. I can help Sean. There's no room for emotions or self-doubt. This is another reason I shouldn't be mixing business with pleasure. Oh well, it's too late to back out now, so I plaster on my game face.

I can do this.

Approaching the glass-walled meeting space, two men come into view. The one wearing an ill-fitting navy suit is pacing. The second man is well put together in his snugly fitting polo and khakis. He's seated, nervously tapping his fingers on the conference table. Hmm.

Sean opens the door with authority, saying, "Good afternoon, I'm Sean Cartwright, owner of the Grand Athena. This is Lowri Upton, our legal counsel."

The suit guy walks over, taking Sean's extended hand and then mine. His hand is clammy and limp. Yuck. It takes all my willpower not to dry my palm on my suit skirt.

"I'm Taylor Williams and this is my client, Troy Galanis. Troy is Mr. Brentwood's heir. Mr. Brentwood was the love of Troy's life. We're here to discuss how quickly you can pay Mr. Galanis the money he's due for his loss."

Sean's eyebrows jump up. I'm surprised as well. What an abrupt way for an attorney to ask for a settlement.

"Mr. Galanis, let me first offer you our sincere condolences for your loss. It was a tragic accident. We understand this is an extremely difficult time for you," Sean says.

"Yes. Immensely difficult," Mr. Galanis says, staring at his clasped hands.

"Please have a seat, Mr. Williams. We're hoping you can fill in some missing details about Mr. Brentwood. Do you know how he came to be at the show that evening?" I ask.

"Why do you care?" Mr. Williams asks.

"He had a special ticket for that performance. Whoever sat in that seat would be invited to participate in the show. We're trying to determine how Mr. Brentwood got that ticket. Do you know?"

"I think someone gave it to him," Mr. Galanis says.

"Why didn't you join him at the show?" I ask.

"He only had one ticket."

"Did he say who gave him the ticket?" I ask.

"No. I had other plans that night. It didn't matter to me," Mr. Galanis says with a flick of his wrist.

"Can we move on from these irrelevant questions and get down to business now?" Mr. Williams asks, leaning forward and placing his forearms on the table.

"Certainly. Tell us what you wanted to discuss today," Sean says.

"Your show killed Mr. Brentwood. Mr. Galanis is Mr. Brentwood's sole heir. It's simple. You owe him," Mr. Williams says.

Sean starts to answer, but I touch his forearm to stop him. This is my territory.

"First, no one killed Mr. Brentwood. He died in an unfortunate accident. Before there can be a discussion of compensation, if any, we'll need additional information. For example, the police need to finish their investigation, and we need proof that Mr. Galanis is the heir."

"Here's Mr. Brentwood's will," Mr. Williams says, shoving a folder toward me.

"Thank you. Who is the executor of the estate?"

"Take a look at the will. Mr. Galanis is the executor and sole heir. That means we can talk settlement now."

"Yes, I want this over with as soon as possible. Dragging this out would be too painful," Mr. Galanis says.

"We're all sorry for what you are going through. Do you have a specific proposal?" I ask.

Before his attorney can speak, Mr. Galanis blurts out, "I want $250,000. Now."

That's not what I was expecting. I'm distracted by Sean's coughing. He was clearly anticipating a much larger demand, as was I.

As I'm handing him a glass of water, Mr. Williams says, "Don't pretend that's a lot of money to you. It's nothing compared to the value of Mr. Brentwood's life."

Is this attorney for real? Does he not know that what he asked for is much lower than we were expecting? Has he ever handled a case like this before? I can't help feeling bad for Mr. Galanis. He needs a better lawyer.

I do my job though, saying, "No payment can be made today. We'll review the will in detail. We'll also need a copy of the death certificate when it's available, along with documents from the court formally appointing Mr. Galanis as executor. If we reach an agreement on a settlement, the details will be put in writing."

Mr. Galanis huffs.

His attorney says, "We understand there are formalities. Can we agree on the amount and the timing for payment?"

"Mr. Cartwright and I will discuss this privately. Leave your contact information with Emily. We'll reach out when we're ready to talk again."

"We can wait here while you talk elsewhere."

"Our discussions will take longer than that, and we require additional time to look over the document you provided. We'll be in touch in a few days. How can we reach you?"

"That's not acceptable. We'll wait," Mr. Williams says.

Sean is busily typing on his phone, which he's discreetly hidden beneath the table. He tilts his screen for me to see, and I nod at his smart move. Security will be here shortly.

"Why the hurry?" Sean asks.

"As my client says, this is horribly painful for him. He's decided to move to the East Coast and leave the horrific memories of Mr. Brentwood's death behind him."

"I see. When are you moving?" Sean asks.

"Immediately," Mr. Galanis says.

"I'm sure that it will take a few days to make arrangements to relocate. That will give us time to review the will and discuss your settlement proposal," I say, standing to indicate this meeting is over.

Sean follows my lead. "Good day, gentlemen. We'll be in touch," he says, holding the glass door open for everyone to leave.

But Mr. Williams and Mr. Galanis don't budge.

"We're not leaving until this is settled," Mr. Williams says.

"You *are* leaving. As Mr. Cartwright said, we'll review your proposal and contact you. Please do not show up unannounced again," I say, walking through the door.

Mr. Williams calls out, "Perhaps we should head to the courthouse and file a lawsuit today."

"Feel free, but that will slow down the process," I call back calmly and continue walking with Sean back to his office. We've only taken a few steps when we hear security guards ushering the visitors into the elevator.

* * *

"What the hell was that?" Sean asks when we reach the privacy of his office.

"The strangest settlement conference I've ever attended," I say, dropping into one of the guest chairs.

"Part of me wanted to accept the offer, pay the guy, and be done, but it was too easy. Something is off."

"I wholeheartedly agree. I'm looking up Taylor Williams in the attorney database now. It's possible he's a recent law school graduate and doesn't know what he's doing."

"What does it say about him?"

"Believe it or not, he's listed as an attorney specializing in estates and wrongful death cases." I'm stunned.

"Are you sure you're looking at the correct person?"

"It's the entry for the only attorney named Taylor Williams in Las Vegas. He's with the Fishbourne Peabody law firm."

"Are you saying he knows what he's doing?" Sean asks.

"On paper, it looks like he should. In person, I'm not sure. If he's experienced in this field, why did he only ask for $250K? I was expecting the starting request would be at least a few million, and you would be lucky to settle for a million, plus or minus."

"Exactly. After all, we are a casino. I've had people stub their toe and ask for $250K. It doesn't make sense."

"No, it doesn't, which has me wondering whether the will is valid and whether Mr. Galanis really is the sole heir."

"Good point. My public relations team wants me to settle with the family quickly to keep the press at bay. However, I can't settle until we're sure it's Mr. Brentwood's actual estate and heir we're dealing with. What's the next step?" Sean asks.

"Investigate further. I'll start by reviewing the will. I'll also try to track down the witnesses to the will. My firm will run a social media and background check on Mr. Brentwood to see if any family turns up. We'll also find out whether Mr. Galanis shows up as his partner. Do you have a way to find out who would have given Mr. Brentwood the ticket to the show? We need to know why he was in that seat on that night."

"I'll check with the ticket office, but people often trade and resell tickets."

"Is Detective Fielder the type to exchange info with us, or will he try to shut down our efforts and tell us to stay out of police business?"

"In the past, he's been reasonably open to working together. Why?"

"We should let him know about the unexpected visit by the supposed heir. He can run a background check to see if Mr. Galanis is who he says he is. Also, Detective Fielder should have Mr. Brentwood's driver's license. I'd like to get a copy and compare it with the signature on the will."

"That's a good idea."

"If the detective is feeling particularly talkative, maybe he'll also share other details of his investigation. His officers would have interviewed the performers and crew as well. I'd like to compare my notes with his. By now, he's also probably spoken with the vendor who built the tree. I'm sure that Fielder would have asked whether the vendor used those latches on other projects and whether they have had any issues."

"That's a solid plan. I'll set up a call with him. I'm not trying to get out of paying what's fair. If the Athena is responsible, then we'll take care of his family. Of course, this is a business. I can't hand out money if it wasn't our fault, but I'll do my best to make sure whoever is responsible pays."

"I understand. First, let's find the cause of the accident and why your safety checks didn't detect the problem. Second, we'll verify who controls Mr. Brentwood's estate. Then we'll know the next steps. I'm going back to your apartment to work."

"I'll walk you to my elevator," he says and guides me toward the flowing waterfall protruding from the back wall of his office.

He places his palm on a panel, causing the entire waterfall to move left a few feet, revealing the hidden elevator.

As we wait for the door to open, he pulls me into a tight hug and gives me a kiss on the forehead, saying, "In the past, we've had the occasional guest die from a heart attack or stroke. We couldn't prevent those tragedies. I never anticipated dealing with deaths at the hotel due to unnatural causes. It's been an emotional roller coaster lately. First, it was the deaths at the cooking competition five months ago, and now Mr. Brentwood. I don't know what I'd do without you right now."

"We've got this," I say, holding him close.

"We make an unexpectedly outstanding team. You were great today. Is it wrong that I have a hard-on for my badass attorney? I have plans for you the next time you visit my office," he whispers in my ear.

The elevator dings, saving me from the need to respond.

I leave, hot from his last comments and thinking we *do* make an outstanding team.

For now.

32
SEAN

Paxton Rossi and, to a lesser extent, his twin brother, Kincaid, hung out with Evan and me throughout college. That was before we learned that our families' businesses were incompatible with our friendship.

At that point, we faced a difficult decision. In the end, Evan went back to Catalinius, so it wasn't as much of an issue for him. Kincaid took off for medical school and wasn't around much. Paxton and I opted to find a way to preserve our friendship. As part of the solution, we agreed to never discuss business, and we never have. It was the only option given the conflict between our two families' occupations. Mine runs a casino; his runs the Las Vegas mafia.

Regrettably, today I must break that pact. We have to discuss business, and it's his fault. His people brought Rossi dealings onto my property. That was beyond unacceptable, and I'm going to find out why and make sure it never happens again.

Arriving at Henri's Bistro ten minutes early, it's obvious Paxton is already here. Two of his security men are stationed by the front door, and another is roaming the parking lot. Knowing him, his security team arrived at least twenty minutes before me to scout the place. Of course, there are more people gunning for his life than mine.

Walking into the restaurant, I scan the dimly lit dining room, immediately noting that it's completely empty. A moment later, the tux-clad maître d' greets me and motions for me to follow him. I do, chuckling to myself that Paxton has taken this meeting request to an extreme. We need to talk, but there was no reason for him to buy out the restaurant. A private room would have been sufficient. He's been a bit dramatic ever since his father's revelation at the end of college. It's probably why he's still alive though. Who knows what I would do in his situation.

Walking through burgundy velvet drapes guarded by two burly linebacker types, I'm greeted by my college buddy, who extends one hand and slaps my back with the other, saying, "It's good to see you. It's been too long."

"What's up with the deserted restaurant? I was starting to expect a body search before I could be in your presence," I say, only half-joking.

"My apologies for the extra precautions. Your invitation was unexpected, and I've received verifiable threats lately. I'm taking extra security measures when I'm in public these days."

"I wanted to meet in person, but I don't plan to cause you bodily harm."

"I know. It's everyone else who worries me. Like it or not, that's the life my father left me. I'm trying to reform our business as much as possible, but change happens slower than I'd prefer when it comes to how others perceive my family."

"Our dads both threw us curveballs when they passed away prematurely."

"They did. Have a seat and let's talk. Mauricio, Macallan for my friend and a vodka martini for me."

"Of course, sir."

"It's been close to a year since we've met. We're overdue for a lunch, but why the emergency meeting today?"

"Let's enjoy our drinks before getting serious. Tell me how you and your family are doing," I say.

"Kincaid's a successful surgeon in Los Angeles. Our little sister, Brooke, is in Europe now, studying art history. Neither of them wants to be near the family business even though I've cleaned it up considerably. We still see each other occasionally. Mom did a stellar job shielding all of us from Dad's world, but you know what happened. In the end, I couldn't escape it. Luckily, they could."

"Your mom made the correct choice using her British citizenship to take the three of you to England for school. I know you hated boarding school, but she gave you a normal childhood, which wouldn't have been possible here."

"That's true. Dad showed up for visits when the other fathers did, so we didn't figure out the family secret."

"I'm surprised your parents let you attend college in the States."

"They tried to convince me to study in England, but I was an adult by then. They didn't have much choice but to let me return to the U.S. Regardless, I didn't learn the real nature of Dad's work until my senior year of college. It was a shitty day when he sat me down and *explained* the family business."

"I'll never forget that day either. I wasn't sure I believed it when you called and shared the outlandish story. I mean, it was unbelievable that my friend's dad was the head of the Las Vegas mafia."

"It felt like a nightmare, and I couldn't wake up. Can you believe that day he asked Kincaid and me to decide which of us wanted to take over for him when he was gone? I'm still shocked my twin got up, said he was going to med school, and walked out, leaving me to deal with Dad by myself. That was the first time I felt alone. Before that, Kincaid and I were inseparable."

"I remember."

"You and I got ridiculously drunk that night trying to figure out what I was supposed to do."

"We never did come up with a solution where you weren't stuck with the business."

"We didn't," he says as food arrives.

As we eat, I remember Paxton wasn't the only one impacted by Mr. Rossi's revelation. It shook my life too.

When I returned home, I told Dad that my friend Paxton Preston just learned he was Marcus *Rossi's* son rather than Marcus *Preston's* son. It turned out that Preston was his middle name. Surprisingly, his parents hid this fact from him all those years. Preston was his mom's maiden name, and the name she'd put on his birth certificate. His dad had gone along with it to protect Paxton and please his wife.

Dad quickly sat me down in his office and explained that my friendship with the eldest son of the mafia don could cause problems for our family's casino business. In recent times, casinos have had to maintain a clean record or lose their licenses. Dad couldn't risk anyone thinking he or his family had mafia ties. That meant publicly hanging out with Paxton was a problem.

I was devastated that one of my best friends was being pushed out of my life. It wasn't fair. Eventually, Paxton and I found a way around the "friendship ban" when we both joined a soccer league in Las Vegas. That meant we didn't completely cut ties with each other —at least not when we were on the field, or the pitch, as our friend Evan calls it.

After a couple of years, I had to quit the team though, and our contact with each other became infrequent. But when Dad passed away, Paxton was one of the first people to reach out to me. A year earlier, he'd been called upon to take over his father's business too. Ironically, we had a lot in common again. We'd both lost our fathers and inherited major businesses to run at much younger ages than we ever expected.

The renewed connection with Paxton came with the problem of navigating the conflict between me being a casino owner and him being head of the mafia. We dealt with it by only meeting in large social settings, not meeting at my casino, and talking on the phone when we had the chance. We've never spoken about our businesses in any detail.

More recently, we've both been busy. It wasn't until I was told Paxton's associates were on my property that it dawned on me how long it had been since we've talked.

Paxton interrupts my thoughts, asking, "What's going on with you?"

"More than I'd like. I'm hoping you'll answer a couple of questions. Do you agree that our families have an understanding that none of your people are ever to come onto the Athena's grounds?"

"Absolutely. The agreement goes back to our fathers' promise not to let their businesses interfere with each other. Then you and I agreed that a line in the sand separating your work from mine wouldn't be sufficient. There had to be a wall, so we don't accidentally step across and interfere with each other. I'm not sure how much that matters now that my business in the U.S. is legit real estate. The agreement stands nevertheless."

"I know you've redirected your gambling business online and offshore and use that money to buy the real estate. You've said that makes it legal, or at least puts it into a gray area that's arguably legal. Nevertheless, you still have associates here who work with you on the gambling side of your business, correct?"

"What if we do?"

"They should never set foot in or around the Athena."

"Agreed."

"Then why the hell were these two guys talking to one of my employees on Athena property?" I ask, handing over a printout of the video image.

He stares at the image, recognition showing in his eyes.

"Those are your men. Don't bother denying it," I say.

"Calm down. I'm not denying it. Where was this photo taken?"

"It's from a camera near a back entrance to my hotel."

"Shit."

"No kidding. That's why I'm upset. Why were they there?"

"I'll find out. They had no business on your property."

"Did you know they came to the Athena or that they were involved with one of my employees?"

"Of course not."

I take a deep breath. My need to protect the Athena and its future can be overwhelming. Paxton's my friend. I should have trusted that he wouldn't purposefully cause my business harm.

"Please forgive my frustration, but you know the problems this could cause for me. I'm already dealing with the police investigating circumstances surrounding an audience member who died while participating in one of our shows. Now I have mafia guys intimidating one of my employees. I don't need the headache of a gaming commission investigation because the mafia is on my property."

"I understand. We'll figure this out before it causes you problems, but my family shouldn't be considered mafia after the changes we've made."

"Your business may be in a gray area, so you can argue it's legit. It may even be one hundred percent legal. But as you said, perception is slow to change. The Rossi family is still a powerful machine in this city, and our connection could cause me problems with the commission. I can't afford to be put in a position where I need to prove your business is above board to keep my casino in the clear."

"It won't come to that. These guys will be dealt with. You have my personal assurance."

"To be clear, I don't want them dead. Just keep them away from the Athena and my employees," I say somewhat jokingly.

"Who said anything about killing them? I'm not my dad. I avoid violence. My best guess is that these guys were trying to collect a gambling debt, but they aren't supposed to facilitate bets for your employees. I'll find out if they took the bet before or after you hired this person."

"If you don't condone violence, why does the video show them threatening my guy?"

"Sometimes these lower-level associates get out of line and turn to old-school tactics to collect. While nonpayment of debts is unacceptable, violence isn't the proper method of persuasion. I'll deal with them. They won't bother you again."

"Good. I also want the name of my employee they were talking to."

"You don't know who is in the photo? How do you know it's even one of your employees?"

"His blue badge showed up on the video. There's no question it was one of my employees. The image doesn't have enough resolution to read the name or ID number on the badge. I need to know which staff member it is and why he's gotten on the wrong side of your guys. You owe me that."

"Of course. Give me a few days. I'll fix this. We've known each other for a long time. Trust me."

"Okay. Can we meet here again in a few days?"

"I have a better idea. I heard you hired Evan's future princess as a chef. I know you don't want a Rossi on your property, but would you consider making an exception for my alter ego, Mr. Simon? I'd love to dine in the new restaurant that everyone's talking about and have a chance to see Evan again. I'll deliver the info you want then."

"She wasn't a future princess when the deal was made. Then our buddy, Evan, proposed. I'm shocked he's giving up his bachelor status, much less this soon. He's a lost cause now."

"That's what I've heard. What about you? Any chance of you tying the knot anytime soon?"

I choke on the coffee I'm sipping.

"You know I've always avoided relationships. What about you? Is there anyone special?" I ask, deflecting.

"No. There hasn't been anyone special for a long time. My family and work are not conducive to relationships with the type of woman who interests me."

"What do you mean?"

"The one woman I fell for walked out when she learned about my family. Let's not talk about that. It's in the past. Now what about dining with the princess?"

"We're doing a private soft opening of Pinot & Pie in a few days. If you promise to have the information by then, you can attend disguised as Mr. Simon. But I don't want my head of security identifying you as a Rossi, so make sure you're not recognizable. I'll explain to Daniel that you're a wealthy friend of Evan's. You can't bring your security though. We'll assign my guys to guard you during the event. If that doesn't work for you, then we can meet here in three days. Your choice."

"It's a risk, but I've asked you to trust me. I'll trust you to have my back at the Athena. Send me the details. You can give Evan a heads-up that I'll be there. Don't tell anyone else, not even your assistant or your security team who I really am. You can tell your security that Evan's wealthy friend recently received various threats. That should be sufficient."

"Done. What does Mr. Simon look like these days?" I never know what to expect when Paxton decides to disguise himself as the mysterious Mr. Simon. In the past, he's shown up as a red-headed rocker, a Hollywood producer, and an archaeologist back from a dig in Egypt. Regardless of the specific cover he picks, it gives him freedom to move around safely.

"It'll be a surprise. Look for my college signet ring. I'll be wearing it."

We shake hands, and I check this off my list for now. Soon I'll know which employee will no longer be working for me, and if he has a gambling problem, we'll also offer him help to overcome the addiction. As for the debt to Paxton, they will have to work it out without my assistance.

33
LOWRI

Back at Sean's apartment, Walter greets me. "Mr. Cartwright let me know you were on your way here to work. I set out snacks and sparkling water for you. Your new laptop arrived. I put it on the dining table, along with the instructions for logging into your new Athena account. It will allow you to access the security videos you requested. I'm told they'll be available in an hour or so. Let me know if you need anything else."

"Thanks, Walter. I can't think of anything."

"I'll leave you to your work then," he says, silently disappearing down the hall.

I quickly text Sean to thank him for the laptop as I drop into a chair at the dining table. While I wait for the security videos from the show rehearsals and performances, I have time to research Mr. Brentwood and his partner, Mr. Galanis.

First, I want to learn more about the attorney. That will help me in negotiations with him.

I Google: *Taylor Williams Attorney Las Vegas.*

The only Taylor Williams pops up at the Fishbourne Peabody firm. That's consistent with what I previously found in the country-wide database of attorneys. Clicking on the link, the page for him appears. That's strange. There's no photo, bio, or phone number for Taylor Williams. He must have joined the firm recently. I'll call the main number.

"Good afternoon. You've reached Fishbourne Peabody. How may I help you?"

"I'd like to speak with Taylor Williams, please."

"May I ask who's calling?"

"It's Lowri Upton. I'm following up on a meeting earlier today."

"Thank you. I'll transfer you now."

After a short wait, I hear, "Hello. This is Taylor. I understand you're following up on a matter. I'm confused as to which matter that might be."

I wasn't expecting a high-pitched voice that sounds nothing like the man we met, so I ask, "Is this Taylor Williams?"

"That's correct."

"Then I'm confused as well. I met with an attorney earlier today whose name is Taylor Williams. That attorney was a man with a deeper voice than yours. Do you have a relative by the same name?"

She laughs. "Not that I'm aware of, and I'm not a man. Whomever you met with was someone else."

"So, to be clear, you don't know of another estates & trusts attorney in Las Vegas by the name of Taylor Williams?"

"No, and it's a rather small community of lawyers in my field here. I'd know if there was one."

"How strange. He must not have been local. I'm curious. Why don't you have a photo on your website? Did you join the firm recently?"

"No. Someone hacked our website last week and posted cartoon caricatures of everyone. Management used that as an excuse to update our real photos. It's supposed to be fixed in a day or so."

"What a pain. Sorry to have bothered you."

"No problem."

"Thanks for your time."

I end the call, more suspicious than before. It's a strange coincidence that their website was hacked the same week someone showed up using her name.

For the next hour, I search every attorney database and website I can find, looking for another Taylor Williams. It turns out there are four. One is dead, one is retired, one is a patent litigator, and another is an in-house attorney at a car manufacturer. None of their photos even faintly resembles the man we met today.

Hmm. Detective Fielder will want to hear about this oddity too.

Turning to social media, I search for info on Mr. Brentwood. He wasn't actively posting anywhere. I don't even find any photos of him with his partner. On the other hand, Mr. Galanis is all over social media, but Mr. Brentwood is missing from the posts. Even more unexpected is that Amelia, the performer from the show, is in several photos with Mr. Galanis.

What does that mean? Is that how Mr. Brentwood got his ticket to the show? If that's the case, why didn't Mr. Galanis know that fact? And why didn't Amelia mention it?

I'm considering whether to have another chat with Amelia when my computer dings with a message. The surveillance videos are ready.

Great. Let's see if any of the accidents before Mr. Brentwood's fatal fall were caught on video.

TALK ABOUT BORING. I'VE CAUGHT MYSELF DOZING OFF AT LEAST THREE times as I go through hours of videos from the theater. I need caffeine and sugar.

"Walter, if you can hear me, please bring me a cup of coffee and something with chocolate for a snack."

If it wouldn't appall Sean's butler, I'd be happy to retrieve the snacks myself. However, when Walter is on duty, he's made it clear that he'll take care of my requests for food, and Jenny will handle anything related to my wardrobe. Apparently, my marriage to Sean meant a promotion for Jenny. She's now assigned to me full time rather than looking after me and VIPs in several other suites.

As if by magic, Walter appears. "Of course, ma'am. It will only take a few minutes."

"How do you do that?" I shake my head.

"It's my job, and if I do say so, I'm quite good at it."

He bows slightly and leaves before I can think of what to say.

Standing, I stretch and walk to the windows to watch the scene below, hoping to process the information I've discerned. Mr. Williams, Mr. Brentwood, and Mr. Galanis pose somewhat of a mystery. The videos haven't revealed anything helpful yet. The only thing remotely relevant is that workers moved the fake wall shortly before it collapsed. But it wasn't clear that they did anything to sabotage it.

The aroma of freshly brewed Kona coffee has me turning back to the table. A steaming cup sits next to a plate of chocolate-covered coconut macaroons. Yum! Looking around to thank Walter, he's nowhere in sight. Somehow, he slipped in, deposited the goodies, and disappeared before I could turn around. With his stealth superpower, he'd be quite valuable to the spy agencies.

Fortified with sugar, chocolate, and caffeine, I play the next video, hitting fast-forward when the stage is empty. It's a painstakingly slow process. I finally locate the third accident.

Aha! There is a common thread. It's time to find Sean.

Me: Where are you?

Sean: In my office.

Me: Can I come there?

Sean: It sounds like you're in need. I'd be happy for you to come in my office.

Me.: Very funny. I found something strange about the accidents and about Mr. Galanis's attorney.

Sean: Great. See you in a few minutes. Use the private elevator. Your palm print should work. If not, text me.

Me: Okay. Be right there.

Sean: I don't have any more appointments today. No one will interrupt us …

Me: Would it be a problem if they did?

Sean: I hope so. Hurry up.

With a grin on my face, I tuck the laptop into a tote bag and retrace my earlier steps to the private elevator that will take me to Sean's office.

Hopefully, we can fit the puzzle pieces together.

Since Lowri texted, I can't stop smiling. It's hard to explain. Something's missing when we're apart. Who knew a temporary wife would make me this happy?

Wife? What a bizarre concept. She *is* sizzling hot. It's no wonder I'm looking forward to her company, and after all, it's not a permanent arrangement, so it's not like I'm stuck married forever. Effectively, I get the best of everything for now—a perfect companion, a savvy lawyer, and mind-blowing sex with no long-term strings.

What else could I want?

A knock on the door grabs my attention. "Come in."

"I wanted to check in with you before I leave for the day. Do you need anything?" Emily asks.

"I don't think so. Lowri's on her way here. She found additional info about Mr. Brentwood's fall."

"What did she figure out?" Emily asks, looking concerned.

"I'm not sure yet. Hopefully, we'll get to the bottom of this soon. We can't reopen the show until we're certain there won't be more accidents."

"I'm good with details. I'd be happy to stick around to help."

"That's not necessary. I'll let you know tomorrow if we need you to follow up on anything."

"I don't mind staying," she insists.

"I appreciate your dedication but not another word. Go home. Your days here are already long enough. We've got this. I'll see you tomorrow," I say, motioning for her to head out. I'm fortunate to have an assistant as efficient and loyal as Emily. I try not to take advantage of her time.

As my office door shuts, the whirring of the elevator signals Lowri's imminent arrival. I'd stand up to greet her except there's a rapidly increasing tightness in my trousers that I'd rather not show off when we're supposed to be discussing business. Too bad we can't start with dessert.

I shift in my chair, seeking a comfortable position while staring intently at the contract I'm supposed to be reviewing. Nothing will deflate an untimely *problem* as fast as the details of a supply agreement for gaming chips.

A ding sounds as the doors open. My head instinctively pops up. Lowri's wide smile mirrors mine as we lock eyes.

"I brought my laptop to show you what I found. Is now a good time, or do you need a few minutes to finish what you're working on?" Lowri asks, sashaying toward me.

"Now's good. Join me around here, so we can both see the screen on your computer," I say, as I stand to greet her.

Lowri sets her tote bag on top of my desk and melts into my arms for a warm hug. Taking a deep breath, my lungs fill with the welcome scent of orange blossoms. Mmm. She's enchanting and addictive.

When we separate, I give her a quick peck on the forehead.

"Before we get sidetracked, tell me what you figured out. Have you solved the mystery as to how the tree's platform collapsed?" I ask.

"Not exactly. I noticed a common thread between the earlier accidents though."

She pulls her laptop out, setting it on my desk.

I'm instantly distracted as she bends over her keyboard to log in. My fingers wander to her inner thigh, inching her skirt up. There are real advantages to being married to your lawyer. It's acceptable to cross lines that would be forbidden otherwise.

Sadly, her left hand reaches for my wrist and yanks it away. "Not now. There'll be time for that later. We have work to do. Don't you want to find out why there have been so many accidents?"

"Sorry about that. You are too tempting. What did you figure out?" I ask, clasping my hands on my desk, attempting to keep them off her for the moment.

"Let me show you the video clips. Here's the first one," she says as a video pops up on the screen.

"What am I looking for?"

"They're getting ready to rehearse the first scene with the fireworks. Watch closely as they finish the setup of the sparklers at the back. Tell me what you see," she says, hitting play.

"Performers are milling around the stage. Some are clustered in small groups chatting. I count six crew members working on props near the back of the stage."

"How do you know they are crew?"

"The crew always wear navy shirts with the Athena logo across the back."

Pausing the video, Lowri zooms in and points to a person in navy, wearing dark glasses and a baseball cap. "Keep an eye on this spot."

"Okay." The video resumes. The crew finishes their adjustments, and the rehearsal begins.

As the music builds, dancers leap across the stage and the pyrotechnic fountains, called gerbs, go off, producing plumes of sparks. The effect is dramatic.

Staring at the spot Lowri pointed out, the effect quickly changes from dramatic to scary. A bush nearby the gerb catches fire and goes up in flames as a dancer cartwheels past. The dancer falls to the ground, ripping off his burning sock. Screaming ensues, the crew runs out with fire extinguishers, and the pyrotechnic fountains burn out—all this happens within a span of about twenty seconds.

"Damn. Why was the bush so close to the sparks in the first place?" I ask.

"I doubt it was supposed to be. As you can see, the bushes in front of the other fountains of sparks are further away. Now, let's look at the other two accidents we know about. The next video shows the wall before and during the fall."

"Is that the same crew member working on the wall who was near the fireworks earlier?"

"I think so. Now, take a look at this last video."

Lowri pops it up, pointing to the screen. "See that person checking the vines. Isn't that the same baseball-capped person who was in the other videos?"

"I think so."

"This final video is from the day of the show we attended. The last vine they checked was the one that ripped and sprained the ankle of the performer. The baseball-capped person is a common thread between the accidents. They were present immediately before each of the mishaps occurred. I suspect they either carelessly or purposefully caused each one."

"Is there any evidence it was intentional?"

"The main evidence is that it's the same person. It's hard to believe one person would repeatedly be that careless or that there would be so many coincidences. It's suspicious."

"Was this same person near the tree that killed Mr. Brentwood?"

"We don't know. The tree was stored backstage. The videos I've seen don't show it before the crew rolled it onto the stage. Can you find out if there are cameras backstage that cover that area?"

"I'll check with IT. We'll also track Ron down tomorrow to see if he can identify the crew member in the baseball cap."

"Great."

"Excellent work. Hopefully, we'll soon know who caused the accidents and who's to blame for the untimely death of our guest."

"There's one more thing. I don't think Mr. Galanis's attorney is who he says he is."

"What?"

"The only Taylor Williams who's an attorney in Las Vegas is a woman."

"He must be from somewhere else then."

"That's unlikely. I didn't find any attorney in the U.S. with that name who looks like him. There's a chance he's not an attorney at all."

"You've got to be kidding. Why would someone impersonate a lawyer?"

"The simplest answer is that Mr. Galanis couldn't afford a lawyer and talked a friend into helping him approach you. The other explanations are more sinister."

"How's that?"

"Mr. Galanis may not be the heir. I found photos on social media of him with Amelia. She's one of your performers. I didn't find any photos of him with Mr. Brentwood though. At a minimum, that's curious."

"He gave us a copy of the will. Do you think it's fake?"

"I'm not sure but plan to find out. Were you able to arrange the call with Detective Fielder? We need a copy of Mr. Brentwood's driver's license to compare with the signature on the will."

"I spoke with him briefly. He didn't have time for a meeting, so I gave him a summary of what we've learned so far. He agreed to email me a copy of Brentwood's license by tomorrow. In the meantime, I'll have security use their high-tech facial recognition software to see if they can find a match for Mr. Williams. Let's hope they can shed light on who the attorney really is."

"How? We don't have a photo of him."

"We have video from the conference room this morning. They can extract a single frame that shows his face. While you shut down your computer, I'll give them a call. I can ask about the backstage videos we want to see too."

"Sounds good. I'll sit down while you call. My feet are aching," she says, starting to pick up her laptop to move away.

I wrap my arm around her waist, pulling her down onto my lap. "That was rude of me not to offer you my lap sooner. We were so engrossed in the videos that I didn't realize how long you've been standing," I say, reaching down to pull off her sky-high heels and massage the arches of her feet.

"Oh. That feels good." She moans.

"Hold that thought while I call security."

"Sure."

I leave a lengthy voicemail for Daniel, which gives me a minute to talk myself out of what I'm about to do.

It doesn't work. I want this, so I return to rubbing Lowri's sore feet and say, "I have an idea."

"Whatever do you have in mind?" She gives a little wiggle of her hips against my legs.

"I'd originally planned to bend you over this desk and show you who's boss. Now, a slower, more drawn-out approach is in order."

"I wouldn't mind your first idea, but if you've changed your mind, should we go back to your apartment?"

My decision made, I stand, setting her bare feet on the ground. Keeping my arm around her waist, I turn us to face the wall behind my desk.

"No need to go upstairs. See that trophy on the bookshelf to the left."

"Yes."

Easing my hold on her, I say, "If you don't mind, lift it off the metal base."

She does, and I press my thumb on the nameplate below my favorite painting that's hanging within arm's reach.

She gasps as the wall pops open, revealing a narrow entrance.

Lowri peers into the secret room, asking, "What's in there?"

"It's a small studio apartment. It comes in handy when I'm

working late and want a quick nap or if I'm running late to an event and don't have time to go upstairs to shower and change."

"Why hide it? Do you keep valuables inside? If someone wanted to steal something, they could take that painting. It's an original Miró, right?"

"You know your art. It is. And no, I don't keep valuables inside. The apartment is hidden because it doubles as a panic room in case things go to hell. It was originally built for my dad after rather unsavory characters threatened him."

"Do you mean the mob? Is there one in Vegas now?"

"That's a complicated question, believe it or not. A form of it still exists. The current version of the 'mob' is quite different than in my father's day. My understanding is that the threats against my dad weren't from the mob though. There was a kidnapping attempt that led him to build this room. Since I took over, security encouraged me to maintain it as a panic room. We recently upgraded it with newer technology."

"It never occurred to me that you would need a panic room. I guess it's no different than Prince Evan. You both are potential targets for kidnapping."

"Unfortunately, that's true, but let's focus on happier thoughts," I say, taking the trophy from her hand. Setting the award back on the shelf, I wrap my arms around her and pull her close, nuzzling her neck with warm kisses.

"Are you okay being stuck inside with me for the next hour or so?" I ask in a whisper.

"Is there a time limit for how long you can stay inside? Do you run out of oxygen after that?" she asks.

I laugh. "No. There's a timer that prevents the door from opening again for sixty minutes. It's one of the panic room's features. I wanted to make sure you were okay with that. If not, we'll go upstairs."

"What if I need to pee?"

"There's a bathroom and fully stocked mini kitchen. You can pee as much as you want, and we won't starve."

"You mentioned napping. Does that mean there's a bed big enough for two?" she asks, coyly.

"Absolutely."

"Then I'd love to be trapped with you."

Leading Lowri through the narrow passage, I shut the door behind us, hearing the sophisticated locks click into place. I motion for her to sit on the end of the bed.

Grabbing the remote from the bedside table, I dim the lights and turn on a soothing playlist—my go-to recipe for relaxing.

Now it's time to make up for my oversights earlier. I should never have let her stand while we watched the videos. So, I gently take Lowri's shoulders and lower her body, resting her head on a plush pillow. Moving a chair to the end of the bed, I lift her tired feet onto my lap and give her feet a thorough massage, eliciting moans of pleasure from her as my thumb applies pressure along her arches.

"I'd let you do that all night. It feels amazing."

"I've only begun," I say, leaning over to kiss each of her ten perfect toes.

Reaching higher, I gently knead the backs of her calves while peppering her ankles with kisses and urging her knees apart. Lowering her feet, I stand between her legs as I shed my suit jacket. Loosening my tie, I toss it on the bed and carefully remove my cufflinks. Never taking my eyes off Lowri, I slowly unbutton my shirt, watching her squirm in anticipation, a frustrated look on her face.

"Can't you do that faster?" she begs.

"Patience, my dear. Patience."

She starts unbuttoning her own shirt. I stop her. "Nope. I'll take care of that when it's time. Give me your hands."

She reaches her arms forward, and I take her hands in mine. Before she knows it, I grab my tie and loosely wrap it around her wrists, finishing with a square knot. She can free herself if she wants. I'm pleased when she doesn't try. At least not yet.

I toss my shirt to the side, unfasten my belt, and slowly lower my zipper, maintaining eye contact. "Do you like what you see?" I growl with my own need.

"I love what I see. That's why this is torture. Why are you making me wait? I need you inside me now."

"Anticipation will only make it better. You know I'm right." I wiggle my eyebrows as I drop my trousers and crawl between her legs, spreading them further.

As her clasped hands grab for my arm, I push her wrists over her head. "Keep them there so I can concentrate on taking care of you. Can you do that for me?" She nods even though I know she's not used to letting someone else dominate her to this extent. It's a sign of trust that pleases me more than I'd expect.

I won't let her regret it.

Reaching for the hem of her skirt, I bend forward to kiss her inner thighs as I inch the material up. Uncovering the thin strip of red lace between her legs, I slip my finger under the delicate fabric. She's soaked for me. "I'm dying to taste you," I groan.

"Please," she whimpers.

I slide the fabric to the side and dive in as she arches against my mouth. She tastes like honey and spice. My tongue and lips explore her, varying the pressure and speed as I search for what Lowri likes best.

I've never been this intent on giving the ultimate pleasure to my partner. Don't get me wrong. The woman always comes first, but this is about more than merely ensuring she gets off. I want this to be the best she's ever had.

My fingers find her opening as my mouth sucks her ultra-sensitive nub.

Her arms fly to the back of my head, holding it in place. "Oh, Sean. Don't stop. I'm almost there."

"Mmm. Come for me, sweetheart."

I let my teeth graze across her clit, and she explodes, pulsing hard against my fingers.

When she finally sags against the bed, I crawl beside her and pull her body against mine.

Letting out a sigh, she says, "That was soooo good." She slips her wrists out of my poorly tied neckwear and places her hands on my chest, resting her head in the crook of my arm.

"It will only get better," I promise.

"I'm not sure that's possible, but I can't wait to find out."

I'm looking forward to it too.

35
LOWRI

Lying here next to Sean, we're both silently luxuriating in our sex comas. I may never move from this spot. Tonight has been perfect.

Sean delivered on his promise. He made our previous nights together seem like mere rehearsals for tonight's concert. And don't even ask me about the curtain calls. I'm tired and sore in a wonderful way.

Unexpectedly, I'm struck by an unwelcome concern. Turning on my side, I prop up on my elbow, staring at Sean.

He must sense the movement because he turns his head toward me.

"How many women have you locked in here with you?" I ask.

"What? None. You're the first. I've never told anyone else about this room," he murmurs without opening his eyes.

That's surprising and reassuring.

"Why me?"

He doesn't say anything at first. I've learned from taking depositions for work, no one likes silence. If someone doesn't answer my question immediately, it's best to wait. They will eventually answer to break the awkward silence, so I keep quiet.

It's not long before he opens his eyes, staring toward the ceiling as he says, "I'm not sure. It felt safe to share this secret with you. Will you share something special with me?"

"You already know my biggest secret."

"What's that?"

"I got drunk in Vegas and ended up married. Nothing will top that."

"That doesn't count. Tell me something personal. Why do you avoid relationships? Most women are the opposite in my experience."

"That's a long story."

"We're going to be here a while. We've got time."

"Okay. My parents had an extremely unhappy marriage. My dad cheated on my mom with his assistant, Bev. Mom and Dad divorced, and he immediately married Bev. She was young—mid-twenties. He was at least twenty years older than his new wife. I didn't see much of him after that."

"It must have been tough growing up without your dad."

"It's strange, but I didn't really miss him. He never showed much interest in me. I was a girl and not into sports. He mostly ignored me, even when my parents were married. After he left, I started referring to him by his first name, Lowell, because he never was a real *dad*. My mom, Rita, was a good mom until Lowell left. Then she turned into a bitter man-hater."

"Wait a minute. Don't tell me that that's how you got your name. Your parents combined the first part of Lowell with the first part of Rita to get Lowri?"

"Ding. Ding. Ding. You win the prize. When I turned out to be a girl, Dad insisted that they pass along his name. Mom refused to name me Lowella. That was his first choice. I'm thankful that Mom stood her ground. Instead, they compromised on putting their names together. They learned that a few random people had named their children Lowri. That was enough for them to decide it was an actual name. The rest is history."

"I'll give them credit for being creative."

"I guess. It sucked as a kid. I couldn't buy the cute stuff with my name printed on it. No personalized glitter pens, hot chocolate mugs, necklaces, or reusable water bottles for me."

"I like the name Lowri. I understand wanting the engraved stuff as a kid, but as an adult, standing out can be useful. You make enough money to have your own personalized coffee mugs made."

"You've got a point. I'll admit that I've come to appreciate the uniqueness now. That took a long time."

"I get it. I'm curious about Rita though. You said she was a good mom before Lowell cheated. I can understand her being bitter about the cheating, but why wasn't she still a good mom to you?"

"She did what she could under the circumstance, but she had to work all the time to pay the bills. When she wasn't exhausted from that, she suffered from repeated bouts of what I now know was depression. As a child, I didn't fully understand what she was going through."

"That's awful. She clearly needed counseling."

"I know. She ignored suggestions to get help until much later. Now she lives in her own world. If that's what she needs to cope, I'm good with it."

"That's tough. You've turned into an amazing person. I'm sorry your parents haven't been there for you."

"Someone gave me good advice when I was young. They pointed out that you don't select your relatives, but you can select your friends, so pick well. I've taken that to heart. I'm closer to Cassie than to anyone else. She's my best friend."

"That was excellent advice. As an only child with deceased parents, friends are my family. Do you have any siblings?"

"One brother. We stay in touch but have our separate lives."

"What's he like?"

"His name is Gerald, but he goes by Jerry. He's a couple of years younger than me. Dad was better to him because Jerry played basketball, Dad's favorite sport. My brother's a stockbroker now."

"Does he share your views on relationships?"

"Absolutely. When Lowell eventually divorced his second wife and vowed to never marry again, it sealed the deal for Jerry. He's a player in the sense that he has no interest in being stuck with any one woman. You two have that in common."

Sean turns his head to face me, a dark sadness in his eyes and his lips curved downward. He says, "That doesn't sound like a compliment."

"It's a fact. You, me, Jerry—we aren't into relationships. I vowed never to let a man cheat on me, and Jerry decided he'd never be happy with one partner for life."

"Those aren't my reasons," he whispers.

I'm not sure he intended to say that out loud. Now I'm curious.

"What *are* your reasons?"

"It doesn't matter. The result is the same."

"Please tell me. I promise never to share it with anyone outside this windowless hideaway. Wait a sec. There aren't cameras in here are there?"

"There are cameras for security in case of a threat. You'll be happy to know that I'm the only one who can activate them, and I didn't."

"Whew. The last thing I need is to be on a sex tape or have had a live audience in your security office."

He glares at me. "You don't think I'd do that to you, do you?"

"Not really. At least, not on purpose. You could have forgotten to turn the cameras off though."

His features soften. "This is where I come for absolute privacy. All the cameras, including audio, are off by default. They only activate at my command. You're safe here."

I roll over and wrap my arm across his chest, planting a kiss on his lips. "Thank you. I'm sorry I doubted that you would protect me. It's not easy for me to trust men after what my dad did to Mom."

As I snuggle closer, he says, "I understand."

"Now will you tell me why you avoid committing to anyone?"

"Yeah. My story is the exact opposite of yours and Jerry's. My parents were the epitome of the perfect, happy couple. They met in college, married when they graduated, and were inseparable from that point forward."

"Wouldn't that make you want what they had?"

"In the beginning, yes. That changed when Mom died suddenly. Dad was crushed. It killed me to watch him grieve. He shut down emotionally and was never the same. He turned into an absolute workaholic and devoted himself to the Athena.

It was devastating to watch as a teenager. I promised myself that I'd never get that close to anyone, so I wouldn't end up broken."

"That's sad. It's odd how our parents' polar-opposite marriages led us to similar views of love and relationships. To avoid what happened to them, we've thrown ourselves into work and vowed to lead commitment-free personal lives. It's our way of ensuring history won't repeat itself."

"Yep. For entirely different reasons, we fear being hurt by love."

"Are we missing out though? Look at Evan and Cassie. Sometimes I envy what they have."

"I honestly don't know."

"Was it Tennyson who said something like it's better to have loved and lost than never to have loved at all?"

"Tennyson sounds correct, but I never bought into that tenet in the past. Despite Dad's pain, he did though. There's always a chance he was right."

"Who knows, but this conversation is getting too serious for my comfort level. I'm not ready to deal with these issues."

"Ditto."

I close my eyes. Insecurities suck. Regret could be even worse though. Sleep takes over and saves me from further self-analysis.

36
SEAN

Lowri is sound asleep, draped across me with her head resting on my bare chest. I don't have the heart to wake her, even though it's morning. It hadn't been my plan to spend the entire night in my panic room. Between the physical exertion and the emotional talk, we were wiped out and didn't have the energy to leave. After I notified security not to expect us to emerge from my hideaway until morning, we turned out the lights and crashed.

I haven't slept that well in ages. Why did I share so much though? Lowri is so easy to talk to that I spoke without my normal filter, which is surprising. It's unusual for me to let anyone in, much less a woman I'm sleeping with. Of course, she's technically more than that.

As I absentmindedly smooth her silky hair that's flowing over the side of my torso, it hits me that I feel closer to Lowri than ever. This relationship is comfortable. Did I use the term *relationship*? Whatever it is, she's wriggling her way further into my life.

Shit.

I wonder if we'll feel awkward with each other after our conversation last night.

After our openness, she's going to kill me when she finds out that there's one secret I didn't share. It's time. Actually, it's well past time for Lowri to know about the requirements of my trust.

I never intended to wait this long to tell her. We've been busy. The timing hasn't been good.

No, those aren't the real reasons. I'm rationalizing because I hate to admit that fear is powerful. What if she won't agree to stay, leaving me without my dad's legacy? It's not that I think she'd purposefully screw me, but I have no right to expect her to remain married to me *and* sleep in my bed the whole time.

A wild alternative invades my thoughts. What if I subconsciously want to her stay even longer, but this is my way of pushing her away and protecting myself? By not telling her about the trust requirements, I've virtually ensured that she'll be pissed off when she finds out.

No, that can't be it.

Anyway, time is passing quickly, but the ninety days are not going to elapse without her finding out. Even if they do, there's a bigger issue. If she learns about the trust requirements later, she'll wonder if anything between us was real. Other than not telling her about the trust, our connection, albeit temporary, has been real to me. She'll never believe that. Lowri will assume everything I've done and said has been a ruse to keep the Grand Athena. She'll never have faith in me again.

My stomach lurches at those thoughts.

I'm so screwed.

Lowri stirs, yawning. Rolling onto her back and stretching her limbs to their full length, she asks, "What time of day is it?"

"Morning. It's five minutes before 10."

"No way. I rarely sleep that late. Without any windows to let in light, my body must be confused."

"Same here."

"It was a treat to sleep in, but I better get cleaned up. We have a busy day."

As she starts to sit up, I pull her back against me. "Hang on a minute. I remembered something else."

"You sound unexpectedly serious. What's wrong?"

"Nothing. It's about the annulment."

"Oh. What's the status?" she asks.

It's strange. She sounds a little sad at the thought. Huh.

"It may take a little longer. There's a delay."

"Really?" She perks up, lifting her head to look at me.

"Yeah. I'll explain. You see ..."

My phone rings, interrupting our conversation.

"You better answer that."

I take the call on speakerphone.

"Hello."

"It's Daniel. I'm sorry to bother you, but it's important. Can we talk?"

I'm surprised that the head of security would call me when he must know I'm in here with Lowri.

"What's up?"

"A red flag came up this morning. I also have answers to some of your questions from last night."

"Okay. What has you concerned this morning?"

"You need to see the videos. It will be easier to explain them in person. Would it be possible to meet this morning?"

"Did you check my schedule with Emily?"

"Um. I did. She didn't know where you were, and I was hesitant to share your current location. My understanding is that she's not aware of the panic room."

"I hadn't thought of that. At some point, I should tell her about it but not now. I'll text her and have her clear my calendar at 11:30 a.m. Be at my office then."

"Will do."

The line goes dead.

"That sounded ominous. A red flag can't be good," Lowri says.

"We'll find out soon. We better hustle if we're going to get upstairs, shower, change, and be back in time."

"Can Walter conjure up a quick breakfast too? We never ate last night, and I'm starving."

"I'll text him now. Remind me to fill you in on the annulment stuff later."

"Sure. A little delay's not a big deal. We have work to finish anyway."

"We do." I smile, relieved at the reprieve.

37
SEAN

Lowri and I make it back to my office by 11:15, coffee and breakfast tacos in hand thanks to Walter. We take seats at the conference table as we hear someone at the office door.

Knock. Pause. Tap. Tap. Tap. Pause. Knock.

"Come in, Emily."

"How did you know it's her?" Lowri asks.

Emily walks in and, hearing Lowri's question, answers, "I wanted a signature knock to signal that I'm alone. If a senior-level employee is pestering me to interrupt Sean, I use a different pattern. If Sean doesn't want to be interrupted, he ignores it, and I tell the visitor that he must have stepped out and offer to schedule an appointment. If they don't know Sean's here, it's easier to send them away."

"It saves all of us time. Too bad we didn't figure out this system sooner," I say.

"Do you need anything before your meeting with Daniel? Did you need me to sit in and take notes?" Emily asks.

"No, we're good. Please make sure we're not interrupted though," I say.

"Consider it done," Emily confirms as she leaves.

I call after her, "You can leave the door open for Daniel."

Daniel arrives five minutes early, laptop under his arm. He joins us at the conference table, saying, "Thanks for rearranging your schedule. It's important that you see this as soon as possible."

He opens his laptop, connects it to the 70-inch display on the wall at the end of the table, and pulls up a presentation. "We have several items to cover. I've organized everything into a few Power-Point slides to make it easier. If you don't mind, I'd like to start with your question about the guy who claims to be an attorney named Taylor Williams."

"Did you identify him?" Lowri asks.

"Yes. We isolated his image, and using our facial recognition software, we found a match. Let me show you. Here's the photo we extracted from the video of your meeting with him. It matched with this image," he says, pointing to side-by-side images on the display.

"Oh my god, that's him," Lowri says.

"Who is he?" I ask.

"He's an actor. His real name is Dylan Greyson."

"That explains why he had such a limited knowledge of the law and negotiation tactics. Someone must have hired him to play Taylor Williams."

"It also explains why someone hacked the real law firm's website —to hide that he's not the attorney. If you couldn't easily find the photo of Ms. Williams, there would be no reason to suspect the person you met was a fraud," Daniel says.

"Exactly. Dylan must have based his character on movies and television shows with a little help from Google," Lowri says.

"How bizarre. Why would Mr. Galanis bring a fake attorney?" I ask.

"My guess is that either he's a fake too, or he couldn't afford a real attorney. I'm leaning toward fake given I couldn't find any online connection between Galanis and Brentwood," Lowri says.

"Someone needs to talk with Greyson today," I say.

"We have an address for him. Do you want us to give him a visit or should we call Detective Fielder and have him follow up?"

"I'd prefer you visit him, but I suspect Lowri will tell us to contact the police. Am I right?" I ask, turning to face her.

"You are. If he's part of a scam, you should inform the police."

"You heard her. Get this to our detective friend ASAP."

"Will do. There's more though. We found additional videos of the tree prop before and during the performance where Mr. Brentwood fell."

"What does it show?" I ask.

Daniel types on his laptop, and a video starts playing on the large screen on the wall.

"We're looking at the area backstage where the tree was kept until it was needed onstage. Keep watching, and you'll see one of the members of the stage crew approach the tree in a minute or so."

With no audio to assist, Lowri and I closely watch the scene unfold in front of us. The dim, grainy video shows various performers and stagehands walking past. No one stops or pays attention to the prop.

"Get ready for it," Daniel says.

A person in jeans and a blue polo shirt, imprinted with the Athena logo, walks up to the tree and opens the door in the trunk, disappearing inside.

"Is he loosening the screws?" Lowri asks.

"Not likely. See what happens next."

A minute or two later, he comes out, shuts the door, and grabs a nearby ladder. He places the ladder next to the tree and climbs up onto the platform. We watch as he appears to inspect the railing, branches, and wiring.

"Oh my god, he's stomping on the platform. Why doesn't it give way?" Lowri asks.

"Because at this point, the platform is secure."

"When was this video?"

"This was about thirty minutes before the doors opened for the audience to take their seats."

"That means the tree was properly inspected before the show started. That's good news," Lowri says.

"So, what went wrong?" I ask.

"Take a look at this next video. It shows what happened about fifteen minutes before the tree was rolled onto the stage."

A crew member, wearing a blue polo shirt like we saw earlier, slowly walks toward the prop, looking left and right. It's not the same person who inspected the tree before the show. This person has a different build.

"That's the person with the baseball cap who we saw in videos right before the other accidents occurred," Lowri exclaims.

"What are they holding? Can you zoom in?" I ask.

Daniels complies and says, "There's your answer."

My jaw drops as I stare at the fuzzy image of a screwdriver.

"As you can see, it appears the platform of the tree was purposefully sabotaged, and this is who did it," Daniel says, closing the video.

Shit.

I'm seething mad, fists clenching under the conference table.

"Who is the scumbag?"

"That's still a mystery. We talked to Ron, and he doesn't recognize the person in the video."

"Did you run facial recognition?"

"We can't. The person was careful to hide their face from the cameras."

"I assume they couldn't get backstage without being an employee of the Athena. Is that correct?" Lowri asks.

"Not unless someone snuck them in, or they work for one of our outside vendors."

"How would they have gotten one of the shirts?"

"Those are easy to come by. They keep a stack of clean shirts backstage. The crew members leave their dirty ones to be laundered and grab clean ones each week."

"So how do you propose we figure out who the killer is?" I ask.

"Everyone who works on the production enters the theater through the same entrance. We're in the process of pulling the videos for all the days where there were incidents involving this person in the baseball cap. We'll watch to see when someone matching this description entered the theater and cross-reference their entrance with the employee ID card that was scanned at that time. It's going to take a few days to go through all the tapes to make sure we have the right person in each video and determine whether they use the same ID each time.

Eventually, this process should lead us to the person who killed Mr. Brentwood. It's going to take time though. You'd be surprised at how many crew members wear baseball caps. We have to sort through hours of video."

"Understood. Also pass this info along to Detective Fielder. It will confirm he's dealing with murder rather than an accident. He also needs to know that this actor—Greyson—may be involved in something more dangerous than a mere money scam."

"Yes, sir. I'll take care of it. Before I leave, there is one other thing. It's the red flag I mentioned."

"I'm not sure I want to hear about anything else but go ahead."

"You know those two Rossi guys who were hassling one of our employees."

"Yes, what about them?"

"They were at the performance. They had VIP tickets to meet the performers after the show."

"How do you know?"

"I had the IT team run a facial recognition program to look for them anywhere on the property in the last month. It's been running continuously, and this popped up overnight. When we pulled up the video, they were sitting in the VIP section at the performance."

"Are you telling me they had something to do with the sabotage?"

"We're not sure. It's certainly suspicious."

"What happened after the show? Did they go backstage?"

"No, the VIPs were told the backstage tour was canceled due to an accident. They were offered tickets to a future show instead."

"Paxton Rossi assured me that his guys were not supposed to be here, so why do they keep turning up?"

"Who knows? It doesn't make sense that the Rossis would be involved in sabotaging your show. It's not their usual type of business. We'll figure it out though."

"Do that and quickly. Also, make sure that those guys don't darken our doors again. Do you understand?"

"Yes, sir. We're circulating their photos to everyone via text. If they show up, they will be thrown out."

"Get answers from them first. Find out why they're here in the first place."

After Daniel leaves, Lowri and I sit in silence, processing what we have learned.

A confused look crosses Lowri's face as she asks, "Why would the mafia threaten your performer and kill someone from your audience?"

"It doesn't make sense to me. I've known Paxton Rossi for years. I met with him recently to sort this out. He swore to me that his family is essentially legit now and that those guys should not be here."

"Do you suspect he was lying?"

"I didn't think so, but we haven't been as close as when we were in college. He could be more like his father's generation than I thought. It's possible that Mr. Brentwood owed him money too and was targeted. If that were true, then I'd be shocked if Paxton wasn't consulted before it happened. However, when we met, I didn't get a sense he was lying."

"What about the earlier mishaps? How do they fit in?"

"Your guess is as good as mine."

"What if the killer, or killers, intended the murder to look like another in a string of accidents? But, if that was the plan, how did they arrange for Mr. Brentwood to be the audience member selected to go on stage?" Lowri asks.

"I don't see how they could have unless someone here at the Athena made that happen."

"If you wanted to arrange for a friend of yours to be the one selected, what would you do?"

"That's easy. I'd have Emily take care of it."

"How much do you trust Emily?"

"Completely."

"There's rarely anyone who deserves that level of trust. Be careful. Watch your back."

"Don't worry. I'm always careful."

"Would a performer in the show or someone in the ticket office have access to the ticket? Could they give it to a friend?"

"Occasionally, that would be possible. It depends on whether we need it for a VIP."

"I see. I'm off to analyze the will. Don't forget to email me Mr. Brentwood's driver's license when Fielder sends it."

"Will do."

I stand and give Lowri a quick hug and a peck on the cheek.

As I enjoy the view of her perfect ass walking toward the elevator, I'm left to wonder about my trust in Emily. She has been asking questions about Mr. Brentwood's death and offering to take an active role in solving the mystery. Is it possible she's trying to steer the investigation away from herself?

I shake my head. That can't be. This isn't a thriller movie where my efficient, dedicated assistant turns out to be a villain. Emily's only trying to help. Besides, she doesn't have any connection to the Rossi family, and clearly, they must be behind this one way or another.

38
LOWRI

With my arm laced around Sean's, we walk into Pinot & Pie for the soft opening. Tonight Cassie is hosting a reception and dinner as a test run before the real opening. I'm stunned, which is surprising given that I've already seen the remodeled space. It was magnificent when I had lunch here with Cassie. Now it's reached another level, if that's even possible. In the dim lights, the purple, gray, and cream décor have a royal vibe. It's befitting of my best friend's soon-to-be princess status.

"Sean, this place is even more spectacular in the evening. It's perfect."

"I'm pleased with the result. We were aiming for a regal, modern look."

"Mission accomplished. It's very Cassie. Everyone's going to love it. Do you see Cassie and Evan? I should congratulate her."

"She's on the far side, surrounded by people. Let's give her time to get through the initial greetings. Then she'll have time to talk. We can grab a drink and try out the appetizers while I thank the guests who received special invites from me."

"Lead the way."

Music and electric energy fill the air as we mingle among the guests dressed in shimmering cocktail dresses and tuxes. Sean said that everyone accepted their invitations to attend. Who wouldn't? They'll forever be sharing stories about the evening that a future princess was their chef. That will be a unique brag for years of cocktail parties to come.

As we slowly make our way around the bar area, Sean shakes hands and introduces me to more people than I could possibly remember. I smile and make small talk, but my mind is on Cassie. This year has been transformative for her. She's gone through such an unexpected metamorphosis from burned-out lawyer to chef to a future princess in a few months.

Her life sounds like the plot of a romance novel, but it's real. I'm ecstatic for her. After losing her parents the weekend of her law school graduation, she's had a tough time. She deserves happiness and security. Everyone does.

A waiter offers us champagne. The rims are dipped in crushed, freeze-dried raspberries, which is one of Cassie's favorite tricks to add a little extra splash to the presentation.

A guy approaches us, slapping Sean on the back, saying, "Hey there. It's great to see you."

"Wes, I'm glad you could make it. Lowri, meet my friend, Wes. He owns one of the best food and beverage distributorships in Las Vegas. He's responsible for sourcing the ingredients that Cassie is using tonight."

"It's great to meet you. I suspect you're one of Cassie's favorite people if you procured the items she wanted," I say.

"She's amazing to work with. It's been a pleasure. Try these crostini," Wes insists, signaling for a passing server to stop.

Taking a bite, my mouth is filled with a lovely mixture of textures and flavors. "These are phenomenal."

"They should be. Cassie insisted on fresh figs for homemade preserves, the best whole-milk ricotta, imported Italian prosciutto, and a delicate lavender honey from France. We're nearing the end of fig season, so it was a challenge to find the quality she wanted, but we did." Wes says.

"I'm glad you succeeded. When Cassie moves to Catalinius, I'm going to miss her showing up at my parties with her creations like this," I say.

"I bet," Wes comments.

Sean has already checked out of this conversation, which is strange. He's been a little off all evening. Nudging him and turning to his friend, I say, "Wes, forgive us. We need to find Cassie and Evan."

"Yes, excuse us, Wes. Thanks again for being here," Sean says, taking the hint and moving us along.

When we're out of earshot, I ask, "What's wrong? Why are you scanning the crowd? Is someone missing?"

"Nothing's wrong. One of my guests, Mr. Simon, is supposed to have information about which of my employees was meeting with Rossi's guys. I'm also hoping Mr. Simon can shed light on what involvement the Rossi guys had in Mr. Brentwood's death. I can't find him though."

"What does he look like? I'll help you look for him."

"That's the problem. He'll be in disguise. He doesn't want to be recognized."

"What's the plan then?"

"He'll be wearing a signet ring and should approach me. I'm impatient though. We need answers."

"I understand, but you'll have to wait. Let's enjoy the party for Cassie and Evan's sake until Mr. Simon makes his presence known."

"I'll try. Let's find the royal couple."

We slowly make our way to the corner where they're talking with a beautiful woman who's a little younger than I am.

Sean smiles broadly when he catches sight of the woman and hurries toward her. They embrace in a long hug as he whispers something to her.

My chest tightens. Is this one of his previous conquests?

I reach Cassie's side and turn to face her with a questioning look as I mouth, "Who is she?"

Cassie hides a snicker behind her hand and whispers, "Jealously is not an attractive look. Besides, she's ..."

Sean steps out of the hug and reaches for my hand, interrupting us.

"Lowri, this is Princess Gabriella Brianna Sofia Caterina, better known as Evan's little sister."

Talk about jumping to the wrong conclusion.

"Lowri, I've heard all about you from Cassie. Please call me Bri."

"It's wonderful you could be here with Evan and Cassie tonight," I say.

"It took a little reworking of my schedule, but the last-minute invitation to the tennis tournament gave me the opportunity to make the trip."

"I'd hoped our parents would join us too. Unfortunately, they already had another commitment," Evan says.

"You know I never expected them to come. I'm thrilled to have all of *you* here. Opening Pinot & Pie is a dream come true and to have the most special people in the world with me is more than I could have hoped for," Cassie says.

The lights blink several times and spotlights draw our eyes to the thirty-foot-high glass wall enclosing the impressive wine room. The music changes to a pounding boom, boom, boom as five acrobats drop behind the glass in dramatic bursts, clinging to unfurling white and lavender aerial silks. The women are wearing crystal-encrusted bikini tops with long leggings. The men are only wearing leggings, showing off their ripped, bare chests.

As the music transitions to a vivacious, up-tempo song, the acrobats go into a fast-paced performance of twists, flips, turns, climbs, and drops.

Bri leans toward me, saying, "Look at the abs on the guy in dark purple."

Nodding in agreement, I muffle a laugh. That wasn't a comment

I'd expect from a princess, much less one I just met. No wonder Cassie and Bri are already friends. She's fun. "He certainly has the muscles to pull off those moves."

Another performer catches my attention. I almost didn't recognize Amelia. Her hair sits in a bun atop her head. Loose blonde curls dangle around her face. She's every bit as fit as the guy who caught Bri's attention. She also reminds me of someone else. I can't remember who.

As the song ends, so does the show. The same deep voice from the pyrobatics show fills the room, saying, "Welcome to the soft opening of Pinot & Pie at the Grand Athena. Tonight you will experience the culinary magic of Chef Cassandra Edwards. It's time to take your places in the dining room. Prepare for your taste buds to be awakened, tantalized, and pleasured."

"That was quite the dramatic introduction. He made it sound like we're about to have a sexual dining experience." I laugh.

"Would that be so bad?" Sean asks, wiggling his eyebrows.

I don't have a chance for a flirtatious retort because Detective Fielder quietly pulls Sean and me away from the crowd that's scurrying to find their tables. "Thanks for including me tonight," he says.

"Of course. Chef Cassie and I wanted you here. We appreciated your help seeking justice during the cooking competition," Sean says.

Detective Fielder chuckles. "I guess that means she's forgiven me for suspecting her at one point."

"Don't give it another thought," Sean says.

"I'll apologize again to be safe. I love her food and wouldn't want to miss out on future invitations. That's not the reason I tracked you down though. We have more info on the fake attorney who showed up in your office."

"What did you learn?"

"We interviewed Greyson. He was scared, so he talked. His career as an actor isn't going well. He was desperate for money and willing to take any job that came with a quick payment. He claims he didn't realize it was a scam. He thought it was a prank and would be good practice for an upcoming audition. He explained that his agent got him a tryout for a role in a new legal drama. He figured the role as Taylor would help him prepare."

"Who hired him?" Sean asks.

"He claims not to know. He was hired through a website where actors can post their credentials and availability for gigs. The website looks legit. He received the cash payment by mail, but unfortunately, didn't save the envelope."

"Did he know whether Mr. Galanis is really Mr. Brentwood's heir?" Sean asks.

"No. He hadn't met Mr. Galanis before that day, and they parted ways as soon as they left the Athena. According to the actor, Galanis wasn't very talkative before or after their meeting with you. He doesn't think Galanis was the person who hired him. Greyson said that after your meeting, he suspected that his role was a scam instead of a prank. He turned down a request to follow up with you about a settlement offer. We're reaching out to the website owner to see if they will share the name of the user who hired the actor. But we're not holding our breath. The website owner will probably insist on a subpoena. Even if we receive the info, the user may have provided fake info."

"Did you arrest Greyson?" I ask.

"We passed along the information to the district attorney. It will be up to her as to whether he's charged, but given the facts, it's unlikely. We can still use the threat to make a deal with him if we need his help."

"Thanks for letting us know. Keep us posted if you learn more," Sean says, shaking the detective's hand.

<h1 style="text-align:center">39</h1>

SEAN

Evan, Bri, Lowri, and I converge on our dinner table and find one of the six chairs is already occupied by a stately, gray-haired man. I can't help laughing as he stands.

"What's funny?" Lowri asks.

"It's an inside joke from college. Play along, and I'll explain later."

"I can do that, but I'll want all the details," she says with a wink.

"Professor Simon, it's been a long time," I say, patting him on the back.

In a weathered, husky voice, the professor says, "It has been. Thank you for inviting me tonight. It's such a pleasure to see you and Evan again."

"We're glad you could join us tonight. Have a seat. Evan and I will take the ones on either side."

We have a round table for six, so I pull out the chair to my right for Lowri, and Bri takes the chair on the other side of my wife. We leave a chair between Evan and Bri for Cassie in case she joins us during the evening.

Evan and Bri know who's hiding behind *Professor Simon's* disguise but don't know why he's making an appearance tonight. In contrast,

Lowri knew I've been looking for Simon, but she doesn't know who he really is. It's going to make for an interesting evening. I hope the good professor has the answers he owes me.

"Excellent. Are you going to introduce me to the lovely lady next to you?" Prof. Simon asks.

"Forgive me. This is Lowri Upton. Lowri, meet Prof. Simon. Professor, I believe you know everyone else."

They shake hands and everyone takes a seat.

"This is a wonderful surprise. Sean didn't mention you would be here tonight," Evan says.

"It was a last-minute decision. Enough about me, let's talk about what's important," the professor says.

"What's that?" Bri asks.

"Food, of course. Have you looked at the tasting menu for tonight? I can't wait to try everything," he says, holding up a printed card that lists each course.

As we're discussing it, Cassie emerges from the kitchen and steps to the center of the room, wireless microphone in hand.

"Welcome. I'm Cassandra Edwards, better known as Cassie. Thank you for joining us tonight. As you all know, I'm here as the result of a cooking competition. The theme for one of the rounds of that contest was 'Comfort with a Flair.' At the time, my mind raced trying to figure out what that meant. The theme could have different meanings to different people. It could refer to comfort food with an unusual twist. Or it could be fancy preparation and plating of a traditional comfort food. Neither of those seemed quite sufficient for the Grand Athena, which represents luxury in everything. That led me to wonder if we were intended to create an upscale experience based on comfort food concepts. Ultimately, I decided the goal was to deliver all three. While I'm not sure that I completely accomplished that goal during the fast-paced competition, I hope we've achieved that special experience for you tonight. Please enjoy!"

The crowd breaks into applause, cheering as Cassie takes a bow and leaves the dining room. Paxton, aka Prof. Simon, uses that moment to learn toward me, whispering, "I have the information you want. Can we talk somewhere private after dinner?"

"We can go to my office when this is over."

Before Paxton can say anything else, Emily approaches me. "Sean, the wine you requested will be brought down next."

"Thanks for giving me the heads up, but you're a guest tonight. You aren't supposed to be looking after me."

"When I ordered your wine for tonight, I told them to give me a heads up when the acrobats were ready to retrieve the bottles. That way, you and your guests wouldn't miss it. But don't worry, I'm definitely enjoying myself tonight. I'm with the group by the far window."

"I appreciate your thoughtfulness. Now promise me that for the rest of the evening you'll leave the work to everyone else."

"I will. Thanks for including me tonight."

As she's about to leave, Emily does a double take when she notices the professor. She opens her mouth as if she's going to say something. Instead, she scurries to her table. How odd.

Turning back to my mafia friend, he looks strangely sad as he watches Emily depart. "Sean, who was that woman?" he asks.

"That's my assistant, Emily. Do you know her?"

"No. She reminds me of the only woman who ever broke my heart. Her name was Lee. Emily dresses conservatively and seems introverted unlike Lee. Otherwise, Emily could be Lee's twin."

"I guess it's possible Emily has a twin. She's doesn't mention her family very often, but I believe she's an only child."

"It's doubtful they're related. It's not important anyway. Lee hasn't been in my life for a long time. So, back to the reason Emily stopped by. What was she saying about acrobats retrieving wine? Are we supposed to be watching something?"

"We are." Catching everyone's attention, I say, "I've ordered special wines from my collection for our table tonight. Emily informed me the acrobats are about to climb the silks to the top to retrieve the bottles for us. Now's the time to watch."

As we watch the acrobats use the silks to climb and descend the wine tower, I pull out my phone, quickly sending a text to the stage manager for the pyrobatics show. We need to make sure that two riggers check these silks every night too. We don't need one to tear while an acrobat drops down the fabric with a wine bottle nestled in a holder strapped to their body. Broken glass and a fall could be a lethal combination.

As we're captivated by the flavors and plating of the food, we chat about a myriad of topics ranging from Evan and Cassie's new charitable work to Bri's tennis schedule for the next year. She's particularly excited about Wimbledon. She may be given a wild card slot to compete in the tournament.

We're finishing dessert when Cassie finally joins us at the table. I raise my glass for a toast. "To Chef Cassie and a wonderfully successful soft opening of Pinot & Pie. The Grand Athena and I are honored to have you as our guest chef this month. Cheers."

"I can't thank you enough. You'll never know how much this means to me. Your faith in me is humbling," Cassie says.

"It was easy. You earned it. Now, if you'll excuse the professor and me, I've promised to show him photos in my office."

I whisper in Lowri's ear, "Take your time here with our friends. I'll meet you in the apartment a little later. Simon has info for us, but he wants to meet in private."

Now it's time for answers.

40
SEAN

"Professor, follow me. The photos we were discussing are in my office," I say, escorting Paxton out a back entrance of Pinot & Pie. As I prearranged, my security guys essentially surround us, maintaining a short distance on all sides. We take the route through the casino even though it's longer than my typical path. I'm not comfortable giving Paxton access to the Maze. I don't know how much I can trust my college friend, given the potential connection between his men and Mr. Brentwood's death.

"I'm sure the photos will bring back fond memories," he says for the sake of our ruse.

As we're walking, I ask, "So what happened to Lee? If she was the love of your life, why aren't you still together?"

A faraway look clouds his eyes as he hesitates before answering.

Waiting, I wonder why I'm asking the question in the first place. But for some reason, I'm curious as to why he let such a special person go, whereas Evan grabbed Cassie tightly and practically won't let her out of his sight.

Am I subconsciously wondering what to do about Lowri? She's certainly become an integral part of my life. Will the desire to be with her fade when it's safe for me to get an annulment? Or if I let her go, will thinking of her put Paxton's look of longing and regret on *my* face?

Finally, Paxton saves me from analyzing my dilemma, saying, "It was my fault. I kept a secret from Lee for too long, and it came out in the worst way possible. After that, it was impossible to restore the relationship. That was the main reason she left me. There were other factors too. I'd rather not talk about it more."

"Understood."

Shit. I have to tell Lowri about the requirements of my trust and the real reason for the delay in processing our annulment. Even if we don't plan to stay together, I'd like us to remain friends.

We walk in silence until we're at my office.

Opening the door, I invite Paxton in, signaling for the security guys to wait outside my door.

"Let's get to business. What did you find out? Which of my employees were your guys hassling and why?"

"You should know that the guys in the video no longer work for the Rossi family. Before we parted ways, we had a productive *talk.* They only knew your employee as A.R. Those could be his initials or something else. They didn't know."

"Are you sure they didn't know?"

"Zero doubt."

"I won't ask how you're sure. Why were they involved with A.R.?"

"Your employee was into us for a large gambling debt. The guys in the video had taken the bets and wanted to collect. The gambler promised that he would have the money shortly. In the video, my guys were emphasizing that it would be bad if he were lying."

"They shouldn't have been doing business on my property."

"Of course not. They no longer work for me."

"Did you know they were also at our show the night an audience member died? They had VIP passes."

"Oh, hell. No, I did not know that. Too bad I can't fire them again."

"We've had a few unexplained mishaps on the show. Mr. Brentwood died as a result of the last one. It's suspicious that your men were onsite with backstage passes that evening."

"Are you suggesting my family had something to do with his death?" he asks sternly.

"I'm merely sharing facts about two guys you recently let go," I say as I turn my palms up.

"Okay, but for the record, I certainly didn't have anything to do with sabotage on your show. No one else in my family would do that to you. If those two idiots who used to work for us did something without our permission or knowledge, then we'll find out. They will not get away with it. That's not acceptable."

He's turning bright red as he punches his right fist into his left palm. I've rarely seen Paxton mad, but he's seething now.

"Thanks for confirming that it wasn't you or your family. I couldn't imagine the Rossis would mess with my family after our long history. It's still strange that your guys repeatedly violated our longtime pact to keep our businesses separate. It's worked for our families for decades. Why would they take bets from one of my employees?"

"In their minds, taking a bet from someone who worked here was unrelated to your family. They have since disavowed that belief."

"You said you've moved away from violence."

"I never mentioned violence."

"Touché. I'm still left with figuring out which of my employees is gambling more than he can afford."

"I have one more thing for you that may help."

Paxton pulls a folded piece of paper from his pocket and hands it to me.

"What's this?"

"A photo of your gambler."

"Where did you get this?"

"The two guys had a habit of taking photos of the people placing bets in case they had to track them down later. Do you recognize him?"

"No. Your guys aren't even good photographers. A shadow covers half his face."

"They didn't excel at many tasks that are useful to me."

"I'll see if our security team can figure it out. Between this mediocre photo and the initials A.R., let's hope they can work their magic."

"Oh, there was one other thing. I'm not sure it means much. They said he wore makeup sometimes. The problem is that it's common for guys in Vegas to wear makeup for personal or professional reasons."

"Thanks. I'll pass the info to our team. Thanks for helping me out with this."

I text Daniel to let him know about the new photo.

"You're welcome. Now that our business is done, tell me about Lowri. You two have more of a connection than is typical for you. I sense she's more than your usual arm candy. What's the deal?"

"You wouldn't believe me if I told you. That's a story for next time."

"Intriguing. Evan and I are getting together in a couple of days. Let us know if you can join us."

"I will. Thanks again. My guys will make sure you make it out safely," I say, opening my office door.

We part ways because Daniel is waiting for me in the security office to look through employee photos.

Then it'll be time for the hard talk with Lowri. By that time, maybe she'll already be asleep, and I can put off the conversation until morning. She's a night owl, so it's doubtful, but I can hope.

41

LOWRI

I've been back at Sean's apartment for over an hour. My mind is racing as it runs on autopilot, processing all the information we've collected. At this point, I'm too tired to process this much data.

Needing a break, I crawl into bed and turn on a movie. That usually helps me clear my mind. Then I can work through the facts with Sean when he finishes his meeting with the friendly, but mysterious, Prof. Simon. I can't wait to hear the inside joke Sean mentioned, and hopefully the professor will provide the remaining pieces of the puzzle.

THE NEXT THING I KNOW, SEAN IS CRAWLING INTO BED BESIDE ME AND pointing the remote control at the television to turn it off. I must have dozed off while watching. Rubbing sleep from my eyes, I ask, "What time is it?"

"It's late. Go back to sleep,"

"No, I'm awake now. Tell me about your meeting with Prof.

Simon. Have you been with him this whole time?" I ask, propping myself up with a couple of fluffy pillows at my back and smoothing the comforter over my lap.

"After talking with him, I went to the security office to meet with Daniel to follow up on the information Paxton shared."

"Wait a minute, you were meeting with Prof. Simon. Who is Paxton? And what was the inside joke about the professor?"

"I did promise to explain, didn't I? I'll start with a story from my college days. Evan and I were friends with Paxton Preston back then. One Halloween, Paxton decided to dress up as one of our professors, Dr. Simon. He looked exactly like him. He emulated the professor's voice and quirks to perfection. It was hilarious."

"So, are you telling me that tonight Paxton was pretending to be Prof. Simon?"

"Exactly."

"Why?"

"He didn't want anyone to recognize him, and for my sake, we needed to avoid anyone linking the two of us with each other."

"I don't understand."

"It's complicated. Do you remember when you were in my office and Daniel stopped by to tell me that two mafia guys were intimidating one of our employees outside a back entrance to the Athena?"

"Yes."

"You've heard me mention Paxton Rossi. He's head of the mafia family in Vegas. Paxton Rossi and Paxton Preston are the same person. When we were in college, Paxton didn't realize his father was the mafia kingpin. His parents hid it from him by using his mother's maiden name, Preston."

"How is it possible he didn't know?"

"His mother shielded him from his father's business from the time he was a child. When he, his twin brother, and his sister were young, his mom moved them to London. They went to school there until they each turned eighteen and returned to the U.S. for college.

It wasn't until his last year of college that his parents told him about his dad's work. He was dumbfounded."

"That still doesn't explain why he showed up as Prof. Simon tonight."

"Now that he's head of the family, he's making efforts to legitimize their business interests. Unfortunately, he's still routinely the subject of threats. That's where the disguise comes into play. His various versions of Simon allow him to mingle in public and reduce the likelihood that someone will try to kill him."

"That makes sense. I can understand why you are worried about being linked with him. You can't afford for the Athena to be seen as having mob connections."

"Exactly. We've found ways to quietly remain friends over the years, but we are extremely careful to keep our business interests separate. That means he's usually not welcome here. I made an exception tonight because we needed information from him. He also wanted to see Evan and meet Cassie. Paxton taking on his alter ego was the easiest solution for all of us."

"It's complicated, but I guess it worked."

"It did. Paxton gave me a photo and some info about my employee who was interacting with his guys. It turns out that my employee racked up a large gambling debt with the Rossi family. Unfortunately, Paxton doesn't know the gambler's full name, only that he goes by A.R."

"Shit."

"No kidding. I gave the info to Daniel. It's possible this guy is an entertainer. The photo isn't great, but security should be able to narrow down the possibilities."

"May I see the photo?"

"I already told Daniel to scan it and send it to us."

"Good. What will you do when you figure out who the gambler is? Will you fire him?"

"Gambling addiction is a serious problem. We'll try to get him help, but he can't keep working here. His debt makes him an easy target for blackmail. We can't risk him using inside info about the Athena to pay off a blackmailer."

"I see what you mean. Is gambling addiction common?"

"It occurs more often than we'd like. I've read studies that say it affects about one to two percent of Americans. It makes me ill to see people gamble away money they can't afford to lose."

"You must make a lot of money from those people though."

"Hopefully not. Certain guests may lose a little more than they intended. When they do, most people don't repeat that behavior, or they spend a little less on something else to make up for it. Those people usually aren't addicts. The Athena doesn't want money from people with gambling problems. We want people here who are having spectacular experiences, not those who believe their next bet will turn their life around. That never works out well for anyone."

"What are you doing about it? How can you tell who's addicted?"

"It's a tough problem. There are signs that we watch for on the cameras. We also train our dealers to look for those gamblers. Then we can cut them off. We also discreetly provide info in all our guestrooms about the signs of addiction and how to get help. Sadly, it's not enough unless all the casinos band together and implement similar programs. Even then, it's only a start. It's a slow process because not everyone shares my belief that we have a moral duty not to take bets from addicts. Some do no more than post the obligatory notices about responsible gambling and where to seek help if you have a problem."

"Did you confront Paxton about whether his family played a role in Mr. Brentwood's death and the other mishaps during rehearsals?"

"I did. I'm convinced he had nothing to do with any of that, but it's still possible the two Rossi guys who were intimidating my employee could have. They may have tried to scare the guy into paying, and the wrong people were hurt. When I hear myself say that, it sounds a little far-fetched though."

"It does, but I'm not ready to cross them off my list of suspects yet."

"Paxton promised to investigate and let us know if those guys had any hand in the sabotage."

"Good. Before you got here, I was thinking we're gradually piecing the puzzle together, but I have a nagging feeling that we are overlooking something important."

"There's other stuff we should go over too. Do you have time to talk in the morning?"

"We can talk now unless you're too tired."

"Would you mind if we wait until morning? I'm mentally and physically exhausted."

"Of course not. Let's get some sleep."

42
SEAN

Waking up, I sense someone staring at me. I crack open my eyelids a smidge, not wanting to face full-on daylight quite yet. Sure enough, Lowri is propped on an elbow with a mischievous grin on her face.

"What has you wide awake and so cheerful this morning?" I murmur.

"Cassie's opening night went great. I slept like a dream. Then I woke up next to your hot hardness, hoping we could start the day off with a bang." She snickers at her intentional word play.

Fuuuck. Playful Lowri is sexy. And my steel-hard cock is in full agreement with her plan. Damn it. We have to talk first. I'm not the jerk who'd take advantage of her offer minutes before telling her I've been hiding something.

Shit, she's going to think I'm exactly that asshole for waiting this long to tell her. I doubt she'll be speaking to me after this.

"Not to kill the mood, but we need to talk first," I say, knowing I'm definitely killing the mood.

"That sounds serious. What's wrong?" she asks, worry spreading over her face.

"Remember I said we needed to discuss the annulment?"

"Yes. I'm still confused as to why it's taking this long. I can always step in and talk with your lawyer if there's a problem."

"The problem is not with the lawyer and not with the annulment itself. The problem is with me. I shouldn't have waited to tell you. I've just dreaded this conversation."

"Are you saying we don't need an annulment? Wait a minute. Don't you dare tell me you're already married. You know how I feel about cheaters. Or do you want to stay married and were afraid to tell me?" she asks, skeptically.

"I've never been married before. Our marriage is valid, and I'm still on board for the annulment. But I need to ask a favor. Can we delay the annulment for a few weeks?"

Her frown deepens as her eyebrows scrunch together.

"Why?"

"I hadn't realized that my dad set up my trust in a screwball way. My lawyer explained that there is a clause in the trust agreement related to my marrying. It says that if I marry before the Athena is transferred to me personally, then I must stay married for a minimum amount of time. If I don't, then the Athena will never be mine. It will remain in the trust, directed by the trustees. They would have the power to kick me out entirely."

Her jaw literally drops open.

"I knew something was amiss. The paperwork should have been ready for our signatures within a few days, and judges usually sign off on annulments within a couple of weeks."

"The lawyer did say that, but contrary to popular belief, annulments aren't regularly granted here."

"That's because there's only a short list of allowable reasons for an annulment. But our situation falls squarely within one of those reasons. We were drunk!"

"Yeah, I know."

"How long do we have to stay married?"

"Only three months."

"From now or from our wedding date?"

"From the wedding. It's only a few more weeks."

"I'm not sure I'd call eight to ten weeks *a few*. Why didn't you tell me? Why would I care if we delayed the paperwork a little longer? I'll go home to San Diego. Your lawyer can let me know when the annulment goes through."

"Well, that's the problem. Umm... The terms of the trust agreement require us to live together the whole time."

"What the hell? Why?"

"As I told you, my dad was head over heels in love with Mom until the day she died. He wanted the same for me and didn't want me to take marriage lightly. If I married, he wanted me to give it a real chance. The younger I married, the longer the requirement to stay married and try to make it work. We're lucky that we only have to stay married three months."

"When did you find out about this marriage clause?"

"Only recently, I swear."

"How recently? Don't lie to me."

"A couple of days after we got married—when I met with my lawyer to start the annulment process."

I see it when it dawns on Lowri.

"Now I understand. That's why you hired me to represent the Athena and insisted I stay here. You didn't specifically want me for the job. And the only reason you agreed to my request for monogamy was to keep me in your bed to satisfy the requirement to live together."

"Don't go there. That's not what happened. I love having you between the sheets with me. Our chemistry is off the charts. You're a great lawyer. We've made a fantastic team. Why wouldn't I want us to work and play together?"

"I don't know that I believe you. Regardless, you should have told me."

"I know. I was afraid of losing everything. Then, after I'd waited to tell you, I was worried you'd think I was manipulating you."

"You were."

"I'm sorry. That wasn't my intention. I've recently seen the havoc that keeping secrets can cause. I don't want that in either of our lives. I promise to be completely open with you going forward. Can you forgive me? Will you stay?"

Silence looms between us for several minutes. I'm staring at her face but can't read her thoughts.

She finally says, "How can I be angry? It's a fake marriage. I'm actually somewhat amused at your predicament."

I close my eyes, slowly letting out the breath I've been holding as the tension releases from my neck and shoulders.

"That's a relief. Thank you."

"No problem. I'll stay, but you need to compensate me."

I bite my lip to remain calm. "Exactly what do you have in mind?"

"My time is valuable, and I'm doing you the favor of a lifetime. Decide what it's worth to you and make me a proposal. I'm flexible —money, ownership interest, property, or a combination. Feel free to be creative. I'm going to take a shower. You can let me know what you've decided when I'm done."

Damn. Damn. Damn.

I didn't think Lowri would be after my money. That's not who I thought she was.

I'm so screwed. She knows what the Athena is worth to me. *Everything*. Does she expect half?

I'd call Evan for advice, but I'm embarrassed to tell him how royally I've fucked up my life.

Now I have about twenty minutes to come up with a proposal to save my future.

43
LOWRI

I hurry to the bathroom before Sean sees how devastated I am. Silly me hoped Sean was delaying the annulment because he was falling for me. But no, he was manipulating me for his own benefit. Rather than trust me, he hid his secret. We aren't the team I thought we were. Instead, I'm being held hostage in a marriage that never should have happened.

Turning on music and the shower, I step under the too-hot water, wanting to feel a different pain than the one that's breaking my heart into tiny pieces.

I knew better than to let my walls down and dream I might have found what Cassie has with Evan. Under the rainfall showerhead, my tears fall freely and disappear down the drain with the cleansing flow of water.

When I arrived here, I wondered if there would be magical moments, mysterious men, or more mayhem. I never imagined there would be all three, and they would lead to heartbreak.

I let myself cry through three songs about love gone wrong. Apropos.

Pull it together. It's going to be okay. I'll leave Las Vegas in the same situation as when I arrived. Everything that happened here was always meant to be temporary. How can I complain?

I have learned a valuable lesson. Never again will anyone talk me into mixing business with pleasure. It hurts too much.

So much for pulling it together. I'm not okay.

I cry ugly tears, knowing the noise of the shower and cranked-up music will cover my sobbing. Sinking to the floor of the shower and hugging my knees close to my chest, the tears start to subside, but my body is shaking.

I don't know what to do next. Where do I go from here? How can I get out of this apartment without Sean figuring out how upset I am?

I'm wiping away tears when suddenly the water is cut off. A fully clothed Sean sans shoes is crouching beside naked me on the floor of the shower. "Don't worry, I'll take care of you. I've come up with a proposal. You can have my apartment in Paris and enough money to be set for life. I don't expect you to have sex with me. Just live with me for the remaining part of the three months. It's not that long."

"I don't want your lousy apartment or your money. I was messing with you for being such a dick. You should've been honest with me from the beginning. I'm such a fool. I thought you were starting to care for me. I lowered my guard and accidentally let you into my heart. But now it's clear. None of this between us was real. You were trying to let the required time pass without telling me because you assumed I might be a gold digger and would try to make a money grab. It kills me to know you see me that way." The tears start flowing again.

I feel Sean turn around and sit next to me on the cold, wet stone floor. He lifts me onto his lap and pulls me against his chest, kissing the top of my head. I'm not sure why I let him. I should push the bastard away.

"You've got it all wrong, sweetheart. I do care about you. I've been wrestling with the fact that my feelings for you are causing me to question my views about relationships. It's scaring the hell out of me."

"Then why didn't you tell me about the problem with the annulment sooner?"

"I'll admit that in the beginning, I was afraid to tell you. I didn't know you as well, and I couldn't predict what your reaction would be. Then as we became closer, I realized how bad it looked that I'd waited to discuss it. I was scared I'd lose the Athena, and I was afraid to lose what we have."

"What *do* we have? How can I trust that you aren't just trying to talk me into staying? It's the Athena you want."

"I won't lie. Of course, I want to keep the Athena. It's my family's business. I don't want to lose our connection either. You are incredibly special to me, but I'm not sure how to prove it to you. I messed up badly, but I'll do whatever it takes. How can I make this up to you?"

"I need time and space to sort through my feelings. But don't worry, I won't let you lose your precious inheritance from your father. I don't want that on my conscience, so I'll stay here until it's safe for you to get the annulment. I'll *even sleep,* and I mean actually *sleep,* in your bed. That way you can honestly say we lived together as required. That's all I can promise."

"That's incredibly generous. I can't ask for more than that after what I've done to make you question me. As difficult as it will be to lie next to you each night and not reach for you, I'll respect your boundaries. Nothing will happen that you don't want.

"Thank you. I appreciate that. Don't think it will be that easy on me either. Despite my brain telling me to run from you, my body hasn't received the message yet." I laugh halfheartedly, stifling the last of my tears.

"Will you still be my lawyer too? We make a powerful team. I'd like to keep working together if you're willing."

"Are you sure? You no longer need that excuse to keep me here. I've already agreed to stay."

"I'm absolutely sure. We work well together, and I have a feeling that we're getting close to solving Mr. Brentwood's murder."

"Okay. If you don't mind, I'm going to dress and go for a walk to clear my head. Text me if we need to meet about work."

"I will. Daniel can send someone with you on your walk."

"That's not necessary. I promise I'm not going to run away."

"I'm not worried about that. I'm worried about your safety. Last time we went for a walk, you were mugged. So, please humor me, and let me have someone watch over you."

"If you insist."

Maybe he does care at least a little.

44
SEAN

Lowri pulled on jeans and a T-shirt and left for a walk. One of our plainclothes security guards was waiting outside my apartment to follow her. I'd texted him with an order to protect her with his life. It's becoming painfully clear to me that I'd be crushed if anything bad happened to Lowri.

In the elevator to my office, my mind continues to process the situation. I'm not sure exactly where we stand, but it could be worse. At least she's still here. What else I want, I'm not sure. All I know is that seeing her hurting and crying tore apart something inside me. The sinking feeling in the pit of my stomach is making me sick.

When the door opens, my assistant is busily arranging papers on my desk at the far end of the room.

"Good morning, Emily. What's on the agenda for today?"

"Detective Fielder called to request a meeting with you this afternoon. Should I confirm for 2:00 p.m.?"

"Make it 3:00 p.m. and text Lowri to make sure she can be here then."

"Will do."

"What else is pressing?"

"Daniel wants to meet later today to discuss the photo you gave him last night. I told him you might fit him in around 4 or 5."

"Either time works."

"Otherwise, you have a couple of calls regarding the contracts I left on your desk."

"Also set up a meeting with the food and beverage director to discuss the announcement that Kai will be our permanent chef of Pinot & Pie. The timing of the publicity is critical. We want to avoid detracting from Cassie's month as guest chef but still showcase his arrival at the Athena."

"Understood. I'll schedule that meeting for this afternoon. Do you need anything else?"

"I don't think so. Oh, there is one more thing. You don't happen to have a twin sister that you've been hiding from me all this time, do you?"

"No. I don't have a sister. You know I'm an only child. Why do you ask?" She tilts her head, looking confused.

"Oh, it's nothing. A friend of mine saw you at the soft opening of Pinot & Pie. He said you could be his former girlfriend's twin. Her name is Lee. He clearly regrets messing up and losing her. If Lee happened to be your sister, I thought we could play matchmakers and arrange for the two of them to meet again."

"Did your friend say what he did wrong?"

"Something about hiding a secret for too long, and then it came out in a bad way."

"Hmm. When someone royally screws up a relationship, it's often impossible to repair the damage. I doubt he'll get a second chance."

"Maybe not. We can't do anything about it. It wasn't your sister."

"No, it wasn't my sister," she says with a faraway look.

"You look lost in thought. I'm sorry if this conversation conjured a bad memory."

She dips her head. "No need to apologize. It just reminded me of someone special from a few years ago. He was the love of my life, but it wasn't meant to be." She sighs as she leaves my office, closing the door.

I've never been able to imagine committing to someone for life and risking the hurt of losing them. That didn't turn out well for Dad. But Paxton and Emily are in even more pain from letting someone go. Their situations are a stark reminder that regret from past decisions and mistakes can haunt you for years.

Is that how I'll feel if I let Lowri go?

45
SEAN

Checking the time, I know Detective Fielder will be here any minute. He's known to be punctual. Hopefully, Lowri will show up a few minutes early. I'd like to gauge her mood and start repairing the damage between us.

No such luck. At 3:00 p.m. sharp, I hear the detective and Lowri exchanging greetings outside the open door to my office. As I stand to greet them, Lowri crosses the threshold, followed closely by Fielder. Anxiety over my relationship issues with Lowri is temporarily replaced with curiosity as to why Fielder called this meeting.

"Greetings, detective. Have a seat and give us an update on your investigation."

"If you don't mind, I'll stand. This should be quick. I have officers waiting for me near the theater."

Lowri's eyebrows pop up in sync with mine.

"That sounds ominous. What's going on?"

"We're here to arrest one of your performers on suspicion of murdering Mr. Brentwood. I wanted to give you the courtesy of a heads-up."

"Which one of the performers?" Lowri asks.

"I'd rather not say until they're in custody, but you are both welcome to accompany me to the theater,"

"Of course, we'll be going to the theater. It's Sean's hotel. You don't get to *invite* him to join you. It's the other way around," she says.

She beat me to the punch. Gotta love that spunk.

"Like she said, *we* will escort you to the theater. First, tell us how you know your suspect is there? And why do you think it was one of our performers?"

"We've tied one of your performers to Mr. Brentwood. They had motive, opportunity, and means. They also have the build and blond hair we can see in the video footage your security department shared. As for how we know they are in the theater, we followed them here. Now, please *take* me to the theater before they leave."

"Why won't you tell us who it is?"

"Walls have ears, and we can't take the chance that someone will alert them, and they will run."

"That's rather insulting," Lowri says.

"Forgive me, but we're dealing with a murderer. I don't care if it's insulting. I'm not risking the suspect getting away," Fielder says.

"Fine. Let's go," I hiss.

I lead the way, with Lowri by my side. Leaning down, I whisper to her, "This is a shit show. Not only did a member of the public die, but also, my employee may have murdered him."

She nods.

46
LOWRI

We're all in a foul mood as we traipse to the theater. I'm pissed that Fielder is being secretive about his suspect, not to mention he's dissing the Athena's security. Sean's worried about the hotel's reputation, and Fielder is grumbling about the lack of respect for authority.

Sean's perfected the art of walking and texting. I assume he's alerting Daniel to the situation, but I doubt that's required. A bunch of police officers lurking about wouldn't go undetected by the massive camera system in the Athena. Daniel should already be on his way to the theater.

I know I'm right when Sean shows me his phone's display.

> Sean: Police are going to arrest performer for murder. Get to the theater NOW!

> Daniel: Already on my way. Who is being arrested?

> Sean: It's apparently a secret. Don't let anyone leave the theater. Make sure all exits are covered.

Daniel: Will do.

I nod. As we continue walking, Fielder makes a call. I strain to overhear the conversation he's having with his team. His short one-word responses aren't helpful.

"Mr. Cartwright, everyone's in place. Call off your security. We don't want anyone to get hurt."

"I will not. My security is here to make sure none of my employees or guests are hurt when you attempt to arrest someone you refuse to identify. We could easily arrange to detain the person if only you would work with us. Given your stubbornness, I have no choice but to have my team protect our people," Sean says.

"Fine. We'll coordinate with Daniel. You and Lowri stay a safe distance back. This person has already killed once. We don't know what they will do in response to our attempt to arrest them."

Fielder places another call to his team and arranges for them to explain the plan to Daniel.

We enter the theater through a side entrance near the stage. Our presence is obscured by the booming music and the darkness of the seating areas. The only light focuses on the two performers on stage. Reese and Amelia are rehearsing an acrobatic scene where they dance together high above the stage, each supported by their limbs entwined in silks. They're mesmerizing to watch.

Suddenly, the music stops, the house lights turn on, and at least ten police officers and Athena security guards storm the stage while Reese and Amelia dangle from their silks.

"What the hell is going on?" Reese yells.

"I'm Detective Fielder and these are members of the Las Vegas police department. We need you both to slowly lower yourself to the stage."

"Why? What's wrong?" Amelia asks.

"It will be easier to talk when we don't have to yell. Please come down," Fielder says in a calm, but firm, voice.

The acrobats comply and both are immediately restrained by the officers. That's confusing.

I watch as panic crosses both their faces, and they writhe, trying to free themselves from their captors. Which one is being arrested? Are they both involved?

Hearing the click of metal, my gaze goes to the steel handcuffs clinching around Amelia's delicate wrists. As she screams in horror, an officer begins reciting her rights. "You are being arrested for the murder of Mr. Brentwood. You have the right to remain silent ..."

"I didn't kill anyone. I don't know what you're talking about. Let me go," she pleads as her anger turns to tears.

In a separate conversation, the officer holding Reese releases him. "Sorry to hold you, sir. We couldn't risk you getting in the way of us arresting her."

Reese looks shell-shocked as he shakes his head and mutters, "No problem. I'm not feeling well. This is too much."

"You're free to go. Grab your stuff and exit via the main entrance to the theater, if you don't mind," the officer says.

"Yeah. Okay," Reese says and hurries away.

Detective Fielder joins Sean and me as Amelia is hauled away.

"Where are they taking her?" I ask.

"We want to question her while she is still shaken by the arrest. Can Daniel arrange for us to do an initial interview in one of your security offices? Then we can transport her to the station."

"Of course, provided that you don't object to Lowri, Daniel, and me listening."

"As Ms. Upton reminded me, it is your hotel," he says with a slight smile before continuing, "And Mr. Cartwright, please forgive me for not sharing that it was Amelia we were here to arrest. We had tried to corner Amelia at her apartment this morning, but she slipped out a back way. We were surprised she made a stop here on her way out of town. We couldn't risk her avoiding us again," Fielder says.

"Why would she come here if she was making a run for it?" I ask.

"We don't know. My officers saw her fill her trunk with bags. That led us to believe she planned to leave Vegas today."

"I get it, but we've worked well together in the past. You could have trusted us," Sean says.

"Yes, but we couldn't afford to lose time while I explained everything to you."

"Are you going to tell us why you think she did it?" I ask.

"I don't *think* she did it. I *know* she's responsible. It turns out she had been dating Mr. Brentwood, and they had a major breakup when she found out he was also dating someone else."

"That must have been Mr. Galanis."

"We don't have a name, but we know he was dating a man."

"Amelia turned up in some photos with Galanis on social media. They must have met through Brentwood. Why was Brentwood at the show if he and Amelia had broken up?"

"We believe she had already given him the ticket and decided to use the opportunity to put an end to him."

"Do you think she was the one in the baseball cap, causing all the accidents?"

"We do. She has the right build, and the blonde strands of hair that show from under the cap look like hers. When she was backstage between scenes, she would've had plenty of time to loosen the screws in the tree's platform. We believe she's the one on video with the screwdriver. She knew Mr. Brentwood would end up on stage. It made it easy to exact revenge."

"What about the earlier accidents? Why would she have hurt all the other performers?"

"Overall, those incidents resulted in minor injuries. We believe she staged those, hoping that when Brentwood was killed, it would look like another of many accidents that were occurring in an unsafe environment."

"She couldn't be sure he would die. If his necktie hadn't caught, he would have fallen about ten feet and likely only ended up hurt, not dead," Sean says.

"It's quite possible that she only wanted to injure him as punishment for what he had done to her. Instead, it went sideways, and he died from the intended *accident*. Regardless, the result was murder."

"It's hard to believe she would do this. When I interviewed her, she appeared open and honest in her answers," I say.

"Criminals are often believable."

"You're not saying she's an experienced criminal. You're saying this was revenge gone wrong," I point out.

"We're still investigating her past. Who knows what will turn up? The good news is that we have the murderer in custody and your theater can reopen."

"That is the best news I've heard in a long time," Sean says.

"Now let's see if Amelia will fill in a few gaps in this mystery," Fielder remarks.

If we're lucky, she'll also shed light on what is going on with Mr. Galanis and his fake attorney.

47
SEAN

It's surprising how often a casino faces the need to question someone or hold them until the authorities arrive and haul them away. We've had to deal with employees who get greedy and pocket gaming chips, gamblers who decide they can cheat, and guests who get out of hand after imbibing too many free drinks at the slot machines.

Dad had the wisdom when he built the Athena to include a couple of police-station-style interrogation rooms fitted with a wall of one-way glass and recording equipment. In sharp contrast to the Athena's sumptuous luxury, Dad also insisted upon cold, bleak furniture: a simple metal table bolted to the floor, a bar across the top of the table to handcuff an unruly guest to, and hard metal chairs. No room for comfort here.

Lowri, Daniel, and I watch through the one-way glass as Detective Fielder questions a crying, shaking Amelia.

After reminding her of her rights, he says, "Please state your full name for the recording."

"Amelia Rae Graham."

Amelia Rae? A.R.? Is she the gambler who's in debt to the Rossis?

It must be a coincidence. Paxton said it was a guy who owed them money.

"Tell me about your relationship with Mr. Brentwood," Fielder says.

"There's nothing much to tell. He was a cheating bastard."

"Is that why you broke up?"

"Yes. I found out that he was also having an affair with a man."

"Was that Mr. Galanis?"

"Yes. He'd previously introduced him as a friend. I later learned what he meant. It didn't matter who it was though. All that mattered was that he lied to me."

"So, you hated him."

"I despised what he did to me. He said we were going to be married, but it was all a lie."

"How did Mr. Brentwood get a ticket to the show?"

"I gave it to him."

"Why did you give him a ticket after you broke up?"

"I gave it to him a couple of months ago—before we broke up. It was a birthday present."

"I see. Did you know that whoever sat in that seat would be invited to the stage to participate in the show?"

"Yes. I wanted him to feel special and be part of the show with me. When we broke up, I tried to get the ticket back, but the asshole refused to return it."

"Is that why you arranged for the tree's platform to break when he was standing on it?"

"I didn't have anything to do with that. He just fell."

"No. Someone tampered with the platform. That's why he fell. It'll go easier on you if you tell me the truth now. You loosened the screws holding the platform in place, didn't you?"

"Of course not. I didn't like Brentwood. He's a piece of shit, but I've moved on. I'm dating a fantastic guy who is a million times better. He's considerate, handsome, attentive, and has more money than he needs. I didn't know it at the time, but Brentwood did me a favor. I never would have met Sergio Martinez if Brentwood hadn't cheated on me."

"When Brentwood didn't return the ticket to you, didn't you see it as a chance for payback?"

"That wasn't important to me."

"Be honest. Who wouldn't want a little revenge after being treated that poorly?"

"He wasn't a nice person, but he didn't deserve to die."

"You staged the accidents, including one where you were supposedly injured. You intended Mr. Brentwood's fall to look like another mishap. He deserved it for cheating on you. But it all went wrong, didn't it?"

"I don't know anything about the accidents except that I was stabbed with a bunch of sharp pins that were left in my costume, and several other people suffered injuries. I'll admit that there were more accidents than I would have expected, but they were the result of carelessness. Regardless, I didn't have anything to do with the injuries onstage. I certainly didn't do anything to harm Mr. Brentwood."

"Come now. You wanted to see him suffer for what he did to you, right?"

"I never wanted to see him again, but I didn't need revenge. Why would I risk screwing up the rest of my life when I have a dream job and a fantastic boyfriend? It makes no sense. Don't you have a video of the person who did this? There are cameras everywhere. No one would get away with messing with the props."

"I see you're aware of all the cameras. We do have videos. Look at this photo. During the show, you were caught on video at the tree with a screwdriver. We've got you. You can't deny what you did."

"That's not me. I don't wear baseball caps."

"Then who is it?"

"There are more than two hundred people involved in the production of the show. It could be any of the performers with blond hair or someone from the crew."

Detective Fielder leaves the room and joins us, saying, "She's a cool one."

"Are you sure you've got the right person? If she's happier now without Brentwood, why would she hurt him?" Lowri asks.

"It's not unusual for someone to seek revenge when they've been wronged, even if their current life is better. The 'accident' was premeditated. She's had plenty of time to prepare a cover story. We'll take her to the station, and her situation will become even more real to her. If she keeps talking before she lawyers up, she'll eventually trip up and say something inconsistent. They always do."

"Before you leave with her, can you ask about her gambling on football? We've learned that one of my employees named A.R. owes the Rossis a rather large sum. We thought it was a man, but since she said her name is Amelia Rae, I'm not sure. Daniel, do you have a photo of the Rossi guys who were at the show? The detective can see if Amelia recognizes them."

"Give me a minute, boss. I'll print one," Daniel says, walking over to a computer as we watch Amelia through the one-way glass. She's fidgeting nervously, eyes darting around the room.

With the printout in hand, Detective Fielder rejoins the suspect. "I only have a couple more questions for you. Who's your favorite football team?"

"Huh? Why does that matter?"

"Just answer the question, please."

"I don't have a favorite."

"Don't you like football?"

"Sergio loves it. I've watched games with him. I don't know much about it though."

"When was the last time you saw these guys," he asks, laying the photo on the table and pushing it toward Amelia.

"Who are they?"

"You tell me."

"I don't know them. I've never seen them before."

"Weren't they at the show to meet you? You owed them money from gambling on football."

"I told you that I don't know anything about football. Why would I gamble on it?"

"Maybe you were placing bets for Sergio. Is he a fan of the LA Tigers?"

"I don't know if he likes the Tigers. He follows the Las Vegas team, whoever they are, but we don't gamble. I don't know the guys in the photo. I didn't harm Brentwood. This is all absurd. You've made a major mistake. Since you won't listen to the truth, I'm not saying another word until I get a lawyer."

"Fine, but you're making this whole situation harder on yourself."

Amelia is true to her word and sits there silently, glaring at Fielder.

Fielder opens the door to the interrogation room and signals for two officers to take Amelia away before he joins us in the viewing room.

"What do you think?" I ask.

"I'd be shocked if she knows anything about football, much less gambles on it."

"Yeah, she didn't know there isn't a team named the Tigers in LA. That was a clever test," Lowri says.

"A simple trick of the trade. It's doubtful that she's your gambler even though the initials match."

"I agree. It would have been too easy for the killer and the gambler to be the same person. At least we no longer have a murderer running loose here. Unfortunately, we still don't know which employee is involved with the Rossis."

"Don't worry—criminals slip up. They're not as smart as they think they are. We'll let you know when this is all wrapped up. In the meantime, your show can reopen," Fielder says as he departs.

"That's good news. Will you open the show tomorrow?" Lowri asks.

"No. They need a couple of days to rehearse and give Amelia's understudy time to practice. Most importantly, they can't use the tree, and I don't want any audience members on stage anytime soon. We've kept Mr. Brentwood's death reasonably quiet, but the idea of reenacting the scene where he died would be morbid."

"I'm glad they're rewriting that part of the show. If you don't mind, I'm going back to your apartment to deal with my other work. I'll have Walter bring me food. I plan to work straight through dinner. Want to grab a drink around 9:00 p.m. or so?"

"That works. While you catch up on work, I'm going to reach out to Paxton. It's time he helps us set a trap for this A.R. person. I'll also meet with Ron to discuss reopening the show in a few days. Rehearsals can resume tomorrow morning, but I want him to walk me through his plans to rework the show without the tree prop. I'll text you where we can meet for drinks."

"Perfect. I'll be ready for a change of atmosphere after being stuck at my laptop for several hours," she says, walking away without any physical contact.

No kiss on the cheek. No quick hug goodbye. Not even a simple squeeze of my forearm. The absence of her touch leaves me with an emptiness. The comfort she's brought me in the last few days is gone. She wasn't cold or rude or even angry, but it's different than before. I don't like it. And it's all my fault for being such a jerk and messing up what we had.

Later tonight, I'll find a way to fix my screw up with Lowri. Now, I must focus on identifying the gambling employee.

If A.R. is a true gambler, he or she won't be able to resist the offer I have in mind for Paxton's guys to put on the table. It will flush A.R. out into the open. Problem solved.

Why didn't we come up with this idea sooner? Of course, there was a murderer to catch.

48
SEAN

Paxton wasn't willing to share the method his guys use for contacting this mysterious A.R. fellow. He *was* willing to tell his men to lure A.R. to the Rossi home with a proposal for a double-or-nothing bet to square his debt with them. Given A.R.'s inability to pay and apparent penchant for gambling, he won't likely pass up the opportunity to make one more bet that could free him of debt.

When A.R. shows up, Paxton will learn the gambler's real identity. Then we can fire him. As for A.R.'s gambling debt, Paxton promised to work out a nonviolent solution. I have no choice except to trust him on that part.

With the plan in motion for catching A.R., it's time to concentrate on convincing Lowri that I haven't been using her, at least not in the way she thinks. She's special to me, and I can't imagine losing her friendship and support. It's going to be difficult enough to let her go at the end of the ninety days, but there's no way I'm letting us part on bad terms.

I'll show her that this short relationship has been real for me. Our marriage may not be destined to be permanent because that's not what either one of us has ever wanted. But every emotion and every moment together have been authentic, at least for me. I'm pretty sure that's true for her as well.

I racked my brain for a romantic idea that not only would wow Lowri but also would demonstrate my sincerity. I have a decent amount of experience with impressing women. I've just never tried to prove my true feelings to anyone. Hell, I've never *had* feelings like this for anyone. It was a wake-up call finding her sobbing in the bathroom. My failure to share the requirements of the trust agreement inflicted more pain than I'd imagined possible. I'd expected her to be mad, not hurt. Seeing her that way gutted me.

Hopefully, the plan I settled on will work. I shared my predicament with Emily and asked for her help with putting my idea into motion. After chastising me for being such an idiot, she got to work and made a couple of suggestions of her own to amp up the evening.

The alarm on my phone buzzes. It's time to meet Ron. Once that's done, I should have enough time to change clothes and meet Lowri.

If I'm lucky, the evening will end with Lowri forgiving me.

49
LOWRI

I've been sitting at the dining table, typing away on my laptop for hours when Walter approaches so quietly that I jump out of my chair when he asks, "What would you like for dinner tonight?"

"Could you work on being a little less stealthy?" I laugh, sitting down again.

"If that would please you," he says, his ever-serious and formal demeanor intact.

"Could I have a small serving of mac and cheese?"

"Of course. Will you be dining while you work?"

"I will. Thank you, Walter."

He disappears as silently as he arrived.

My food cravings are a giveaway to my feelings. Mac and cheese is one of my go-tos when I'm down. Despite my best efforts to bolster my mood, I'm disappointed about what happened with Sean. He hid crucial details from me. Now the warmth between us is gone.

My body is confused though. His six-feet-plus of gorgeousness still gets my core tingling. It doesn't matter if he's naked or wearing one of his custom suits that hugs his perfectly toned body like a glove, my hands yearn to roam over every inch of him. Those hours he spends in his private gym have paid off.

Remembering running my fingers through his thick blond hair with its whiskey-colored highlights while staring into his intense, sparkling blue eyes makes my heart pound. When he smiles at me, I'm captivated. There's a smirk that hints at a touch of arrogance, or maybe it's just confidence. Regardless, it's magnetic and draws me in.

It's true we never planned on anything except a couple of fun weeks helping Evan and Cassie. That all changed when we got married, started working together, and grew closer. I'd never tell him, but for the first time in my life, I was feeling love for a man. I shared intimate thoughts and history with him that only my best friend knows about me. That's why it hurt deeply to learn that he was only using me to keep his hotel.

But, unlike Amelia, I'm not into revenge. Besides, Sean and I never promised each other anything—other than when we were drunk and got married, which doesn't count. I'll bury my emotions and help him keep his hotel. It's enough that I've had fantastic experiences in Las Vegas, along with bringing a mega-client to my firm. Even if that last part was just Sean's way of manipulating me to stick around, the partners at my law firm will still credit me for the win.

Unfortunately, this pep talk to myself doesn't prevent a tear from rolling down my cheek. Hastily wiping it away, I stare at my laptop, attempting to focus on the contract I'm editing.

Unexpectedly loud footsteps interrupt me. Looking up, Walter is hilariously stomping his way toward me, carrying a large tray. I laugh, quickly covering my mouth with my hand. He either truly aims to please me or is pointing out how inane he thinks my request for a louder entrance was. Regardless, I appreciate the smile it puts on my face.

With great fanfare, he says, "We have an individual casserole dish with lobster mac and cheese drizzled with chili oil, a side salad of baby greens topped with slices of Asian pears, and warm dinner rolls. Please enjoy."

"This looks delicious. You went to too much trouble though."

Of course, Walter took my request for a simple bowl of pasta and raised it to the sky. What did I expect? It's the Athena, and technically, I'm still Sean's wife. I'm learning we don't do simple. But I'd be a fool to complain about food this good. That would be silly. Instead, I enjoy every bite, emitting a few moans of delight along the way. This dinner redefines the term comfort food.

I finish my late dinner and continue editing the contract until my alarm goes off, signaling it's time to meet Sean for after-dinner drinks. I'm not sure that was the best idea. A long hot bath and a glass of wine by myself would have been the smarter move. Instead, I opened my big mouth and suggested drinks.

It's time to don my carefree, fun-loving mask again and pretend everything is fine. I've been wearing it as protection for years. I'll need it tonight.

As I'm closing my laptop, Walter reappears, saying, "Pardon me, Ms. Upton. Mr. Laurent is here to see you."

Looking up I see Christian holding a large box tied with a giant red and gold bow.

"Good evening, Ms. Upton. Mr. Cartwright sent this to you. He also asked me to wait while you change and then take you to meet him for drinks."

"How strange. Sean said he would text me where to meet him."

"I gather it's a last-minute change of plans. I'll wait here with Walter."

I shrug and take the box to the bedroom. My guess is that Sean has a business event that popped up and is inviting me to join him rather than cancel our plans for drinks. Or he could be kidding himself that a glamorous evening out will serve as an apology for the way he manipulated me. Either way, his plans must require me to wear a new cocktail dress. It's too bad because I'm tired and was looking forward to simply relaxing over a glass of wine.

Untying the wide satin bow and tossing the box lid on the bed, I wonder what color Sean picked this time. The cobalt blue one from the first night was gorgeous. He does have exceptional taste, or at least someone who works for him does.

My jaw drops as I push aside the tissue paper to reveal lavender pajamas and fluffy house shoes. What the heck? There must be a mistake.

A small envelope stuffed into one of the shoes catches my attention. Opening it, I read the note inside.

Lowri,

Yes, I sent you PJs. I know it's a little odd, but I figured we both could use a relaxing evening, and nothing is comfier than PJs. We've had a lot of stress lately, the worst of which has been my fault. Hopefully, this will help. Christian will wait while you change. The drink I promised will be ready when you get here.

Please take one more reckless chance and join me tonight. You won't regret it.

Sean

Damn. How can I stay annoyed at him? But I have to. I'm not falling again. I'm not over the hurt yet, and I'm not letting myself be subjected to that type of pain again.

I can't let myself forget that Sean is still manipulating me to ensure I stay here. He can't fathom losing his beloved Athena. I should turn down the invitation.

But why deprive myself of whatever indulgent evening Sean's planned? Joining him doesn't necessarily mean forgiving him anyway. Or does it?

A hot shower is in order. I need time to think.

It won't hurt for Sean to wait a little while.

50
SEAN

I'm pacing back and forth across the wide expanse of the Athena's rooftop. It's been forty-five minutes since Christian texted that he gave Lowri the gift box. She should've been here by now. What if she's not coming?

I get it. She has every right to be upset with me. But the spark between us is still there, and we were getting along fine earlier today. She was the one who suggested drinks. There's no reason for her to change her mind. It's not like I sent her something provocative from one of the lingerie boutiques. PJs were meant to signal that I wasn't expecting anything other than a relaxing evening.

Looking at my phone for the millionth time, only one more minute has passed. It feels like ten times that.

I can't fix the friction between us if she's not here. I could text Christian for an update. I don't want to come across as worried though. He might clue in on the fact that there's trouble between Lowri and me. What the hell! Why do I care what *he* thinks?

Me: What's your ETA?

Christian: 5 minutes.

Me: What took so long?

Christian: Not sure. She didn't say.

Me: Okay. Thanks.

Hmm. I'm not sure what the long wait means. Did Lowri hesitate to accept the invitation? Is she making me squirm? Or is there a chance she took extra time to get ready for the special evening? I can only hope.

Supposedly, actions speak louder than words. *Operation Show Not Tell* is moving forward.

Knowing Lowri's on the way, I pop the cork on the champagne that's been chilling and take one last look at my surroundings to make sure nothing is missing. Reflections from the neon lights on the Strip take the place of stars in the night sky. There's a slight chill in the evening air, providing a positive energy that will hopefully lead to forgiveness, if not more.

Hearing the ding of the elevator at the far end of the roof, I take a swig of liquid courage. Here goes everything.

The doors part, revealing Lowri in the soft satin pajamas that hug her perfect curves. Even in PJs, she's a goddess.

Our eyes lock but neither of us says anything. I'm hypnotized by the sway of her body as she walks toward me along the candlelit path that's strewn with lavender, white, and pink rose petals.

Meeting her halfway, I open my arms, inviting a hug. Relief washes over me when she closes the space and wraps her arms around me. "You're extremely huggable in your soft, plaid PJs. Flannel looks good on you," she says.

"Everything looks good on you." I kiss the top of her head, not wanting to push my luck.

As I tighten the hug, her supple, perky breasts crush against my flannel shirt.

Shit. She's not wearing anything under her top. I barely manage to separate us before it becomes horribly obvious that my cock is at full attention. Down boy. Not now. We're apologizing, not seducing—well, at least not yet.

"What is all this? We were supposed to meet for a drink." She waves her hand around the scene I've set for the evening.

"Change of plans. Movie night in PJs. We have a giant screen, a lounging bed with loads of pillows and blankets, and mountains of snacks to munch on while we watch. Are you up for it?"

"How fun. I haven't taken time to watch a movie on a big screen in ages. This doesn't seem like you though." She laughs.

"I thought we'd try something different. We don't have to party full-throttle all the time. We've been subjected to loads of stress, so a little relaxing downtime would do us both good. What do you think?" I ask, handing her a glass of champagne.

"Thanks. I could use a break."

"Okay, let's toast to watching old movies under the night sky. Cheers," I say, and we clink glasses.

"Did you say old movies? What are we watching?"

"*Casablanca.*"

"I love *Casablanca*, but I haven't seen it in years."

"Let's get comfy and start the movie. It was one of my parents' favorites."

Lowri crawls onto the outdoor bed and nestles her back against a pile of pillows as I cover her with a plush blanket and place a bucket of caramel popcorn drizzled with white and dark chocolate on the side table near her. Settling in beside Lowri, I'm careful not to crowd her. Any intimacy tonight will be her choice.

"How did you know that's my favorite popcorn?" she asks, moving the bucket to her lap and popping a few kernels into her mouth.

"I may have asked Cassie for snack suggestions." I grin.

Turning to me, she says, "You've got to try this. It's crunchy, sweet, a little salty—simply the perfect mouthful of snack heaven."

Her animation over it is adorable. A warmth flows through me knowing she's happy. Not many women I've encountered, other than my mom, would find such pleasure in something as simple as popcorn. Most expect diamonds and extravagant dinners. Even those gifts don't always elicit such pure appreciation and delight as I see on Lowri's face now. She's simply different in such an amazing way.

I try a sample, reminding myself to thank Cassie for her help.

"I hope you're sharing. That stuff is something else," I say, grabbing the remote control to start the movie.

Lowri kindly puts the bucket of gourmet popcorn between us.

The movie starts with chaos erupting on the screen.

We're engrossed as Ingrid Bergman and Humphrey Bogart portray the story of Ilsa and Rick reconnecting.

Despite knowing the ending, I can't help rooting for their love. Turning to watch Lowri's reaction, I wonder what we're rooting for with each other.

As the movie nears the end, a cooling autumn breeze picks up, so I toss another blanket across us.

"It's getting chilly," she says, snuggling against me for the first time this evening.

I wrap my arm around her shoulder, pulling her closer. Leaning down, I kiss the top of her head.

When Rick and Ilsa say their final goodbye, Lowri clutches my PJ top as tears gently roll down her cheeks. I wrap my other arm around her and whisper, "Don't cry. I've got you, sweetheart."

"I'm okay. It's just so romantic. Rick put everything on the line for his former love. Why doesn't love like that exist in real life?"

"I'm starting to believe that it does," I murmur, barely audible.

"What?"

"The movie's a classic."

When her breathing slows, I reach to my side table and snag a chocolate-covered strawberry. "Chocolate makes everything better.

Take a bite," I say, placing a giant strawberry against her luscious red lips.

She opens her mouth, allowing me to slip the tip in, and bites down. Chocolate bits drop onto the blanket and strawberry juice dribbles down her chin. I smile.

Lowri quickly sits up, covering her overfilled mouth. "I'm making a mess." She giggles as she finishes chewing.

"Here, let me help." I reach over and wipe her lips with my thumb and bring it to my mouth, unable to resist the elixir of chocolate, strawberry, and Lowri on my tongue.

She watches me closely, her eyes longing and wistful.

Reaching forward, I gently pull her back against my side and stretch a warm blanket over her shoulders. "Are you enjoying movie night?"

"I am. This is such a treat. How did you ever come up with this idea?"

"Dad. This is what he used to do when he screwed up with Mom. I hoped it would help mend things between us too."

"What do you mean? We're staying together for a couple more months. You'll get to keep the hotel, and I'll go home. What happens in Vegas stays in Vegas. Isn't that the promise?" she muses sadly.

"This isn't about the hotel. This is about us. You and I have avoided relationships, but that doesn't mean we don't have feelings for significant people in our lives. You are extraordinarily special to me. I haven't been pretending. I've wanted to be with you. It wasn't about the hotel. Every minute we've spent together, every date, every night, every *everything* has been real to me."

"It has? How can I be sure you're not just trying to make sure I stay?"

"Shit. I'm so sorry I waited to tell you about the trust agreement. If I'd told you immediately, you never would have had reason to doubt our time together."

"But you didn't. Now I don't know if I can ever trust you again."

"I understand, but I'll work to earn it back. You already promised to stay, so tonight is not about that. My only reason for planning this was to demonstrate that you're important to me irrespective of the marriage and the ridiculous trust agreement. You're the most amazing woman I've ever had the pleasure of being with, and I'm sorry I made you feel otherwise."

"Are you sure you're not trying to get into my pants again?"

"I wouldn't have sent pajamas if that had been my goal tonight. Don't get me wrong—they are sexy as hell on you. But I hoped the PJs would convey there are no expectations along those lines tonight. This was about spending time together and apologizing for being such an idiot."

"Sometimes you surprise me. You're always confident and don't care what others think. Tonight I'm seeing another side."

"I wasn't confident tonight. I was afraid you wouldn't show up."

"I almost didn't."

"What changed your mind?"

"The truth?"

"Always."

"It was a combination of curiosity and wanting to enjoy whatever was planned. I figured it would be something spectacular to ensure I stay and help you keep the Athena. Ultimately, I decided that showing up didn't mean I had to forgive you. I never expected this level of sincerity. It's as if you really do care about my feelings."

"I do," I say, leaving off that I never dreamed it was possible to care as much as I do.

"Are guys in security watching us?"

"No. I ordered them to turn off the cameras."

"Aren't they worried about your safety? Don't tell me you have security guards hidden somewhere in the shadows."

"No. We compromised on security tonight. They gave me a panic button," I say, pulling it out of my pocket.

She bursts out laughing. "Put that somewhere we won't set it off accidentally. Walter walking in on us was bad enough. The last thing I want is your security team surrounding us with guns cocked."

"Yes, ma'am." I set the device on the side table despite Daniel's orders to keep it on me at all times.

"Sean, you are special to me too. But I can't handle secrets or being manipulated."

"No more secrets. It crushed me to see how much I hurt you. Can you forgive me?"

"We have an undeniable connection. I'm working on the forgiveness part. Now, please pour me some champagne so I can make a toast," she says.

I continue following orders, happy this is going in a positive direction and anxious to hear what she has in mind.

"To us—whatever that means and for however long it lasts."

"To us," I toast without the added qualifiers.

Lowri moves to sit sideways on my lap, wrapping her arms around me. We kiss. We cuddle. I want to smother her in pleasure but not tonight.

As sleep starts to take hold, Lowri softly asks, "Did movie night work this well with your mom?"

"It did. Dad even had a few additional tricks up his sleeve. Sometimes he hid air fans nearby to make sure it was cool enough that Mom would eventually snuggle next to him to stay warm."

"You're kidding. Did you do that tonight?"

"No, I wasn't going to risk you thinking I was manipulating you."

"Good call. You're learning."

Ironically, it's been one of the most intimate nights I've ever spent with a woman, and we barely kissed.

51

LOWRI

I wake up on a rooftop, my back spooned against Sean's heat, his muscular arms engulfing me. Memories of last night fill me with a warmth and sense of security.

But my mind is restless. An unrelated, nagging thought is vying for attention. I can't let go of the feeling that Detective Fielder arrested the wrong person. Rather than jump out of bed, I stay nestled against Sean as I mentally work through my concerns.

Not that I'm an expert, but I don't see Amelia as the vengeful type. Even if Mr. Brentwood's tie hadn't caught on the lever, the fall might have caused a serious injury. He could have ended up with a painful sprained back or broken bones. While Amelia was understandably pissed at Mr. Brentwood, it takes another level of anger to plan and carry out a revenge plot that would cause that type of physical injury.

And what about the risk of being caught? Why would she risk going to jail? She claims to be dating someone new named Sergio Martinez. Based on their social media posts, he appears to be successful and handsome. She's better off without the cheating

Brentwood. So why would she go to this much trouble for revenge? It feels off.

I'll see what I can learn about Sergio. She said he's a real estate developer. It should be easy to look him up. I'll find out if he's as wealthy as Amelia suggests.

Even if Sergio is the one for Amelia, I'm still bothered that she didn't mention knowing Mr. Brentwood. Why did she hide that fact?

The saboteur hid his or her face from the cameras, meaning they were aware they were under surveillance. Amelia admitted to knowing about the cameras. It could have been her.

But would she have risked everything for a little revenge when she has a better life now? Maybe she didn't think it was that much of a risk if no one could identify her, and if Brentwood wasn't badly hurt, no one would spend much time investigating.

I'll rewatch the videos from that night. If Amelia was onstage and staring at the tree when Brentwood fell, then she likely knew he would fall. If not, then maybe there's another clue we missed that will confirm or refute Amelia's guilt.

Content that I'm on the right track, I close my eyes, deciding to sleep another ten minutes before going back to the apartment to dive into the videos. Just then, Sean stirs and peppers the back of my neck with slow, soft kisses. Groggily, Sean whispers, "Good morning, beautiful. Did you sleep well?"

"Mmm. I did. Last night was the best."

I'm not exaggerating. He didn't push for anything sexual. Instead, he lobbied for a chance to apologize and reconnect with me. He succeeded. We needed to clear the air and share our feelings.

"I wouldn't mind spending the day this way, but I have a meeting with Daniel this morning for an update on our elusive, gambling employee."

"I have a project needing attention this morning too. Can we have another movie night this evening?"

"Sure. What should we watch?"

"It doesn't matter, maybe something with soft music. I suspect it'll be background entertainment tonight," I say, rolling over to face him.

"It's a date."

The giant grin on his face and steel rod digging into my thigh tell me he's going to be counting the minutes until tonight. With the ache between my legs, I will be too. But satisfying our needs is going to have to wait until after I watch the videos from the last performance. I think we missed something.

Work first, then play hard.

52
LOWRI

Back in Sean's apartment, I open my laptop at the dining table and start watching the videos of the performance where Mr. Brentwood died. Switching between views from different cameras, I start following Amelia throughout the evening as she moves on and off stage.

She's nearby Reese when he falls. I replay that part to see if Amelia had the opportunity to damage the dangling vine that tore, causing his fall. As the video plays again, Reese's facial expression catches my eye. He winces *before* he falls. He must sense the silk giving way. That must have been scary.

As I continue following Amelia through the videos, she dances off the stage a few minutes before the baseball-capped person shows up next to the tree, which is backstage. Then another camera shows Amelia dancing back onstage after a costume change. It's not clear that she had enough time to change into crew clothing, sabotage the tree, return to her dressing room, change into her next costume, and return to the stage for her next scene. I need Ron's opinion. This is something the stage manager will know.

With an arrest made, the show is back in rehearsals today, so Ron should be in the theater now. I grab my purse and phone, intent on resolving this quickly. It's almost noon. If I hurry, maybe I'll catch him before they break for lunch. If I'm correct, Amelia is innocent, and a killer is still lurking in our midst.

———

OPENING THE DOOR TO THE THEATER'S BACKSTAGE ENTRANCE, I'M MET BY AN unexpected quietness rather than the usual clamor of rehearsals. I look around and spot a woman organizing a rack of costumes down the hall. I walk close enough to be in earshot and ask, "Excuse me, where can I find Ron?"

"I haven't seen him yet. Rehearsals don't start until 1:00 p.m. today. I'm leaving to grab a bite to eat now, but you can wait. Rob should be here in the next twenty to thirty minutes."

"Thanks. I'll wait outside his office. That way I won't miss him."

The woman takes off, and I type a quick email to Sean summarizing what I saw in the videos. That done, I go in search of Ron's office. It's dimly lit backstage, requiring me to move with caution as I step around racks of costumes, props, and lighting equipment on my way.

"Ouch," I mumble as I bump my arm against something big and rough. To my surprise, it's the infamous tree. I rub my sore elbow where the bark cut into my skin. With the light from my phone, I take a closer look at the gigantic monstrosity. The trunk must be eight feet across. Sean said they're not going to use it in the show going forward, but I guess they haven't had time to get rid of it.

The police tape surrounding the tree has been cut, and the door on the far side of the trunk stands open. Curiosity getting the better of me, I step inside. During the night of the tragedy, we were focused on investigating. I didn't notice that the interior is so large. You could fit four or five people in here.

I start looking around, not sure what I'm expecting to find. Metal posts, spaced a few feet apart, run from the floor to the platform above. Looking up, the opening Brentwood fell through has been sealed shut. I'm about to step out when I hear footsteps and a male voice. I turn to look and catch a glimpse of Reese coming toward me with a scowl on his face, talking into his mobile phone.

"That's not the plan. They're going to figure it out. I have to get out of here," he hisses.

Shit. I carefully pull the tree's door almost closed, leaving only a small gap to peer through. I watch as he draws nearer.

Grabbing my phone, I hit record as Reese starts talking again.

"Galanis, you better keep your fucking mouth shut. The money is the only way out of this for both of us. You *will* go through with the plan."

He paces while listening to the response.

I had no idea he knows Mr. Galanis. Did he know Brentwood too?

Peering out the door gap, I anxiously await what he'll say next.

"Cabo San Lucas. I should be safe there. I'll lay low, maybe find a job at a hotel or somewhere until you send my share of the money."

Silence.

"No, I'm not worried about the dumb actor. He doesn't know anything."

More silence.

"I'm not talking about this now. Someone could overhear. You and Brentwood signed up for this deal. Let it play out, and we'll both be fine."

Shit. He did know Brentwood.

"No. I got a new ID. I'm flying out today—can't risk staying here any longer. I'll contact you when I get to Cabo and tell you where to send the money. Don't try to call me again. I'm dumping this phone."

The call ends, but he's still pacing. I quickly send the recording to Sean. I can't let Reese know I overheard him, so I pull the door completely closed, plunging me into total darkness. I'll stay hidden here until he leaves.

Not willing to risk the light from my phone giving away my presence, I stuff it into my crossbody purse. As I fumble in the dark, searching for the outside pocket, the phone slips out of my hand, landing with a loud thud.

Whoosh!

The tree door flies open, dimly lighting the space. An angry hand grabs my shirt, slamming me against the wall of the tree. With his other arm, Reese tosses his backpack to the ground, grabbing my flailing arm with his freed hand.

"You bitch. Fuck. You overheard everything."

"I don't know what you're talking about. I've been inside here."

"Don't play dumb. What were you doing in the tree if you weren't eavesdropping?"

"I was just looking around. Let me go!" I scream, attempting to knee him in the balls. Unfortunately, the agile acrobat easily jumps aside without easing his grip on me.

"Right. You were looking around in the dark. That's a good one."

With a sweep of his leg behind my knees, he knocks me to the ground. I land hard on my ass, barely missing his backpack.

I try everything to free myself—kicking, biting, hitting—but he stomps his other foot onto my diaphragm, knocking the wind out of me, and uses his foot to hold my left arm captive.

As I gasp, trying to catch my breath, he warns, "Hold still. I'm not going to harm you. I just need time to get away."

Without oxygen, I can't tell the jerk that he's already hurt me. He's delusional if he thinks I'll trust anything he says.

Keeping my eyes on him, my mind spins, trying to concoct a way out of this.

He reaches for the hem of his shirt, raising it upward. As I attempt to push myself up with my free arm, the metal chain on my purse clangs against a nearby metal support. That gives me an idea. Unclipping the electronic luggage tracker from my purse, I quickly stuff it into the outside pocket of his backpack as Reese pulls his shirt over his head with one hand and rips his belt from his pants with the other.

Sweat seeps from my pores, not knowing what he's going to do next. The way he has me pinned, I can't reach to hit him. Summoning help is my best shot. As air begins to refill my lungs, I open my mouth to scream, but he stuffs his shirt in it. Bending over, he manages to flip me onto my stomach, pull my wrists above my head, and binds them together with his belt. I have no idea how he did that so quickly. It must be his kickass acrobatic skills.

His foot is now firmly planted on my lower back, preventing me from getting up. I'm not finished fighting him though. I frantically kick my useless legs, hoping to land a blow somehow.

Keeping me pinned to the floor, he opens the main part of his backpack, extracting a couple of exercise bands. In a split second, my feet are bound together. Despite my twisting and flailing, he rolls me to my back and ties my wrists to one of the metal supports and my ankles to another. I'm stuck.

"I need you to stay quiet for a while. Now where did your phone go?"

"Ahh. There it is. I'll take this with me—can't have it ringing and risk someone coming to find you too soon. This is the second time I've had to take your phone—sorry about that. At least I don't have to take your laptop again this time. I know they're expensive, but last time I had to destroy your notes and recordings in case Amelia had shared that Brentwood and I hung out together."

I watch as he takes a spare shirt from his backpack and pulls it over his head. He gives the area a quick scan, hoists his pack onto his shoulder, and peeks out the door. With a last warning to keep quiet, he slides out and shuts the door.

Reese takes off, leaving me stranded, bruised, and unable to move. Darkness surrounds me again, and a sense of claustrophobia overwhelms me with his shirt stuck in my mouth and my legs and arms bound. It's even worse than the paralysis that happens when you're partially awake but can't move.

Closing my eyes, I try to calm myself with logic. It's doubtful Reese will return. My situation could be much worse. I'm safe. I inhale deeply, counting to four, and breathe out slowly. Repeating this a few times, my breathing and heart rate gradually return to an almost normal state.

It could take forever for anyone to find me. Who's going to look inside this tree?

Think.

The performers and crew should be here soon. There must be a way I can draw their attention.

When I hear footsteps and talking nearby, I quickly work through a laundry list of ideas. I squirm to bang my head against the metal support behind me, hoping someone will hear the noise. Damn it. The way Reese tied me between the two supports, I'm stretched out so much that the top of my head barely taps the support.

I scream in frustration and desperation. That doesn't work. The shirt in my mouth muffles it. No one can hear me.

I'm about to give up from exhaustion when my butt connects with a lump on the ground. It's too dark to be sure, but it must be my purse. A light bulb goes off in my head. I need to work it up my body to reach it with my hands.

I'm not sure how long I've been squirming and wriggling my butt, back, and shoulders trying to inch the purse upward along my body. I've already had to stop a couple of times to rest and quash my frustration at the slowness of my progress.

Finally, it's near my neck. If I can move it two or three inches closer, I can grab the leather with my fingers. Rotating my upper body slightly, I give the purse one final shove with my shoulder.

Success!

Taking a deep breath, I re-center myself, being careful not to accidentally push the purse out of reach. I turn my wrists as far to the side as possible and reach to let my fingers gently touch the leather. Working slowly, I pull the bag on top of one hand while using the other hand to locate the strap.

Yes! I got it.

Moving the second hand, I secure the strap with all ten fingers and work them along its length until the cold, hard metal is within my grasp. As I begin banging the metal part of the strap against the support, I swear to never badmouth the weight of the heavy chains they put on crossbody purses again.

A minute later, the door to the tree opens, and a panicked Sean stares at me in disbelief.

I sag, exhausted and relieved, as he and Daniel rush in.

"We heard the recording you sent and have been looking everywhere for you. We didn't recognize the voice. Is that the man who did this to you? Are you okay?" Sean asks, kneeling to remove the gag from my mouth. He searches my body for injuries while Daniel hurriedly unties my arms.

"Yes, it was Reese. I'll be fine. I just hurt all over." My mouth is so dry, I barely can talk.

"What else did he do to you?" Sean asks, helping me sit up.

I groan from the bruises on the front of my torso and lower back. Reese's foot did a number on me.

"There'll be time for that later. Reese is getting away. He's flying out to Cabo now under a fake name, but I don't know what it is. Find my laptop quickly and follow my luggage tracker. I stuffed it in his backpack. It's the only way you can stop him."

"Daniel, call Detective Fielder and get Lowri's laptop. I'll take care of her. Go. Now."

"Got it, boss. Text me Lowri's password."

Daniel's already on his phone as he sprints away.

"Now, let's focus on you. Clearly, Reese did more than tie you up. What happened?" he asks as he unties my feet.

"I survived the fight with only a few bruises—nothing major. I'll be fine."

"First, I'm going to call an ambulance, and then I'm going to kill that bastard when I get my hands on him."

"No ambulance. I'll take something for the soreness and get a good night's sleep."

"Are you sure? At least let the hotel doctor look you over. Will you do that for me?"

"If you insist, but that's overkill."

I listen as Sean calls Emily to arrange for a golf cart to meet us at the nearest Maze entrance, which I learn is underneath the stage. He also instructs her to have the Athena's doctor waiting for us in his apartment.

"Let's go via the Maze. Can you walk if I help you?"

"Maybe."

Sean helps me up. He catches me when my legs give out and the muscles near my waist spasm.

"That's not going to work," he says, reaching down to pick me up.

Hugging his neck, I smile, knowing I trust him to take care of me.

53
LOWRI

I wake up in Sean's bed, surrounded by billowy pillows everywhere—under my head and back, around each arm and leg, even between my legs. I can barely move because there's so much padding. It's like I'm a fragile sculpture packed and ready for shipping. This is hilarious. I'd be laughing uncontrollably if it wouldn't hurt my ribs.

This must be his way of protecting and cushioning me to ease the pain inflicted by Reese. It's way overkill, but I'll admit, it's not just funny; it's sweet.

Last night, Dr. Stewart assured Sean that while I'm badly bruised, my injuries aren't serious. The doctor prescribed rest, pain relievers, and ice packs—not pillows. Those were entirely Sean's idea. When I went to sleep, there were pillows tucked under my head and supporting my lower back. He must have added the ones around my arms and legs as I slept.

Despite the painkillers, I had trouble falling asleep last night. It wasn't until we heard that Reese was in custody that I finally relaxed enough to doze off. This morning I'm feeling better, except for the soreness and bruises. Those will take time. Of course, when I can actually move, who knows what else will be hurting. Maybe immobilizing me with padding really did help me sleep through the night.

I've never seen Sean this attentive, and it's not just the multitude of pillows. Between the continual offers of food, drink, and fresh ice packs last night, Sean smothered me in attention. I'd swear that he purposefully woke me up at least twice to make sure I was alright. Finally, I told him he had to let me sleep.

Ironically, I felt loved for the first time since I was a young child. That's when my parents were still happily married, or at least pretended to be.

Oh, I know Cassie loves me. She's my bestie, but it's different. This is a different type of love. It's deep and intimate. I swear Sean stared at me all night long with a mix of worry and adoration.

Wait a minute. Careful with those emotions. Otherwise, I risk being hurt yet again. It may

feel like love to me, but this isn't a love that's meant to be forever. We're temporary, even if I'm wishing for more.

"Sweetheart, are you awake?" Sean asks when I turn my head toward him. It's obvious he didn't sleep a minute, based on the bags and dark circles under his eyes this morning.

"Uh huh. But I'm stuck. Please unpack me."

"Okay, but It's going to hurt if you move around."

"I'll be careful, but not being able to move is making me claustrophobic now that I'm awake."

"Got it. I'll remove the pillows. Give me a minute. I've asked Jenny to stay with you for the next hour or so. Detective Fielder called. He wants to give me an update. Will you be okay while I'm gone for a little while?" Sean asks as he frees me from the pillow packing.

"No. I'm going with you." I laugh. Oww. No more coughing or laughing until these bruises heal.

"You should stay in bed. Dr. Stewart said you need rest."

"I slept all night. A hot shower and I'll be fine. There's no way I'm going to miss hearing the detective's update firsthand."

Slowly maneuvering myself out of bed, I hobble my way to the bathroom and savor a hot shower. Emerging, Jenny has clothes ready for me. I'm starting to understand why Sean likes having a butler. She saved me from the painful steps and movements that would have been required to retrieve my underwear, clothes, and accessories. I won't admit it to Sean now because I'm going to the meeting, but my body hurts like hell, and without her help, I doubt I could dress myself.

When I'm dressed, Jenny hands me a couple of the pain relievers and a glass of water. I thank her and carefully walk to the living room to meet Sean.

"Are you sure you're up to this meeting? You don't have to go. I'll tell you everything," he says, handing me a cup of steaming coffee.

"I'll be okay. I'm moving a little slower than usual, but after yesterday, it's important to me to be at this meeting. I need to hear the final update in person."

"I understand. You need to know the threat is gone."

"Exactly."

Gently wrapping my arm around his for support, he says, "Fortunately, my office is only an elevator ride away."

THE CAFFEINE I CONSUME ON THE RIDE TO SEAN'S OFFICE GIVES ME A welcome energy boost. We exit his elevator as Emily is showing Fielder into the office. Perfect timing.

"Good morning, detective. We understand you have news for us. Let's sit by the window. It'll be more comfortable for Lowri after her ordeal yesterday," Sean says, ushering us to a sitting area in his office. With Sean's help, I sink into the comfy sofa with a pillow at my back for support. He and Fielder choose the nearby chairs.

"Ms. Upton, I hope you're feeling better today," Fielder says with a nod in my direction.

"I'm recovering. Thank you. I'm anxious to hear what you are here to share."

"We both are," Sean adds.

"I thought you would be. Once we had both Reese and Galanis in custody, they were tripping over each other to be the first to make a deal. It didn't take long to piece together the rest of the puzzle. It turns out that Reese and Brentwood ran into each other in a bar one night soon after Amelia dumped Brentwood. They'd met a few times when Brentwood picked Amelia up after work, so they recognized each other and started talking. That led to drowning their sorrows over their money problems."

"We pay our performers well. Why did Reese have money problems?" Sean asks.

"Reese owed a small fortune to the Rossi family for gambling debts. He's the gambler you've been trying to identify."

"So, the gambling and murder are related after all?" Sean asks.

"Yes. Brentwood was also in financial trouble. He didn't have a job and was mooching off women he conned. Somehow, he learned that Amelia was from a rich family and hooked up with her for the free ride. In reality, however, he was romantically involved with Mr. Galanis, who was also broke. Amelia found out about Brentwood's affair with Galanis and dumped Brentwood, leaving him in need of money again."

"How did that lead to Brentwood's death?" I ask.

"As they drank, Brentwood mentioned to Reese that he had a ticket to the upcoming show and that he wasn't going to give it back. He'd always wanted to appear onstage, and this was his chance. That's when Reese cooked up the idea for Brentwood to fake an injury to extract a quick settlement from the Athena. Then they would split the settlement. Reese would pay off his debt to the Rossis, and Brentwood and Galanis could pay their bills until they found another mark to con."

"So, Brentwood wasn't supposed to be hurt. He was going to fake his injury?" I ask.

"The plan was for Brentwood to stand on the edges of the tree's platform and pull the lever to set off the pyrotechnics for the show's finale. Then he'd kick the platform underneath him. That would cause the screws Reese had loosened to fall out, exposing the opening. Brentwood would drop to his knees quickly and lower himself down into the tree's trunk. When he was found after the curtain went down, he'd feign extreme pain from severely spraining his back. It was supposed to be a fake fall. He certainly wasn't supposed to die."

"Reese must have been in shock that night," I say.

"Absolutely. Not only was he upset that his friend was dead, but also his only hope for paying back the Rossis was lost."

"Let me guess, Reese and Galanis then decided to team up and still come after money from Sean. Am I right?" I ask.

"You are. The original plan went to hell when Brentwood died. The problem was that Galanis still needed money and figured someone should pay for the death of his lover. So, he and Reese decided to go through with a modified plan and demand compensation from the Athena for Mr. Brentwood's death."

"That explains why they hired an actor to play Galanis's attorney. They couldn't risk a real attorney investigating the accident," Sean says.

"Exactly. Reese also admitted that he staged all the accidents, including his own, essentially for the reason we suspected. He wanted everyone to believe Brentwood's accident was one more mishap resulting from ongoing negligence by the stage manager and the Athena. Reese also worried about being caught. The earlier accidents were experiments to see if he could get away with them. He wanted to make sure that if anyone checked the videos from the cameras, they wouldn't recognize him. That's why he opted for the crew shirt and baseball cap. Lots of people wore those. He figured he'd fit in, and he did."

"Why didn't Reese arrange for his own accident to be more

serious and collect money for that? Why involve Brentwood in the first place?" Sean asks.

I respond, "That's easy. Reese was one of your employees. He wouldn't be entitled to anything except workers' compensation for an on-the-job injury. That wouldn't be nearly enough to pay off his debt to the Rossis. He needed a guest who could claim an injury and sue the Athena for enough money to solve his problem."

"Of course. I should have thought of that," Sean says.

"Detective Fielder, did Amelia know what they were planning?"

"No. She had no idea. She really had washed her hands of Brentwood entirely."

"Then why didn't Amelia mention that she knew Brentwood? That still bothers me," I say.

"The answer is simple. The night Brentwood died, the police officers only interviewed people directly involved with the tree prop. She wasn't one of them, so no one spoke to her. Later, she learned we suspected sabotage, but she didn't want to get involved. Had she been forthcoming, she might have avoided arrest."

"Or you might have arrested her sooner," Sean says.

"Well, there's that. I need to get back to the station now."

"One last question. Why had Amelia packed her car to leave town if she wasn't involved?" I ask.

"She hadn't. That morning, she cleaned out her closet. The bags of clothes in her trunk were for charity."

"Oh no. Has she been released?" I ask.

"Yes."

"Detective, thank you for your help. We appreciate you coming in person to give us the update," Sean says.

When we're alone again, Sean joins me on the sofa, commenting, "It's a relief to have the murder and gambling issue solved. I'd contemplated they might be linked if Rossi's guys were to blame. When they weren't responsible, I was sure we were looking for two separate people: a murderer and a gambler."

"I know. If I hadn't gone to the theater to meet Ron when I did, I'm not sure we would have ever figured it out."

"But you could have been killed. Next time, take backup."

"What's this about next time? I don't plan to be involved in any future murder investigations," I chastise, playfully slapping him on the shoulder.

"Good point. Neither do I. Let's focus our energy on enjoyable pursuits."

"What do you have in mind that will avoid my bruises?"

"I know a safe spot to direct my attention. Part those gorgeous legs and let me show you."

He does exactly that.

54
SEAN

Lowri and I are standing in the Athena's VIP driveway, waiting for Justin to pick us up in the limo.

She's beautiful as always. Her burgundy business suit and cream, cowl-neck, satin blouse show off the confident lawyer that she is.

While she's busy checking emails on her phone, I'm straightening my shirt cuffs. It's a habit I picked up from my dad and has become a pet peeve of mine. The cuffs look best when they have three-fourths of an inch showing past my jacket sleeves. When my fingers brush across Dad's cufflinks, it reminds me of his strength and his belief in me. That reminder is reassuring today.

The last few days have gone by in a blur. Lowri has been catching up on her work while I've been busy in my office. As far as she knows, I was way behind on hotel and casino business due to the murder investigation. While somewhat true, I've been busy with plans for today as well.

When we found her tied up, bruised, and in pain, I was both relieved and horrified. Her life was put at risk because of me and my hotel. If she had been killed, I'd have been devastated. Given a second chance, I was determined to get this right, so I called my lawyer first and then Evan.

As we climb into the back of the limo, Lowri says, "I thought we needed to wait two more months for the annulment. What changed?"

"My lawyer did more research. He learned that the judge can issue an annulment that takes effect on a future date. That makes our case a little different than the norm, so the judge insisted on a hearing. He had an opening on his calendar today, so my lawyer grabbed it."

"But what about the Athena? I don't want you to lose it."

"I won't. If we stay together until the official date, then I won't lose the hotel."

"Okay. Let's get this over with then."

My lawyer is waiting for us in the courthouse lobby. "Hello, Sean. Ms. Upton, I'm Gabe Santini. It's a pleasure to meet you. The judge is expecting us."

We enter the judge's empty courtroom. His clerk is there to greet us. "The judge will see you in his chambers. Please follow me."

"What's the deal? Why isn't the hearing in the courtroom?" Lowri asks.

"I requested privacy, if possible. Ideally, we'll avoid the tabloids catching wind of our situation."

"Thanks for that."

We walk through a door at the back left side of the courtroom and enter a beautiful office with dark wood paneling and walls of books. A black-robed man sits behind a massive desk.

We stand before the desk, and our lawyer says, "Good afternoon, your honor. I'm Gabe Santini, here on behalf of Mr. Cartwright and Ms. Upton. They are seeking to annul their marriage."

The judge nods, saying, "I have a few questions for the parties.

According to the papers that were filed, you two did not intend to be married. Ms. Upton, is that accurate?"

"That's correct, your honor," Lowri says in her all-business, lawyerly voice. I'm not sure why that turns me on, but it does.

"Then how did you end up married?"

"We participated in an event to set a world record for the most wedding photos of couples taken at the same place on the same night," Lowri explains.

"So, you were aware that you were having wedding photos taken?"

"Yes, sir. But we didn't realize that they were *real* wedding photos. We thought everyone was dressing up for fake wedding photos."

"Then why is there a copy of your signed marriage license in the record? Do you deny signing it?"

"No, sir. We didn't read what we signed."

"Ms. Upton. Aren't you an attorney?"

"Yes, sir."

"And Mr. Cartwright, you're an extremely successful business-man. Don't you typically read what you sign?"

"Yes, sir."

"Then please explain how you didn't know you were getting married."

"We were drunk, your honor," I say.

"I see. But I'm confused by one of the other requests in your filing. It says you do not wish the annulment to take place today. Instead, you want it to be effective seventy days from now. Why? Most couples who seek to end a marriage want out immediately."

"You see, due to an unusual clause in a trust agreement, Mr. Cartwright will lose the Athena unless we stay married another seventy days."

"Are you okay with that? Is he compensating you for delaying the annulment?"

"I'm fine with it. And, of course, he's not paying me, your honor.

He's a wonderful person. I don't want him to lose his legacy from his father because we drank copious amounts of alcohol one night and took a reckless chance. That wouldn't be fair."

"Mr. Cartwright, you are one lucky man. I don't know that I would have let you off the hook this easily."

"I know, your honor."

"Have you exchanged anything of value during your marriage? Any personal property?"

"Only our wedding rings," I say.

"Sean paid for both of them."

"Do you have them with you?

I pull mine from my pocket, and Lowri removes hers from the chain she wears around her neck.

"Please place them on the desk. We'll have them placed in trust until the annulment becomes effective. At that time, they will be returned to Mr. Cartwright."

I watch Lowri gently run her thumb over the diamond one last time before setting it on the edge of the desk next to mine.

"Do you wish to say anything to each other before we proceed? Ms. Upton, ladies first."

"Sean, I never intended to marry anyone, but the last weeks with you will be wonderfully ingrained in my memory forever. Thank you."

"Mr. Cartwright. Would you like to say anything?"

"Lowri, I don't know where to start. When Evan told me you were on your way to help me plan a party for Cassie, all I could think about was how fantastic it would be to see you again. Then when I set eyes on you in the bar, you were better than any memory. This strange journey is one neither of us planned. You know that relationships have always been a hard no for me. But these last few weeks have had me questioning that. I've wondered if a special relationship might be worth the risk. The idea of you leaving made me wish marriage was meant for me because the thought of you going back to San Diego is upsetting."

Lowri reaches for my hands, her eyes moist with unshed tears. "Oh, Sean. That's so sweet. I've had some of those same thoughts, so I understand. I'm going to miss you too."

Squeezing her hands, I continue, "When I saw you tied up in that tree, I wanted to make sure no one ever has the chance to hurt you again. I knew then that losing you would be painful."

I reach for Lowri's ring on the desk and kneel. "That's when I could no longer deny my feelings for you. I want to work with you, protect you, and cherish you every day for the rest of our lives. I love you with all my heart. Will you marry me for real today?"

Her hands fly to cover her mouth as tears stream down her cheeks. "Are you serious?"

"I've never been more serious."

"Yes, I'll marry you. I love *you* too."

I put the ring back on her finger where it belongs and stand, pulling her into a tight hug.

"Your honor, we'd like to get married," I say.

"To be clear, you are already married. I'd be happy to preside over a renewal of your vows if you would like."

"Yes, we would like," Lowri says as Cassie and Evan burst through a side door, followed by a guy playing the violin, a photographer, and someone pushing a cart covered in miniature cupcakes with white icing and topped with tiny lilac rosebuds.

Cassie runs to hug Lowri, handing her a bouquet of white roses, as Evan slaps me on the back with one hand, shaking mine with the other.

"Oh my god! You had this all planned. How did you know I would say yes?"

"I didn't. I just hoped you would be willing to take another chance on us and stay married to me."

"I knew it was odd to have an annulment hearing. Your honor, you were in on this too, weren't you?"

"It's rare that I'm able to help a couple turn a separation into a happy occasion, so I went along with the plan."

With a quick pounding of his gavel to begin the impromptu ceremony, the judge says, "Mr. Cartwright and Ms. Upton, you both appear sober. That means an annulment will not be an option after today. Do you understand?"

We both nod.

"Then let's get started."

The violinist plays softly in the background as we exchange vows, meaning every word this time.

Once the judge says, "You may kiss your wife," I take her in my arms and press my lips to hers.

When we come up for air, Cassie insists that Lowri and I feed each other the champagne cupcakes with cream cheese frosting. I'm careful not to smash it into Lowri's face. That wouldn't be her style, but I have other ideas for the sinfully delicious frosting when we're alone later. Hopefully, there will be leftovers.

Lowri looks at me, grinning, as if she can read my dirty mind and likes what I'm thinking.

As we're about to leave the judge's chambers, Evan says, "Cassie and I have a surprise wedding present for you. My royal jet is waiting to take you to France for your honeymoon. Walter and Jenny packed your bags and put them in the limo. Your driver knows to take you to the airport."

"Really?" Lowri asks.

Cassie nods.

"Thanks, man. I mentioned taking Lowri to France for a honeymoon, but I didn't want to jinx the proposal by preplanning the trip."

"That's why we did it for you. Now take off. Enjoy," Evan says.

"Can we take cupcakes with us?" Lowri asks.

"There's a boxful in your limo," Cassie says.

Yet another reason Lowri is perfect. We're both thinking of cupcakes.

EPILOGUE
LOWRI

"Welcome aboard. I'm Kimberly, your flight attendant today. Let me give you a quick tour."

Cassie told me about the royal jet, but her description didn't do the real plane justice. The main cabin is decked out with overstuffed leather reclining seats, a dining table, a sofa, and an entertainment center. If that isn't enough, my jaw drops further when Kimberly opens a door in the back, revealing a bedroom and lavatory with a shower.

I notice Sean doesn't react. He's probably flown with Evan before.

"Please take a seat in the main cabin for takeoff and landing, but otherwise, the entire plane will be at your disposal," she says.

"How soon will we be taking off?" Sean asks.

"Within the next fifteen minutes or so. The pilots are doing their final safety checks now. Would you like a drink?"

"A French martini for me and Macallan for Sean."

"I'll bring them to your seats."

We settle into the plush leather seats. While we wait for our drinks, Sean is busily texting someone.

"What are you doing?" I ask.

"Letting everyone know I'm going to be away."

"When you finish, we should toast Cassie and Evan. They were the first to figure out how to make a relationship work. We beat them to the finish line though." I laugh.

We accept our drinks from Kimberly and clink glasses.

"Also, cheers to my dad and his bizarre trust agreement. Otherwise, we wouldn't have spent enough time together to figure us out." He smiles, leaning over and kissing me.

I'll never tire of his lips on mine.

The flight attendant appears again. "Excuse me, we're ready for takeoff. I'll take your glasses so you can buckle up."

Our seatbelts snapped in place, I pinch myself as the plane shoots down the runway and lifts into the air. It's hard to believe this is my new life.

When the seatbelt sign is extinguished, Kimberly offers us a snack. Instead, we opt to retreat to the bedroom for a nap. At least that's what we told her.

Once the door clicks closed, Sean steps within inches of me and gently pushes my hair behind my ears. One hand on each side of my face, he bends down and softly kisses me. Pulling back, he stares into my eyes, saying, "This will be the first time I've ever made love to anyone."

"What do you mean? We've had sex more times than I can count."

"Sure, we've had sex. But I've never *made love* to anyone before you. Be patient. This will take a while. I'm going to find every single place on your body that makes you moan. I'm just trying to decide where to start."

It's getting hot in here.

"I've always heard that sex becomes boring after marriage," I tease.

"Sweetheart, the two of us will never be boring. Let's see. Where are those cupcakes? I have an idea."

Whew! We've had fantastic sex before but nothing like this. Tonight we're combining all the passion and chemistry with love and attentiveness to detail that I've never experienced before.

Propped on an elbow, I trace my finger over Sean's chest as I ask, "When did you start planning to make our marriage a real one?"

"That's a hard question to answer. I'm not sure I can pinpoint a specific moment. Each day we were together, the idea of you leaving bothered me more. I started questioning whether letting you go would be worse than sharing my life with you for as long as possible. I watched Dad suffer when he lost my mom, but they had decades of happiness together. I watched people around me hurting from having missed a chance to be with someone they cared about. Emily and Paxton each let a love go or messed up a relationship in the past and years later are still in pain from the loss. When I found you beaten and tied up in the tree, the reality that I might have lost you was the final straw. I vowed to do whatever it took to convince you that we were meant to be together."

"What would you have done if I'd turned down your proposal today?"

"I figured I'd still have a couple of months to change your mind."

"That's funny. I was dreading the end of our time together but didn't know what to do about it. I'm glad you figured out the solution."

"Me too."

"By the way, when will we get to your apartment in Paris?"

"That's not where we're going."

"It isn't? When Evan mentioned France, I assumed that's what he meant."

"Didn't I tell you that we're not a boring couple? Don't assume."

"Then where are we going?"

"It's a surprise. You'll find out soon enough. In the meantime, let's enjoy the cupcakes."

He knows how to spoil me.

EPILOGUE
SEAN

An hour before landing, Kimberly knocks on the bedroom door to let us know that it's time to return to the main cabin for touchdown.

We've only been seated a few minutes when the captain announces, "Welcome to Saint-Tropez. Your transportation will be ready when you deplane."

"We're in Saint-Tropez?"

"We will be in a few minutes."

The advantages of flying private and royal are innumerable. Passport control and customs take mere minutes.

A man approaches, saying, "Mr. and Mrs. Cartwright, I'll take you to your helicopter."

"Helicopter?" Lowri asks.

"It's the easiest way to get to our destination."

"Does it belong to Evan's family too?"

"No. He knew what I had in mind and arranged it for us."

In the air again, we put on headphones with microphones that allow us to communicate with each other as we skim hills and dip into valleys on our way to the beach.

"Are those vineyards?" Lowri asks.

"Yes. There are a number of small wineries around here."

"Where are we going to land?"

"You'll see. It's part of the surprise."

The beach comes into view, and the pilot guides the small helicopter over the clear turquoise water.

"Is there an island nearby?"

"You might call it that. It's a floating island of sorts," I say, pointing at the mega yacht outside the window.

"Are we going on a cruise for our honeymoon?"

"Yes."

"How many people does the ship hold?"

"I don't remember the exact number, but we'll have it to ourselves except for the captain and crew."

"You rented an entire ship?"

"It's a private yacht named *Reckless Chance*, and no, I didn't rent it."

"Are you telling me you own it?"

"No. You do."

"Huh?"

"It's your wedding gift."

"Have you lost your mind? It must be worth a fortune. Who would give a yacht as a wedding gift?"

"Me. Don't you like it? If not, you can have the Paris apartment or the beach house in Maui instead."

"What have I gotten myself into? This must be a dream."

"Sweetheart, I can't make you a princess, but I can certainly afford to treat you like one. Get used to it."

"I didn't give you anything."

"That's not true. You gave me everything when you said, 'Yes.'"

Now it's my turn to give Lowri even more.

Check out the first standalone book in the spinoff series, Royal Spies.

Evan and Xander's little sister, Brianna is leading a secret life that they know nothing about. Get ready for a high-stakes game. The players include billionaires, royals, spies, athletes, and criminals. Money, love, and life are on the line in *Risky Match*. It's the first standalone book in the Royal Spies series. *Risky Match* is available at

https://geni.us/RiskyMatchAMZAUD

STAY IN TOUCH

I love to hear from my readers. The easiest way to keep in touch is by joining my newsletter and following me. That way you won't miss out on the latest info on new releases, bonus material, and other updates.

Facebook: facebook.com/JDCarothersAuth
Instagram: instagram.com/jdcarothersauth/
Amazon Author Page: bit.ly/amazon_author_jdcarothers
Goodreads: bit.ly/goodreads_jdcarothers
Bookbub: bookbub.com/authors/j-d-carothers
Website: jdcarothers.com
Newsletter: jdcarothers.com/#subscribe

Also, if you enjoyed Sean & Lowri's story, please consider posting a review on your retailer's site, on Goodreads, and/or other sites where lovers of books look for their next read. Posting reviews helps other readers find new authors and titles, which is appreciated.

ALSO BY J.D. CAROTHERS

Want more contemporary billionaire romance with a guaranteed HEA?

Don't miss the other books by J.D. Carothers

Love Over Murder Series
Rival Secrets (Book 1, Standalone)
Royally Deceived (Book 2, Standalone)
Reckless Chance (Book 3, Standalone)

Royal Spies Series
Risky Match (Book 1, Standalone)
Flawless Match (Book 2, Standalone) coming soon

The Holiday Series
Christmas Assignment in Paradise (Book 1, Standalone)

ALSO BY J.D. CAROTHERS

ACKNOWLEDGMENTS

I am extremely grateful to everyone who helped and encouraged me to write *Reckless Chance*. Thank you to my husband for willingness to listen to me talk about the plot and his proofreading of the drafts. Thank you to Suzi. I couldn't have done this without you. Thank you to my editors and proofreaders for their hard work in helping me make this story shine. And thank you to my friends and family who cheer me on.

The audiobooks for this series would not be possible without East House Productions, including the talented cast, engineers, and team assembled by Shane East. They did an exceptional job. I know you'll enjoy the audiobooks.

And thank you to everyone who helped with the launch of *Reckless Chance*.

JD

ABOUT THE AUTHOR

When not immersed in her law career, J. D. Carothers loves to cook for her family and friends, read or listen to romance novels and murder mysteries, eat chocolate, and sip wine while watching the sunsets in the Southwest.

Late at night or early on weekend mornings, she finds a quiet place to write her next contemporary billionaire romance and trade the stress of real life for a fantasy world where twists and turns lead to happily ever afters.

9 781957 997148